Rachel

Rachel

THE SEQUEL TO MCKENNA

A NOVEL BY
Kathleen Sherwood

TATE PUBLISHING & ENTERPRISES

Published by Tate Publishing & Enterprises, LLC
127 E. Trade Center Terrace | Mustang, Oklahoma 73064 USA
1.888.361.9473 | www.tatepublishing.com

Tate Publishing is committed to excellence in the publishing industry. The company reflects the philosophy established by the founders, based on Psalm 68:11,
"The Lord gave the word and great was the company of those who published it."

Book design copyright © 2007 by Tate Publishing, LLC. All rights reserved.
Cover design by Kristen Polson
Interior design by Stephanie Woloszyn

Published in the United States of America

ISBN: 978-1-60247-900-5
1. Christian Fiction: Romance

07.10.25

Books by Kathleen Sherwood

Pioneer Romance

McKenna

Rachel

Contemporary Fiction

All My Tomorrows

Acknowledgments

Michael, thank you for being by my side and for putting up with me when I type during all hours of the night while you try to sleep. You have seen me at my best and my worst, and still you love me. The years have passed swiftly on this rollercoaster we call life. One wonderful thing about getting older is that we can look back and enjoy it a second time. Now, however, a new chapter is unfolding, and we are blessed anew with our two granddaughters, Abbie Grace and Emmy Claire, and as we look forward to another grandchild in December. It is with great joy that we watch them grow and develop more each day. I pray that this will continue not only in the physical realm, but in the spiritual one as well; that they will be able to know the plans God has for them and enjoy the walk, even in the trials, with Him by their side. Thank you for being a part of my life.

Jeremy, our firstborn. I remember the unexplainable happiness as we watched you begin to grow and stretch your wings, even when you snuck out the window of your room to run across the road to be with your grandparents while being punished. Your dad and I both knew that usually a spoken word was enough to discipline you because of your tender spirit. You have blessed us with your strong commitment to both God and your family. You are the quiet one of the family, like your dad; quiet in manner, but loud in actions. Your love shows through the many things you do behind the scenes not only for your dear wife, Tracie, and daughter, Abbie Grace, but for the many that are fortunate enough to know you. We were blessed when God gave you to us. Through you, I have seen that deep waters do run strong and am exceedingly grateful. We love you now and forever.

Jeff, our middle child. You have brought much laughter to us with your many anecdotes throughout the years. Whether it was riding a moped that didn't want to start while your brother pushed stead-fastly from behind, or padding your bottom with dish towels before a spanking, smiles always seem to be present when you're around. God gave you this wonderful, appealing personality, and I pray that you will use it for His honor and glory throughout your life. As I think you already know, draw near to God and He will continue to guide, bless, and be with you every step of each and every day with your precious family, Jessica and Emmy Claire, for only then will life have true purpose and meaning. We love you now and forever.

Jodi, our only daughter. Where has the time gone? It seems only last week that you were playing on the steps of our home in Indiana with your babies lined around you on each side, or the many times you stood near the greeters at church, welcoming everyone by their name, even though you were only three years old. You have always been wise beyond your years, and we know this has been from God. We have seen you stay strong in your convictions when others have fallen. Your potential, as with your brothers, sisters-in-law, and nieces, is bound-less. Let God continue to guide you throughout your life not only as you undertake a new role called marriage with Matthew, but as you serve Him at church and at the hospital with your patients. We love you now and forever.

Mom and Dad, once again you support and encourage me, and for this I am grateful. God blessed me when he let me be a part of your lives. You continue to be my role models in this short journey of life. How much brighter the world would be if all had your positive outlook, due, I know, to your close walk with God. As with the kids, we love you, now and forever.

To my co-workers at the hospital who kept offering suggestions for this book until God opened the floodgates and poured ideas into me once again. Thank you, Pam, Bridget, Jonnie, Rose, Edna, Barbara, Sandra, Gayle, Monica, Glo, and Sherry for your continued support. We have shared a lot of laughter over the years and I am grateful.

To each and every one of you who have asked repeatedly for this sequel, may God richly bless you as you once again step into the lives of the Parker and the O'Malley families. My prayer is that something will leap from these pages to touch your heart and life in some way, drawing you closer to God.

And most of all, to our gracious God, not only the author and finisher of our faith, but of our very lives. The journey has been incredible, and I am truly learning that indeed, with You, all things are possible.

Chapter One

McKenna smiled as she watched their oldest daughter, Rachel, stand near the window in the front room. She had been there for at least fifteen minutes, her eyes scanning continuously for sight of a wagon.

"I don't suppose there is a particular reason why you are so impatient for the O'Malley family to arrive this afternoon, is there?" she quietly teased her.

Turning to beam a brilliant smile at her mother, sapphire blue eyes shone as she replied, "He's finally coming home to stay."

While she finished the final preparations for their supper, McKenna thought about whom Rachel was referring to. Mark O'Malley had finished his schooling as a doctor and had been offered a temporary position as Dr. Hill's assistant. The elderly physician had difficulty making house calls now due to his age and was glad to let someone help him for even a short time. He knew retirement was not long in coming but was not quite ready to relinquish his duties as of yet.

Mark and Rachel had formed a closer relationship since his sister, Laura, had been married almost three years. The two were almost inseparable when he had been home lately for visits the past few months.

Feeling the arms of her husband slip around her from behind, McKenna raised her chin for his kiss on her cheek and smiled.

"What's put that smile on your face?" Tucker asked.

"I was recalling how things have changed. Can you believe that it has been fourteen years since we traveled by wagon to come here?" she asked him in wonder.

"In some ways it seems like we've lived here forever, and in other ways it seems as though it can't be possible that it's been that long. I remember when I first laid eyes on you while you were cleaning tables at Mama's restaurant."

Shifting so she could look into his wonderful eyes, the same vivid, beautiful shade of blue as Rachel's, she asked, "Isn't it incredible how the Lord can turn a bad situation, like the one I was in with my uncle, to something good? I remember feeling so hopeless one day and filled with such promise the next."

"And you were an answer to my prayers, although it did take Mama to point that out to me," he replied with a small grin.

"I do wish she'd join us here."

"We all do. Maybe we can talk her into giving up the restaurant. She did say in her last letter that it was becoming a lot of work."

"I'm going to pray extra hard that she'll come. The kids love her and always hate when she leaves. Besides, I miss her."

"She seems to linger a little longer each time," he told her with a small measure of encouragement, "so maybe next time it'll be to stay."

"That's true. She was here all summer last year."

"Mama!" they heard Rachel exclaim. "They're here!" Running toward the door, she flung it open and waited for Mark to gather her in his arms and swing her around.

"Hello, my little shadow," he told her as he planted a kiss on her cheek.

"Will you never call me by my given name?" she implored of him.

"Of course not. You and Laura were Matthew and my shadows for years. You followed us everywhere we went, and we didn't get a moment's peace because of the two of you."

Looking over his shoulder, she saw his older brother, Matthew, grin at her and nod his head in affirmation.

"It's true, Rachel. We had to sneak out if we were to have any time to ourselves at all."

Hearing this, she had a look of shock on her face before exclaiming, "You mean you did things without us?!"

Laughter erupted as they walked through the doorway.

Although brothers, they looked little alike. Matthew, who was almost twenty-five years old, was taller than Mark with a more muscular build. He had followed in his father's footsteps and had also taken to farming. His hair, which at one time was a deep red, had lightened to a dark blonde with shades of red evident only in the sunshine, while Mark still held the true redheaded features. His auburn hair was slightly curly and his complexion was fair. Both had the intense blue eyes of their father and were considered handsome by the single girls in the area. Their personalities, too, were as different as night and day. Matthew was very laid back and easygoing with a sharp sense of humor, while Mark was the more reserved, quieter one. Their youngest brother, John, who was now almost nineteen, was rather shy and more timid. He and Laura, who was twenty, looked like their mother with dark, shiny black hair and almost midnight black eyes.

"I hope everyone is hungry," McKenna said as she directed their guests to the large dining area.

"Now, lassie, when have ya' ever known me to pass up a meal?" Ian O'Malley asked her.

"Never," Genie piped in with a grin, glancing toward her hostess.

She and McKenna were still the best of friends and felt more like sisters now than ever, although there was an age difference of almost fifteen years. The two regularly visited one another and shared both the good times as well as the bad.

As everyone found their respective seats, it was obvious that Mark and Rachel were eager to be alone and catch up on all the latest news. They whispered frequently and smiled little, knowing smiles. McKenna and Genie, observing the two, grinned at one another. Neither one minded that the two seemed destined to be together one day.

During the meal, the adults began to reminisce about their long trip from Missouri.

"Mark," his mother asked him, "do you remember how much you loved collecting little critters?"

"Yes, I distinctly recall how you and Papa wouldn't let me bring any into the wagon, and you repeatedly checked my pockets."

Laughing, she said, "That's because you snuck a frog in one night and all we heard was croaking. No one could get any sleep. We ended up looking everywhere until we found that fellow. I'm glad you changed from animals to people. Think how handy it will be to all of us to have our very own physician."

Groaning, he told them in a light tone, "And those are calls I won't be getting paid for, I'm sure."

Hearing his words, his papa chipped in and told him with a snicker, "Ach, no, son. 'Twill be a privilege for ya' to take care of your friends and family."

"And I know you'll remind me of that from time to time."

"For sure, me laddie, for sure," he told his son with a crooked smile and a quick wink of his eye.

After the meal was over and the table was cleared, Rachel went to stand in front of Mark, asking him, "How would you like to take a stroll down by the stream?"

"That sounds mighty fine indeed," he told her as he rose to his feet, taking her hand in his own.

Watching them leave, Matthew felt a tugging in his heart.

As the couple walked down the steps and set off in the direction of the crystal-clear water, Mark placed his arm around her shoulders and squeezed.

"I missed you."

"Probably not as much as I did you," she replied back.

"You mean you haven't been seeing anyone since I've been gone?"

Wrinkling up her brow, she said, "No, although Kenneth Murdock did ask if he could call."

"What?!" he called out in a shocked tone. "The man is fifteen years your senior."

"I think he wants a mama for his little ones more than a wife."

"I hope you set him straight on that."

"I didn't have to. Papa handled the matter for me."

"I'll have to tell your father thank you for me."

"Would you mind if I was seeing someone?" she asked, daring to hear his answer.

Thinking about what she had asked, he stopped her and turned to look into her eyes before saying, "Do I honestly need to answer that question? If I do, then I've not been making my intentions very clear lately."

"And what intentions might those be?" she asked softly, lowering her eyes to stare at the buttons on his shirt.

"Give me a little while to get settled and I'll share them with you. But let me add that my future has plans with you in it."

Quietness surrounded the couple as they turned once again and began to walk.

Reaching the stream, Rachel began to take her shoes and stockings off. Watching with inward amusement at how discreet she was not to reveal anything, Mark heard her say, "This warm sunshine and cool water are too inviting to sit still. Come on, let's wade."

Mark, too, began to remove his own shoes and socks, rolling up his pant legs, following her into the brisk, chilly water. Seeing how careful he was to prevent his trousers from getting wet, she couldn't resist and began to splash him. Feeling the cold water trickle down his cheeks, his eyes gleamed as he grinned, and soon they both were dripping from head to toe.

"And here I was trying so hard not to get wet," he said as he assisted her back on the bank to sit and dry in the warmth of the afternoon sun.

"I know, and that's why I splashed you. You looked like a city boy who couldn't stand to get a drop of water on him, and I know the real you was just waiting to come out."

"Honestly? A city boy?" he asked her as he glanced down at the town clothes he had on. "I guess I do, don't I?"

"You did," she told him with a small laugh, "but you don't now. You look like the old Mark with wrinkled clothes and wet, curly hair."

"And you approve, I take it."

"Definitely," she said as she leaned over to brush his hair off his forehead.

Sitting and basking in the glorious sunshine of the summer day, he asked a few minutes later, "Have you decided if you are going to take the teaching job yet?"

"Yes, I am pretty sure right now that I am. The extra money would be useful, and Hannah and D.J. could ride with me. I have to let the board know in a few days."

"I think you'll enjoy it. You have a way with children. They all seem to love you. Plus, you certainly put in some hours studying for your teaching certificate."

"I know. I guess for a little while I had taken the notion toward nursing." She didn't add that she had considered this so that she could assist him when he needed her.

"What changed your mind?"

"When D.J. fell and cut his head open last winter, he bled all over, and I wasn't sure that I could handle that on a daily basis. I thought Mama was going to have two patients to take care of instead of one."

A chuckle arose from him and he told her, "You'd get used to it in time."

"I'm not sure I want to get used to it though. I think I'll leave that expertise in your capable hands."

"And I'll leave the teaching end up to you. I think that arrangement will work fairly well for us in the future," he told her in a satisfied tone.

With a small chuckle, Rachel asked, "Do you remember the first teacher we had after we got settled?"

Both of their minds dwelt back to years ago when the young fellow had arrived. He was tall and thin and didn't look as though he had done a day's work his whole life. His long, gaunt face and thick, bushy brown hair gave him a somewhat unique appearance.

He also wore thick, gold-rimmed spectacles that kept slipping to the end of his nose. Over the first few weeks of the school year, he had become smitten with one of the older students to the point of writing poetry to her and keeping her after the others had left.

"Yes, how could I forget him?" Mark asked her with a smile of his own.

"I don't think Mary Wilson will either. He sure had a crush on her, didn't he?"

"I'll say. Her papa had to remove her from school. I heard that he also had to tell him not to call on his daughter or write to her anymore. I guess he thought he could woo her with his poetry."

"At sixteen years of age, I don't think many girls are interested in poetry," Rachel said, recalling how she would have felt about it a few years ago herself.

"He wasn't here for long, thank goodness," he told her with a sigh. "I know I didn't learn anything from him."

"Mm, somehow I don't think he was interested in teaching. He was looking for a prospective bride," she replied with a grin. "Although he would have loved to tutor Mary, I'm sure."

"He thought he had found his true love with her. Once he discovered that she wasn't interested, he was gone."

Wrapping her arm through his, she laughed quietly. "Those were good days, weren't they?"

"Yes, nothing quite like being a child. Of course, we did have great families, which helped."

The two sat on the small bank and talked for some time before they returned to Rachel's home. It felt so good to catch up on everything that had happened since he had left several months ago. They had always been able to share their thoughts and feelings with one another. It just seemed natural that they should be together now that they were older.

Matthew, sitting on the sofa in the large room, felt his eyes travel frequently to the door, waiting for the couple to return. After more than an hour, he dismissed himself by telling the others that he was going to work on his house. His mother, watching out of the corner of her eye, knew something wasn't right but couldn't quite figure out what it was. He had been very quiet throughout the meal and didn't join the men for the usual small talk and coffee afterwards. If she had the chance, she would ask him about it later. It bothered her when something wasn't right with one of her children.

As he reached the two-story structure that sat between the Parkers and his parents' houses, Matthew reined his horse to a stop and let his eyes linger on the structure. He had been working on it for over six months and it was coming along fine. In the recesses of his mind, he had hoped that it would some day become a home for him and Rachel, but since Mark's arrival, he wasn't overly optimistic about those plans.

Dismounting his horse, he led the gelding to the small post near the front and tied him securely. Taking the stairs two at a time, he let his mind wander once again, picturing a swing on the large wraparound porch and children playing nearby. Shaking his head, as if mentally trying to dismiss these thoughts, he entered into the spacious living area. Walking toward the large window, he sighed when he saw the beautiful view it offered as it looked over the valley. It would be a picturesque site in the fall when the leaves turned their different shades of colors and in the early spring when God's hand touched the ground and brought everything back to life following the cold winter months.

Shrugging his shoulders with a frown on his face, he stepped toward the kitchen and began to work on the hardwood floors that would grace the room.

Matthew had scrimped and saved for over four years to be able to afford to build, and he had no intention of not doing it right the first time. He wanted a place to live where he could bring his wife and have enough room to raise as many children as God blessed them with. *Why, oh Lord, do my thoughts and heart keep returning to Rachel if she is to be Mark's wife?* he struggled inside again.

Yes, he knew that several other young women would be readily available should he show an interest their way, but somehow, none seemed to measure up to the Parkers' oldest daughter. She had grown from a gangly, young girl into a beautiful woman. He grinned as he recalled her blue eyes that lit up as though hiding something and the way her dimples flashed when she smiled. Her blonde hair, which had been almost white when she was a child, had darkened to a golden shade. It had a fetching way of curling up on the ends, much to her dismay. She frequently wore it down when she was at home, tying it loosely with a ribbon to keep it from her face. Only in the last few years had she begun to wear it up when she went to church or to town. As far as personality wise, she was always happy and her cheerful attitude was catching. She would be any man's dream to come home to each evening. *God,* he prayed, *You are going to have to remove these thoughts and feelings for her if I'm not supposed to have them, if it isn't in Your will. You will either have to change me or change her. I leave it in Your hands, Father. But please, God, don't let Mark suffer because of me.*

Picking up his tools, he focused on the job before him, placing his and Rachel's future in the hands of the almighty.

Several weeks later, McKenna felt, more than saw, the presence of her husband as he stood behind her in the kitchen.

"Hello," she whispered as she turned to face him. "You're home early today."

"Yes, for some strange reason I had to see you," he told her as he cocked his head to one side to see her reaction, wondering if his intuition had been right.

"Truly? And why would that be?" she asked with a small grin appearing, lighting up her deep brown eyes.

"I'm not sure. I just know that I needed to feel your arms around me and hear you tell me that everything is all right. You have been acting a little preoccupied lately."

As he pulled her closer, he kissed her before he continued, "You know, after all these years, my love for you has only grown deeper. You are more beautiful to me now than ever."

"I know exactly what you are talking about. I feel the same." Pausing, she told him teasingly, "Although in a few months, you may not be thinking that."

"What is happening in a few months?" he inquired.

"I'll be getting as big as that barn of yours, I'm sure; especially come November," she added with a twinkle in her eyes.

"I knew it!" he exclaimed. "There has been something different about you, I just couldn't quite figure out what it was. I had to come and talk to you. I don't know why I didn't think of it before. You acted the same way with the last pregnancy."

"This one is somewhat of a surprise to me. Hannah is almost six years old now."

"She and Rachel will be thrilled to hear the news. Now, D.J., well, that could be another matter."

McKenna smiled as she thought of their son. Donovan James was almost fourteen years old, and girls and babies were not his favorite things at this stage in his life. They had shortened his name to D.J. after he had been born because Rachel had been unable to pronounce it. The young man looked like his papa but had his mother's sable brown eyes and long, dark eyelashes. He was a fine looking young man who could only think about fishing and farming. He was quiet and a little more on the serious side but was tenderhearted and would fiercely protect his sisters should the need arise. His dry sense of humor would break through frequently, and although he didn't smile often, his eyes sparkled, belying the serious look on his face.

"Maybe the baby will be a boy and he'll take an interest this time."

"Maybe," he told her with a tone that said *don't be disappointed if that doesn't happen*. "When did you discover you were with child?"

"I've been feeling differently the last few weeks but wasn't certain until a couple of days ago. My body is definitely beginning to change, and I was a little nauseated yesterday morning."

"Does Genie have an idea?" Their friend always seemed to have a premonition about these things.

"You know Genie. She has a way about her with women expecting babies. She asked me the other day while we were cleaning up when I was due."

Emitting a soft chuckle, he asked, "Do you want a boy or a girl?"

"A boy would be nice for D.J." she replied, dwelling on his question. "But then a girl would be wonderful for Hannah. She'll be happy with either though. She loves babies of any kind."

Hugging her once more, he asked with a glint in his eye as he searched the house, "And where is everyone now? It's very quiet here for a change."

"Rachel and D.J. have taken Hannah over to see the new puppies at the O'Malleys'. They left a short time ago."

Seeing the smile present on his still very attractive face, she heard him ask, "How would you like to rest for a little while? I think you look a little tired."

"Rest?"

"Well, yes, later," he told her as he led her down the hallway.

As the Parker family gathered around for their evening meal, Tucker stood to his feet and walked around to stand behind McKenna.

"Your mother and I have an announcement for you. We are going to have a new member in the family come November."

Before any further words could be said, Rachel and Hannah jumped to their feet to hug their mother.

"Really, Mama?" the six-year-old asked in wonder. She was the spitting image of her mother, except her eyes tended to be more hazel. She had light brown hair, and the soft curls framed her petite, oval face.

"Yes, honey, really."

"How many will you have, Mama?"

Laughter filled the air as McKenna told her, "Just one, sweetheart. Not like the O'Malleys' dog, where there are five."

"I'm glad," she told her solemnly.

"And why is that?"

"Because if there were five girls, Rachel and I would have to share our room."

The frank, honest answer of the little girl brought snickers from the rest of the family members. Hannah tended to be the thinker and spoke whatever popped into her head at any given moment. Although loving, she wanted to know the answers to all the questions that seemed to plague her young brain. She more than made up for her brother's quietness with her frequent chatter.

"I don't think you'll have to give up your room, honey. I'm going to straighten up the sewing room and make it a baby's room for later."

"When Rachel and Mark get married, the baby can stay with me," she answered, still obviously in deep thought about the sleeping arrangement of the new baby. All eyes turned to the oldest daughter after the seemingly innocent statement. Rachel felt warmth creep up into her cheeks and only shrugged her shoulders in reply, staring downward at the plate before her.

"We'll see about that when the time comes. Why don't you finish your supper now like a good girl," her mother told her, hoping to draw attention away from Rachel. She had said nothing about her intentions concerning marriage, and until she did, McKenna would say little herself. Recalling how the couple had acted together, somehow she didn't think it would be too long before the subject was mentioned.

Chapter Two

The letter came in the post three weeks later. It was from Tucker's mother. Hurrying to get supper on the stove, McKenna opened it quickly to hear the latest news. Her letters were usually cheery, filled with the woman's keen sense of humor, and everyone loved to hear what new story she had to tell them. As she began to read, however, a frown appeared on her face and she felt an old fear steel its fingers around her heart. She had written to tell her that her uncle was very sick, and it was only a matter of time before his impending death.

Resting the letter in her lap, tears began to fall before she was aware of them. How long she sat and grasped the letter securely with clenched fingers, she wasn't sure. The memories she had buried deep inside now rose as if they had occurred yesterday.

Tucker, having finished the chores, entered the house and found his wife absently staring out the window, the paper still clasped in her hands. Noticing her red eyes and tear-streaked cheeks, he walked toward her and bent down, the concern obvious on his face.

"What is it, sweetheart?"

Turning to look into his eyes, she whispered, "It's my uncle. Your mama says that he is gravely ill and dying."

Hearing these words brought an array of feelings. Anger and a need to protect her rose from within him. Reaching over, he stood to his feet and pulled her into his arms. Hearing the sobs against his shoulder, he held her without words until she spoke.

"I know you won't understand this, but the Lord has told me to go to him."

The shock that flooded through him was quickly masked as he listened to her continue. His first reaction had been to vehemently deny her of doing this. Scenes from the past flashed before him as he recalled the treatment she had received at her uncle's hand.

"I've been sitting here for probably the better part of an hour. I don't want to go, but I know I have to. Maybe it's to bury that part of my past with him. I don't understand why."

"I won't stop you if that's what God has told you to do, but I will not let you go back by yourself. You do understand that, don't you?" he asked in a no-nonsense voice.

Feeling her grip his arms tightly, although unaware of her actions, she replied in a quiet, fearful voice, "I couldn't go without you. I don't know what to expect."

Resting his head lightly on hers, he let her relieve deep-rooted emotions before she stood back and smiled through her tears.

"Do you think we could leave in a few days? I think time is of the essence, according to your mother."

Contemplating all that needed to be done beforehand, knowing in his heart he would do this for her, he said, "Yes, I don't see why not. I'll talk to Ian about one of his boys helping D.J. with the chores. He's got a lot of work to finish out in the fields. Rachel can handle Hannah, and I'm sure Genie will pop over to keep an eye on things also. I'll go into town tomorrow and get the train tickets."

"If I know Genie, she'll jump at the chance of being able to have Hannah stay with them. She loves that little girl like one of her own." Pausing, she looked gratefully at him and added, "Thank you for understanding."

"You're welcome," he replied in a voice he hoped sounded more convincing than he felt.

The next few days were busy ones as they made preparations for the trip back to Missouri. Tucker knew that his wife was having trouble sleeping. He would wake up to find her reading her Bible quietly or sitting in the rocker praying. He had been sending a lot of prayers toward heaven lately also. Both were uncertain of what they would face in the days ahead. He only hoped that with her emotions in such a fragile state due to the pregnancy, she would be able to cope. He knew he tended to be overprotective of her while she was with child, but like McKenna, sometimes the past resurfaced quickly. Letting his mind wander to many years ago, he could still recall the painful time of losing his first wife in childbirth. Rachel had only been a small child, and instead of having a wife and two children, his world was suddenly filled with pain and confusion, and his family consisted of only Rachel and himself. Only when McKenna and he were somewhat forced into marriage did the days become better. With a lingering smile, he remembered that it didn't take long for him to fall in love with her. God had placed her in their lives. He had known they needed her as much as she needed them. Turning his thoughts to their return to the small town, he was very thankful of God's promises to be with them. He relied heavily on the fact that their heavenly father would not give them any more than they could handle, as He told them in the book of 1 Corinthians.

The whole family, the O'Malleys, as well as Pastor Keller, were at the train station for farewells. Genie had insisted that Hannah stay with her and Ian while they were gone. She had added that it would be one less thing for McKenna to worry about, knowing that she would be well cared for. Rachel and D.J. would remain at the homestead to keep it running smoothly. Genie knew that Rachel was beginning to work on lessons for the new school year, and having a busy little girl around would hinder her progress.

As Tucker and McKenna boarded the train, they noticed it was rather empty except for a few other people in attendance. An elderly, heavyset man sat across the aisle from them, and a younger couple was several rows in front.

Taking their seats, Tucker placed their bags in the seats next to them and turned to face his wife.

"How are you?"

In complete honesty, McKenna answered, "I'm not sure. I think I'm exhausted from thinking about this and waking frequently during the nights."

Taking her hand in his, he caressed it as he told her, "It will be different this time. He wouldn't dare lay a hand on you while I'm there."

Shivering at his words, she only nodded and turned to look out the window as the train began to depart. As the miles slowly ran together, she noticed Tucker lean his head back and close his eyes. He had been up early that morning to make sure everything was ready for the O'Malley boys to help D.J. with all the livestock. It was a busy time as they were getting ready to round up the cattle to be sold, but that would have to wait until he returned.

Watching the dry, flat land pass before her eyes, she let her mind roam back to the time when her mother was dying. She was sixteen years old and the ache squeezed her heart as if it were yesterday. How she missed her kind voice and gentle spirit. Before her death, her mama had arranged for her only child to go and live with her deceased husband's brother and wife. He was the undertaker in a nearby town, and they had not had any children of their own. She could remember so vividly getting off the stage and the emptiness engulfing her as she walked the lonely trek to their house. It had not been the welcome she had hoped for when she had arrived. Her aunt, although kind, was timid and controlled by her uncle. He allowed them little money, although he squandered his on drinking and gambling. The young girl, needing to find comfort to aid her in grieving, had received none from her only relatives. Only when she began to work at the restaurant that Tucker's mother owned did she find a small measure of consolation in loving arms. The two were immediately drawn to one another not only because of their strong beliefs, but also because of their kindred spirits.

What began as verbal abuse with her uncle, however, soon changed to physical abuse after her aunt's death later that year. His drinking sprees became an everyday occurrence, and he took his frustration at his gambling losses out on her. Remembering the bruises and injuries she had suffered from him, she felt panic begin to well up from deep inside. She had thought these things would remain in her past, but she realized that going back provided the key to unlock this dark door in her mind. Tears began to trickle down her face as she recalled the last awful night that he struck her. She had refused to be married to the banker, even after the two of them had agreed on a bride price. He exploded in rage and she feared for her life. Only when Tucker rescued her did she feel protected and safe.

Leaning her head back against the seat, she wiped the tears from her face and began to pray for strength to get through the days ahead. The gentle, lulling motion of the train soon worked its way into her tired body and weary soul and she fell asleep a few moments later.

"No!" she cried out. "Please stop!"

"McKenna." Tucker shook her arm to awaken her. "Honey, it's only a bad dream, wake up."

Straightening herself into an upright position, she recalled where she was as she glanced around her. Terror was still evident on her face and Tucker placed his arm around her and pulled her into a close embrace, swaying gently with the rhythm of the train.

"I'm sorry," she whispered against his shoulder.

"It's all right now," he told her in a hushed tone. "You're safe with me. You haven't had those dreams for a long time."

"I know. I think returning has stirred up everything."

"I only hope we won't be gone too long and can return home soon."

"I know God wants me there, but I don't want to go," she told him in an anguished voice. "It's been so long, but somehow it's still so fresh. Is it something I'll ever forget? "

"No, it's a part of your life, honey. But we both know that God can and will take the bad and make it something good."

"Yes, but how does He take something like this and make it good?" she asked.

"I don't know. That is where our faith and trust in Him comes in."

Holding her, neither spoke for a few minutes. Each was recalling in their own minds the darkness held by the town they were moving closer to with each passing mile.

After eating the lunch she had packed, McKenna began to take in the scenery once more.

"Feeling better now?" Tucker asked, noticing a more peaceful look on her face.

"Yes, I'm remembering our first night together as husband and wife. I was so afraid, but I loved you so much."

"I knew that, that's why I made myself wait until you were ready."

"And I was," she told him with a twinkle. "I think those were some of the first things I loved about you, your kindness and thoughtfulness. You always put me above yourself."

"Because I only wanted what was best for you. That's how much I loved you. I didn't want to scare you off. I knew it had to be in your time, not mine." Chuckling, he added, "Although, I'm not saying it was easy, because it wasn't."

Thinking about how affectionate he was, even after all the years together, McKenna could understand. He still couldn't pass without touching her lightly or kissing her.

"Remember how excited we were about the soddy?" he asked.

With a small smile, she told him, "Yes, my first real house. Our home," she added. "I loved it...well, everything but those dirt floors. I have to admit, however, I was ready to be in the new house the next year. With the addition of D.J., we were becoming a little cramped."

"You have made both places homes."

"That was the easy part. I had you by my side," she whispered as she took his hand in her own.

"It's been a good life for us, hasn't it?"

"The best possible. I never imagined that when I married you, I was just beginning to live my dream. And I wouldn't trade one day of it with you for anything. God gave you to me and I'll always thank Him," she whispered for him alone.

Unable to stop himself, he leaned over and stole a kiss. Glancing around the train, he told her, "Sorry, I couldn't help myself."

"I didn't mind."

Peering around her husband, she noticed that the elderly man was snoring softly with his mouth hanging open. His long handlebar mustache wiggled as he exhaled. A giggle almost escaped before she could stop herself.

"Guess this rocking motion tends to put everyone to sleep," Tucker said, noticing the gentleman also.

"Yes, and a quick nap does sound good," she replied as she snuggled up into his solid shoulder. "I'm so drained emotionally that I feel worse than if I had worked all day."

As she became still, Tucker prayed that God would prepare her for whatever awaited them in the small town. It was easy turning something over to God, he had learned. The hard part was leaving it there. He also prayed that God would help him control the deep-rooted anger that wanted to seep to the surface. He knew how easy it would be to let his sin nature control him as he recalled how the man had hurt his wife.

The next morning, as the train pulled into the station, McKenna and Tucker noticed the new buildings that had been erected since their move. The bank had been enlarged and now had a welcoming feeling to it. The banker, Mr. Harrison, had died in a mining accident three years earlier. Thinking of the man, McKenna shuddered, recalling the agreement that had been made for her to marry him. How different her life would have been had such a marriage taken place. He was an evil man several years her senior. After she had run away with Tucker, the banker arranged for her to be kidnapped and returned to him. She would never forget the relief she felt when she saw Tucker and Ian O'Malley appear in the cave to rescue her. She had God to thank for that; He had led them to her.

Heading hand in hand toward the restaurant, they smiled as they entered and saw Tucker's mother waiting on tables with her back to them.

Following behind her quietly, he wrapped his arms around her. Knowing who was holding her, they heard her squeal in delight and she turned to engulf him tightly.

"You're here early!" she exclaimed in a voice overflowing with happiness.

"Yes, we didn't have to make one of the stops and it saved us a few hours."

"McKenna, come here," she told the younger woman, taking her into her arms tenderly. "I have missed you so much."

"And we have all missed you."

"I've got so much to fill you in on. Let me tell Dorothy that I'm leaving. I think she can handle the rest of the customers. I've got a lovely supper waiting for us at the house."

Watching her bustle away, the two smiled.

"She never changes, does she?" McKenna asked.

"No, and I wouldn't want her to."

"Me neither."

Sitting around the table after supper, Mrs. Parker leaned back in her chair before telling them, "I've got some news for you both. Whether it will make you happy or not, I'm not sure though."

Glancing at each other, husband and wife looked back into her twinkling eyes and heard her continue, "I've sold the restaurant and am going back with you both to live."

Of all the things they expected to hear, this was not one of them. McKenna, jumping from her chair, ran to wrap her arms around the dear woman.

"Mama Parker," she exclaimed, "that's wonderful! We were praying that we would be able to convince you, and it seems that our prayers have already been answered."

"What changed your mind?" Tucker asked with a satisfied smile present.

"I had another offer on the restaurant, along with the house, and decided it was time to move on in my life. The future suddenly seemed bleak with no one to share it with. Besides, I can't have my grandchildren grow up anymore without me there to watch. I've already missed enough. I'll have lots of catching up to do. I want to be a part of this new little one's life from the start."

Facing her son, she warned him, "Guess what you'll be helping me do until we're ready to go?"

"Packing, no doubt," he told her with a grin. "And I don't mind one bit. It's about time. Hannah has threatened several times to come and visit her grandma. We told her to pray that God would show you that you needed to move."

"Now, son, you know that everything happens in His timing, not ours. Although I have to admit, I'd sure like to help Him along sometimes."

Laughter filled the small kitchen as they made plans. Only when McKenna crawled into bed beside her husband much later did she dwell on the next day and seeing her uncle. She had no idea what to expect or if he would even welcome her. She didn't know how she would face him if she saw the old hate from years ago in his eyes. Cuddling up close to Tucker's warm body, she felt him entwine his arms around her.

"Thinking about tomorrow, love?" he asked intuitively.

"Yes."

"Pray, ask God for His guidance and the right words."

"I already have, but I'm still afraid of the old ghosts that will be there to haunt me."

"Ghosts that have been laid to rest long ago, I hope," he whispered against her hair.

Eating little for breakfast, McKenna felt her stomach begin to knot up as she and Tucker walked the long, dusty road toward her uncle's place—the house that had never become a home for her.

They had learned that there was an elderly woman coming every day to take care of him now. He was bedridden with little strength left.

As they knocked on the door, thoughts of the many times she had run home to prepare supper before he returned from the saloon flooded her thoughts. She had been so afraid to displease him in any way. Squeezing her hand for reassurance, Tucker nodded his head as if to say, *It will be all right, I'm here.*

A moment later, an older, slightly stooped woman answered the door. Her gray hair was matted and her appearance was one of an unkempt state.

"What ya' sellin'?" she asked in a sneering voice.

"Nothing," McKenna told her. "I am here to visit my uncle."

"Your uncle, ya' say?" she asked loudly, as if her hearing was poor.

"Yes, may I come in and see him please?"

"Don't matter one way or the other to me. Please yourself."

As they entered the filthy, dark house, McKenna felt sorrow fill her. *Is this what her uncle had been reduced to?* Obviously, he had not had a good life the past fourteen years. Lightly rubbing her fingers over her palms and feeling the moisture present, she realized how nervous she was about the visit.

Walking past the woman, they entered her uncle's bedroom and were shocked to see the frail appearance of a once-robust man. His gray hair was overly long and tangled. He looked as if he hadn't shaved in weeks. He was like the skeleton of the uncle in her memories. Pity for him trickled through her and her heart broke. This was not the man who had physically abused her years ago.

Opening his eyes, eyes that seemed hollow to McKenna, she heard him gasp as he recognized her. He studied her intently for the length of almost a full minute with little expression present. Unsure of herself, McKenna gazed into his eyes, hoping to find some sort of a bond between them that could bridge the past into the present.

Without saying a word, she walked toward him and picked up his hand in her own. His eyes followed her every move.

"Uncle Hilton, it's me, McKenna," she whispered softly.

"Yes, girl," he told her in a raspy voice, his eyes never leaving her face. "I could never forget you."

Watching, she saw him try to gather enough breath to continue. After a moment of silence, he asked her, "Why did you come back?"

"Because God told me to," she answered in honesty.

Not sure of his reaction to her words, she saw him close his eyes and a lone tear slid down his lined cheek.

"I don't deserve you to come back." A hacking cough filled the room several seconds before he continued, "I treated you badly and I'm sorry."

McKenna, overcome with emotion, knelt beside his bed and knew the tears were falling silently. Hearing the words she thought would never pass his lips, she felt a freedom filter through her for the first time in many years, a freedom that offered peace.

"Yes, you did. But God loves you and so do I." McKenna wanted to say she had forgiven him, but she knew at this time that she couldn't bring herself to utter the words. She felt like she was an infant learning to take one step at a time.

Turning to hide the emotion he was feeling, he clutched her hand weakly as pain passed through him. She waited until the wheezing eased enough for him to speak.

"I know…That's what changed me. God lives inside me now."

"Oh, Uncle Hilton!" McKenna cried out in relief. "When did you accept Christ?"

"Pastor Schaffer came over last week and told me to get ready to meet my maker. He also said that if I didn't ask Jesus into my life, I would be going to hell for eternity…a hell that would be much worse than the prison of the bottle for most of my life."

Joy leapt inside her as she turned and smiled in amazement at her husband. "Uncle, do you remember Tucker Parker? The man I married."

Nodding his head in affirmation, she saw a small smile break through his scraggly beard for the first time.

"Bet he remembers me too," he told them with the hint of amusement.

"Yes, sir, very well," Tucker returned, also with a small grin.

"I'm sorry," was all the older man said.

Realizing that he was getting tired, McKenna asked, "Can I come and stay with you during the day and help take care of you?"

"You'd do that for me?" he asked quietly, surprise filling his pale face.

"Yes, I would."

Nodding his head again, she saw him close his eyes. The deepened breathing a minute later told her he had fallen asleep. Gently unclasping her hand from his, she placed it under the blanket and turned to leave the room.

Seeing the woman watching from a chair at the table, McKenna told her, "We won't be requiring your services anymore."

"What ya' mean? I need the money," she asked in a raised tone.

Reaching into his pocket, Tucker extracted a small amount of money and handed it to her.

"This should help for a while."

Turning abruptly, she spat in the fireplace and stomped from the room.

"By the looks of this house and my uncle, I don't think she did anything."

"No. Are you sure you are up to this?"

Smiling with a new radiance, she answered, "Oh, yes. I'll start this afternoon after lunch."

Seeing her determination, he took her hand in his and they proceeded toward the restaurant. Both her heart and feet felt as though they were weightless as they entered the dwelling to tell Mama Parker of the news. *Was the sun shining this brightly when we left this morning?* she asked herself. *If it was, I sure didn't notice it.*

Laden not only with cleaning supplies, but clean towels and bedding, McKenna eagerly approached her uncle's house. *This is the first time I've ever been anxious to come here.*

Praying as she walked, she said, "Thank You, Lord, for changing his life. You never cease to amaze me at how You work in each one of us; how You can take a lump of clay and make something beautiful out of it, because that's what we are, Father, unformed clay. Do whatever it takes, God, to form us to be what You would have us to be. I know that I can place the past at Your feet now. I also know that whatever the future holds, You are in control, always working to mold us to be like You, and I thank You. Help me to always keep my eyes focused on You and Your will."

Climbing the steps and walking to the front door, she opened it slowly and felt the familiar heaviness of long ago flood her. A smile broke through her features as she realized that God was present now. Placing her first thoughts in the back of her mind, she set her items on the table and walked to her uncle's room. His breathing was irregular and each breath seemed to be a struggle. Hearing her footsteps as she approached his bed, he turned to look into her face and smiled.

"I thought I was dreaming after you left."

"No, I really am here to help you," she said as she returned his smile.

"Still don't rightly know why after what I did to you," he told her in a hoarse, wheezing voice.

"That is all in the past. You are a child of God's now, you're different. I can tell."

Nodding his head, unable to converse anymore, she watched him close his eyes to rest. Walking back through the doorway, she quietly shut his door and began the task at hand. Tucker was coming over shortly. He had agreed to help bathe and shave her uncle. First, he was going to the mercantile to buy him a new set of clothes; the ones he was wearing hung on him and looked as though they hadn't been washed in weeks.

After cleaning for a short time, she heard footsteps on the porch and smiled when she saw her husband enter the door.

"I tried to hurry," he told her as he returned her smile. "I don't like you being here alone."

Walking toward him, she wrapped her arms around him. "It's all right now. God has changed him. There's a new feeling in this house, the spirit of God's love."

"I guess I've been thinking of your earlier words, that sometimes the past is hard to leave in the past."

"But that's all it is now," she answered honestly. "It's time to make new memories for the future."

Hugging her tightly for a moment, he was amazed at how special this woman was. She had a pure heart and always looked for the best in everyone. Her nature was one of forgiveness, and he knew he was indeed a lucky man to have her by his side.

"I love you," he told her simply, although the words held a depth of truth.

"I know, and I love you too."

Working side by side, the two quickly and efficiently had her uncle bathed, clean shaven, and in new clothes. It had worn the ill man out, but he never complained while they worked. After they had finished, in a rasping voice he told the couple, "Thank you."

Taking his wrinkled, thin hand into her own, she smiled before replying, "You're welcome. Later, after you've eaten supper, I'll try and trim your hair for you."

Hearing his wife's words brought a quick grin from Tucker as he recalled her first experience cutting her own papa's hair and leaving him with what looked like two eyes in the back of his head. Feeling her gaze upon him, he saw her flash a knowing smile his way.

"I think I've improved since then."

Reaching up to run his hands through his own dark hair, which now had a tinge of gray at the temples, he said, "I could use a trim myself."

"Maybe in the next few days I can work you in somewhere," she told him with a hint of mischievousness.

Glancing toward her uncle, who was now fast asleep, he came to stand near her and whispered in her ear, "You'd better save some time for me. I'd be lonely without you."

Kissing him quickly, she said, "I'll always have time for you."

McKenna was standing near her uncle and watching him sleep. Although his breathing was still labored and his color pale, he looked immensely better. Gone was the long, shaggy hair and beard. The ragged, dirty clothes had been replaced and he now had a peaceful look on his face. The doctor was to stop by at anytime and check him over before starting his own day at his small office by the post office.

As she reached to adjust the covers more snuggly around him, she heard a soft knock at the door. Stepping as quietly as possible, she opened it to the waiting physician.

"Good morning," she told him cheerily.

"Good morning, yourself. How is he today?"

"I think he might be better."

"Mm…Let's just have a look and see," was all the man said as he moved to the sick man's bedroom.

After several minutes of examining him, he slowly and methodically put things back in his bag. Gesturing with his hand that he would talk to her in the kitchen area, she nodded in understanding. McKenna saw concern on his face as she followed him from the room.

"He's not better, Mrs. Parker. His heart is giving out and he can barely breathe normally. I fear it won't be much longer now."

Hearing these words filled McKenna like a shroud.

"I think I knew it in my mind, but my heart didn't want to accept it," she told him with sorrow.

Taking her small hand in his larger one, he said, "I understand. He is ready to go and meet his maker in heaven. He'll have a new body there. This one is tired and worn out from all the abuse over the years. Besides, somehow I think his wife will be mighty anxious to see him now."

"Yes, you're right," she returned, feeling the sadness leave her with the comforting words.

"Call me if I can do anything," he told her as he walked toward the door.

"Thank you."

Watching him walk away, she returned to her uncle's side and sat in the chair near his bed. A few minutes later, she saw his eyes open and a small smile appear on his face.

"Not good news, I take it?" he asked.

"No," she replied with eyes downcast.

"It is good news," he whispered raggedly, reaching for her hand. "I will be with God soon…and my Mattie, my poor, poor Mattie."

Looking into his eyes, she, too, felt a smile creep onto her face. "Yes, and what better place to be than there?"

"Could you read to me from the Book of John? The fourteenth chapter has given me comfort lately."

"Of course," she told him as she rose to retrieve her Bible off the kitchen table.

Sitting down again and turning to that particular passage, she began to read verses one through six in a soothing, quiet tone.

Let not your heart be troubled;
ye believe in God, believe also in me.
In my Father's house are many mansions;
if it were not so, I would have told you.
I go to prepare a place for you.
And if I go and prepare a place for you,
I will come again, and receive you unto myself;
that where I am, there ye may be also.
And whither I go ye know, and the way ye know.
Thomas saith unto him,
Lord, we know not whither thou goest;
and how can we know the way?
Jesus saith unto him,
I am the way, the truth, and the life;
no man cometh unto the Father, but by me.

Glancing up, McKenna saw that her uncle had once again fallen asleep. Although his chest rose and fell with difficulty, the peace that was present on his face offered her a small measure of that very peace herself.

How ironic, she thought, *that the very verses that bring him comfort now brought me peace and assurance so many years ago in my own small room in this very house.*

Tucker was afraid to let McKenna go alone each morning for fear that she might find her uncle already passed away; therefore, he walked her to the house before returning to help his mother. After she had cleaned him up following breakfast, she watched him sleep; the extra exertion tired him out easily.

He woke himself up not long after that as he gasped for his breath. She saw his eyes flutter open and turn to look at her with a tenderness she had often prayed for.

"The time is near, McKenna," he told her as he lightly stroked the hand that held his. "I need to speak to you before I am gone."

Without words, she nodded and waited patiently for him to tell her what was on his mind. Reaching for the nearby chair, she sat down, leaning forward to listen.

"I would like to share with you my story, if you'll let me. Maybe it will help a little," he continued with his voice low and gravelly.

"Of course," she replied, watching him inhale as deeply as possible before he began.

"Your Aunt Mattie wanted children so badly. After three times of miscarrying babies before she was very far along, we were beginning to lose hope of ever having a child of our own." Pausing again, he tried desperately to catch a breath. McKenna helped him sit up and placed a pillow behind his back for support.

"Finally, she carried one the full nine months and we were thrilled.

After a long, hard labor, the child was born dead. I think a piece of my heart was buried when they laid our son to rest that cold, rainy morning. It changed your aunt. She became withdrawn and despondent."

Tears slid down his weathered, wrinkled cheek, and he didn't even seem to be aware of them. Taking a minute to gather his breath, McKenna could see the grief etched on his face as he recalled those days in his mind.

"I soon began to drink heavily to keep the hurt from surfacing. One thing led to another, and I couldn't seem to help myself. Your poor aunt was brokenhearted and needed my comfort, and I wasn't there to help her. I couldn't console myself, let alone her."

The intense pain was evident on his face as he clutched his chest tightly for the length of several minutes; pain not only from his illness, but from deep inside. Turning to face her, the anguished look on his face spoke volumes to his niece. He had been suffering and had lashed out at her and Aunt Mattie instead of turning it over to God.

"I did things that weren't right. I hurt you and Mattie and am ashamed of my behavior. The bottle became my demon; it was the prison, and Satan held the key."

Stroking his hand, she placed a hand on his forehead to brush a strand of gray hair that had slipped down.

"I wish I had known God then; maybe things would have been different. Mattie tried to talk to me several times about needing Him, but I wouldn't listen. I figured I didn't need a God who would take our children. I didn't realize that He was the one who could help me… that He was the one who was cradling our small ones in the palm of His hand."

Pausing for a few minutes, not only to regain breath, but composure as well, he continued, "I don't rightly know if you can, but I'd like to ask your forgiveness."

With tears streaming down her own face, she whispered, "I do forgive you. I know now that this is why God had me come. It is time to lay the hurt and sorrow to rest. We can be filled with His hope and promises now."

"I just wanted you to know that I wasn't always a bad person."

With eyes that were heavy, but a heart much lighter, the older man drifted into a restless sleep.

McKenna and Tucker, arriving early the next morning, found him in the same position as when she had left. He had died during the night. As she wept near his bedside, she couldn't help but notice the look present on his face. He had a small smile on his cold features, and he had the Bible laying on his chest. He had gone home and was finally at rest. He was not only in the very presence of his savior; he was with his wife and children. She could only imagine the joy he must be experiencing—joy that he had not had during most of his life on earth. *How happy a reunion it must be.*

Chapter Three

The warm, hot sunshine beat down on those gathered around the gravesite the following day. *It's ironic*, McKenna thought, *that Uncle Hilton is buried in one of his own coffins. I wonder if he built this one himself or if his partner did.*

The undertaking business would be sold to pay past debts the man had accumulated over the years. There would be no profit in its sale. The house was in such shambles that almost any offer at all would be entertained by McKenna and Tucker. As friends and family of the Parkers gathered to offer condolences, it was with mixed emotions as they said their final goodbyes. Food had been brought into the restaurant for a meal afterwards, and then they would go back to Mrs. Parker's house to make plans for the future.

Walking back a few hours later, Tucker noticed that his wife looked exhausted. The last two weeks had been emotionally draining to her.

"You are going to go home and take a nap," he told her with concern.

"I am feeling a little weary."

"Yes, honey," Mama Parker interjected, "you need to rest and take care of yourself and the little one you are carrying."

With a smile, McKenna placed her hand over her stomach and said, "Yes, I can definitely tell that I'm with child. I think I could crawl back in bed and sleep for a week."

"That's just what you are going to do when we get back to the house. The sheets are nice and clean, and I want you to rest until supper. Plans can be made after that."

With a grateful smile toward her mother-in-law, McKenna said, "That does sound wonderful."

"And you, Tucker," his mother continued, "can help me pack up things in the kitchen that I need to have shipped out."

"I'd rather take a nap," he told her with a smile.

"Sorry, not this time," she said, looping her arm through his as they walked up the stairs into the kitchen.

Mrs. Parker, Tucker, and McKenna were gathered around the table after the dishes had been cleared and began to decide what their next course of action would be.

"I will go tomorrow and begin to sort through some things at Uncle Hilton's. I don't believe there will be very much of value, and it shouldn't take very long. Tucker, why don't you stay here and help your mama?" McKenna suggested.

"Are you sure you don't want me to go with you?" he asked with a slightly worried tone.

"No, I'll be fine. If I get tired, I'll come back and rest, I promise."

Still not certain of this arrangement, Tucker eventually agreed. He knew from past experience that when his wife set her mind to something, she would follow through until it was finished.

Laughing, McKenna said, "I can't believe I slept for two hours and I'm already tired again."

"You have a good reason to be, dear. This past week has been emotionally wearing, and sometimes that is harder on a body than physical labor. Now, son, take your wife and go to bed. You both have a big day ahead of you tomorrow," Mama Parker told the couple.

Before they could rise to their feet, there was a rapping noise at the door and Mrs. Parker rose to answer it. With a dreadful feeling in her heart, she saw that it was Amos Williams.

"Hello, Amos," she greeted him.

"Susan," he said almost curtly. Before he could speak any other words, she told him, "My son and daughter-in-law are here visiting."

"Would you care to take a stroll then?" he asked in a softer tone.

Turning to face her family, she stated, "I will be back shortly. Goodnight to you both if I don't see you before breakfast."

Goodnights were said and the couple moved to their room. As he shut their door, Tucker looked questioningly toward his wife and asked, "Who do you suppose that was?"

"It sounded like a gentleman caller to me," McKenna told him with amusement, noticing the stern look on her husband's face.

"Surely she wouldn't leave if she was in love with someone here."

"Maybe she has plans to take him with her."

For some reason the thought of this bothered Tucker. His mother had never spoken of this matter before. He would discuss it with her in the morning. He knew nothing of the man and would not let her do something in a quick fashion.

Tucker arose earlier than usual the following morning and walked into the kitchen to find his mother humming softly.

"Good morning, honey," she told him as she reached for a coffee cup to pour him some of the hot, steaming liquid.

"Mama, who was that man last night?" he asked straight away.

"My, not even a good morning first," she said, teasing him.

Seeing the look of concern on his face, she pulled the chair out to sit next to him.

"His name is Amos Williams, and he has been trying to court me for two years now."

"Trying?" Tucker asked.

"Yes, I have found him to be a very persistent caller."

"And you don't return his feelings?"

"No," she told him as she looked away briefly. "It's hard to explain. He is a very prominent member of the community and also a solid church-going man."

"What is the problem then?" he asked, pondering her words.

"I feel nothing for him other than friendship. Maybe I want to experience the same thing I did for your papa and James, I don't know."

James was the man whom she had married after Tucker's father had died. He, too, had passed away almost twenty years ago, leaving her a widow yet again.

"There is no attraction whatsoever. He is kind and has always been a perfect gentleman in all of our outings."

"I distinctly remember you telling me to let the little seed of friendship grow in my heart and develop into love," he reminded her, thinking about his marriage with McKenna.

"That's true, but the seed has been sitting there for quite sometime without sprouting," she told him with amusement. "Besides,

50

you can't tell me you weren't drawn to that sweet wife of yours from the very beginning. It didn't take too much watering from what I can remember."

Recalling their first meeting, Tucker could not deny that he had felt a bond between them immediately.

"No, I know what you are talking about. It was as if we shared something without even knowing one another."

"Yes, and it's missing with Amos. I figure that after two years, if it's not there by now, it never will be."

"Does he know about you moving?"

"He does now," she told him with a chuckle. "He was mortified to think that I would turn down his offer of marriage. He reminded me of how many women would be happy to have him for their husband."

"And what did you tell him when he said that?" he asked, almost afraid of hearing the answer.

"I told him, 'Well, if that's the case, you'd better be knocking on some of their doors, 'cuz this woman just said no.'"

With laughter filling the room, McKenna smiled as she entered the cozy atmosphere of the small room.

"I guess things are all right down here now," she enquired.

"Perfect, dear, just perfect," her mother-in-law told her with a wink toward her son.

"So does that mean you will be traveling with or without a companion?"

"Definitely without," Mama Parker replied with a smile. "And until the good Lord Himself tells me that I need a husband, that's the way it will stay."

McKenna sorted through items in her uncle's room first. Most needed to be thrown out, and the prospective pile of unwanted things was growing rapidly. By lunchtime, she had become fatigued and realized that she was hungry. Just as she placed the last article of clothing from the dresser onto the bed, she saw her husband enter with a picnic basket.

"How would you like to take a break and eat lunch with your favorite person?"

"I would love it," she told him as she walked toward him with a beaming smile, her large brown eyes shining.

"Good. There is a quiet little place at the edge of town with a stream nearby. It looked like it might do. I thought maybe you'd enjoy sitting outside for a change."

"Lead the way," she told him as she took his free hand in hers, feeling love for him flow from her fingers to her heart. Glancing at his profile, she felt blessed to have been given such a man for her mate. He was a good provider, a loving father and husband, and most importantly, he was dedicated to serving God.

"And what are you thinking?" he asked as he turned to face her.

"How blessed I am to have been a part of your life."

He set the basket on the porch and placed both hands on her arms and replied, "Not as blessed as I have been. God knew I needed you as much as Rachel did long ago."

Leaning down, he placed a kiss on her cheek. McKenna was so full of love that she could not have spoken if she had wanted to.

As they neared the edge of the gently flowing water, they found a fallen log and sat down on it.

"I don't know what Mama has thrown together for us to eat."

"I don't care, I'm hungry," McKenna told him as she began to sort through the various items of leftover chicken, rolls, fruits, and apple pie for dessert.

"This is a feast," she told him in wonder.

"Remember who prepared it. She has always thought that the answer to most things is food."

"She is in the right business, that's for sure."

After prayer, as the couple ate, they discussed when they would leave to return home.

"I miss the children," she whispered with longing. "I need to see them. I know I had to come back here, but it doesn't stop the ache from not being near them; to hear Hannah ask one hundred questions a day or D.J. and his quiet presence. To observe Mark and Rachel as they develop their new relationship...and I miss those stupid chickens," she added as an afterthought. "I can't imagine Rachel gathering eggs from those grumpy hens. You have to have a firm hand with them or they become too protective."

"Me too. I miss it all. And most of all the children," he told her as he thought of them in his mind. "Maybe D.J. or one of the O'Malley boys will take pity on Rachel and deal with the hens." Sitting there quietly, each let their thoughts linger on their lives. McKenna heard her husband ask, "What if I line things up to try and return by the end of the week? Can you be ready by then?"

"Yes, I will. Please," she told him as she looked into his eyes, "let's go home."

"I'll tell Mama of our plans, and hopefully we can wrap things up on her end by then too. Well," he told her as he stood to his feet, "if we're gonna be all packed up by then, I'd better get back now. I never realized how much she has accumulated over the years."

Bending over, he looked into her eyes and planted a kiss on her forehead before telling her, "I love you and am so proud of you. You were obedient to God by coming back, and look how He has blessed you for it."

"I won't say that I was happy with the idea at first, because I wasn't. But I know now that it was His will for us to be here." Touching her hand to her heart, she said, "I feel as if I am whole in here now. I haven't felt like that for a long time."

Tucker took hold of her hand, and the couple walked toward her uncle's house, knowing that they were indeed where God had called them to be.

Before they reached the front steps, they were greeted by a young couple with eager faces.

"Mr. Parker," the young man began, "my name is Chad Culver, and this is my wife, Lucy. We are interested in buying this house if it's for sale."

Slightly taken aback, Tucker told him seriously, "It is in dire need of repair, son."

"We know, sir. We don't have very much money and hoped you would sell it to us cheap and we could fix it up ourselves."

Reaching up to stroke his chin, blue eyes locked with McKenna's brown ones, he asked, "What price did you have in mind?"

The small amount named caused Tucker to raise his eyebrows. Turning an anxious face to his wife, the young man added, "Lucy just found out she is having our first baby. We would really like to have our own place before it's born."

McKenna's smile beamed from ear to ear. After years of neglect and abuse, she could envision the love the house would feel. She swiftly said, "Sold, Mr. Culver."

Tucker heard her reply and turned to her with a look of surprise. Noticing the happiness radiating from her, he looked back to the couple and held out his hand to shake on the deal, confirming it.

"Really?" the man asked in amazement.

"Yes, it's my wife's decision to determine what becomes of it. If she wants you to have it, then it is yours."

"We'll be right back with the money," the man said as he grabbed his wife's hand and rapidly turned to leave down the road.

Shifting to face his spouse, he said with a gleam in his eyes, "Remind me, Mrs. Parker, to never let you handle the business side of our farm."

"Oh, Tucker, did you see the look on their faces? Now this house will have a future filled with love and happiness, not sorrow and pain. It will hear the echo of a child's laughter instead of angry words from the past."

"Yes, and I think it deserves that," he told her as they entered the dilapidated building.

McKenna had just finished her uncle's things and began to sort through her aunt's belongings. It looked as if nothing had been touched since her death many years ago. Dust was evident on everything.

Stepping over to the cedar chest in the corner of the room, she sat down on the floor and lifted the lid. A strong, musky smell filtered through the air and almost made McKenna wretch. After taking a few deep breaths, she turned her attention back to the items in front of her. Several knitted shawls were on the top. Gingerly lifting them out, she realized that her aunt had probably made these herself. One was rather ragged, and she could faintly recall her aunt wearing it on chilly evenings. The wool was frayed and it was worse for the wear. Setting it aside to be discarded, she reached for the second one. It looked almost new. It was pale green with a small amount of fringe on the edges. With a smile, she knew that she would keep the shawl for herself for special occasions, as well as in remembrance of the kind woman. She placed it lovingly against her cheek and felt a moment of sadness. She recalled her uncle's words and could only imagine the pain Aunt Mattie must have felt at losing not only her children in death, but her husband more each day through his withdrawal from her.

As she laid it aside, she saw a small wooden box inside the chest. Lifting it out carefully, she placed it on her lap and removed the lid. A picture of her aunt and uncle, yellowed with age, sat on the top. Evidently it had been taken on their wedding day. The two made a striking couple. All vestiges of unhappiness and bitterness were not evident on their faces. Only hope and love shone from each of them. *Lord, how can things go so wrong in our lives? Is it because we don't know You or, if we do, choose not to follow Your guiding hand?*

Beneath the picture was a deed to the small building where her uncle had worked most of his life as well as the deed to the house. She would find the Culvers and make sure they had it in their possession. Placing them nearby, she saw a piece of cloth that had been folded neatly and tied with a piece of twine. Curiosity getting the better of her, she concentrated for a few seconds on untying the knot that held it securely. Finally able to undo it, she opened it to reveal a letter of some sort with something laying underneath. Lifting the paper carefully, she saw a pearl necklace. All color drained from her face as she remembered her mama's beads. *What are they doing here and why?* She had tried to recall over the years what had become of the beads but to no avail. McKenna had thoroughly searched their small home after her mother's death.

Holding the letter in her hands for several seconds, she was almost unable to read its contents. With fingers shaking, she slowly unfolded the paper and stared at her mother's familiar handwriting. The words *To my darling daughter* leapt off the pages to her. In shock, she leaned back against the chest and closed her eyes. Tears began pooling and she wept softly for several minutes before being able to continue. She could still hear her mother's voice in her mind, and the last few days before her death flashed before her.

Finally, after gaining some of her composure, she read again.

> *To my darling daughter,*
>
> *I am writing this letter knowing that my time left with you is short. It is not my desire to leave you; however, it is God's, and He knows what is best. We have to trust Him and walk by faith and not sight at times, and this is one of those times.*
>
> *As you read this, I pray that you will find a measure of peace, knowing that a small portion of me remains in your heart and in your mind. I have always been proud of you, McKenna; any parent would have been pleased to call you their child. Always continue to be steadfast in your love for God and He will always direct your steps.*
>
> *I have sent this letter and my pearls over to your Aunt Mattie with my desire of her sharing these things with you on your wedding day. It grieves my heart to know that I will not be by your side when you exchange vows with the man I trust that God has brought into your life. I am also saddened by the knowledge that I will never be able to hold your children or hear their laughter; that I will not see how wonderful a parent you will be. But rest assured, I am in the very presence of God, and what greater place could there be for me than to be with my savior and former loved ones who have gone on before me? I, too, will wait for you to join us one day. Your father and I will eagerly anticipate when you will be with us for eternity.*
>
> *I pray that you will have a good life, one filled with both joys and sorrows, for that is truly how we grow stronger in our faith. Life cannot and must not always be a mountaintop experience, for it is in the valleys that we are able to look up and draw strength and guidance from God. Always remember, my*

child, it is through the difficult times that our faith grows, and
we can see His almighty hand at work.

My strength is ebbing away and I must close my words to
you. I love you and will always love you. May God richly bless
you on this day and the many days ahead.

In our loving Christ's name,
Mama

The tears had coursed down her cheeks, blinding her several times to the point that she had to stop and wipe them away. How long she sat letting her mind dwell once again on her childhood and parents, she wasn't sure. Tucker arrived a short time later and found her in the same position on the floor, the letter firmly held in one hand and the necklace in the other.

"McKenna, what is it?" he asked as he knelt down beside her.

Unable to reply, she handed him the letter and watched his face as he read it.

"Oh, darling," he told her as he finished and gathered her into his arms.

Shifting her position to look into his face a few minutes later, she said, "All I can think is that if I had not been obedient to God and returned, I might never have seen this or found her beads."

"But you were obedient, and now you have a small inheritance of your mother's to keep with you. This is something that you can pass on to our daughters as a remembrance of the grandmother who would have loved them."

"And she would have loved them, Tucker, she would have," she replied in a choked voice.

"Come on, honey, it's time to call it a day. We are almost through with Mama's things and can finish up here tomorrow."

Helping her stand to her feet, the two began the trek back; each had their mind filled with the same thought. They were thanking God for yet another miracle. Not only was McKenna able to remember the last days with her uncle and how he had changed his life, but she now had a small legacy from her own mother to treasure and pass down to her own children.

Chapter Four

Rachel had climbed up into the loft to study the lessons for school tomorrow. It had always been her quiet retreat to get away from the hustle and bustle of the house. She could think, read, and pray without being disturbed. Hearing someone enter, she scooted toward the edge of the hay loft, knocking off some loose straw down below. Peeking over, she smiled when she saw Matthew below her brushing off the fallen straw.

Hearing her soft giggle, he looked up into her twinkling eyes and asked, "Did you do that on purpose, or was I just at the wrong place at the wrong time?"

"I'm sorry. I didn't realize you were standing below."

Watching her climb down the ladder with agility, she came to stand in front of him. As she reached to remove a few pieces from his hair, Matthew had to refrain from pulling her into his arms. Her hair had been pinned up for school earlier that morning and several strands had come loose to frame her heart-shaped face. She looked adorable to him.

"And what brings you here today?" she asked.

"I promised your papa that I'd help D.J. with the chores."

For some reason, his words and the nearness of him brought an unfamiliar quickening in her heart.

"And where is my little brother now?"

"He's moving the cattle to the south pasture and repairing fences. I told him I would feed the livestock. What were you doing up in the loft?"

With a humorous look appearing on her face, she said, "This is my special retreat to get away from an inquisitive little girl, and it has somehow become a habit," referring to Hannah.

"Mama is keeping her busy. The house has been livelier since she's been there, that's for sure."

"She could have stayed with me and D.J.," she told him with a worried look.

"No, my parents are enjoying her thoroughly. I heard them say last night that it's nice to have a little one around again."

Nodding her head, she asked him, "Promise me you'll tell me if she wears out her welcome. She can get rather rambunctious at times."

"I will."

With a lopsided grin appearing on his attractive face, he asked, "Want to take a break and help with the chores?"

Hearing the challenging tone, she replied, "Of course. What do you want me to do?"

"You gather the eggs from the chickens, and I'll get their feed."

"Really?" she asked him quickly. "Mama insists that is her job. She's always loved it and won't let anyone else do it. D.J. has been doing it since they left."

"Today, it's your turn," he said with a smile as she headed in the direction of the chicken coop.

As she began to leave the barn, she heard him chuckle and say, "Uh, Rachel, aren't you forgetting something?"

Seeing her lovely features pucker as she tried to think of what he was talking about, she saw him walk toward her and grab the basket off the wall of the barn.

"Oh, that might help," she told him with a giggle.

As he watched her leave, he felt his heart tug inside. His feelings were growing stronger, not lessening, as he had prayed.

As he reached for the latch on the door, he heard Rachel cry out. Rushing into the coop quickly, he smiled when he saw her holding her finger.

"That bird pecked me," she told him in disgust.

"You have to let them know who is boss. Sometimes they tend to become a little protective of their eggs."

Saying this, he walked over and swiftly moved the hen to the side. Standing back, he grinned and told her, "There you go; yours for the taking."

Placing the eggs in her basket, she had a determined look on her face as she stood in front of the next chicken. Doing exactly as he had done, she quickly pushed the bird aside and gathered the egg.

Her face was filled with accomplishment and she looked beautiful. Her eyes glowed, dimples flashed, and Matthew felt his heart race.

"You were right. I must have shown them I was afraid."

Nodding and grinning, he watched her make short work while he filled their water trough and put corn in the feed bin.

They worked side by side and had all the chores done except milking the two cows. After feeding the horses in the barn, Matthew walked over and replaced the grain can.

"You want to milk one while I milk the other?" he asked her with a grin.

"Do I detect a hint of a challenge in that tone of voice?"

"Of course," he replied as he handed her a bucket.

Setting the bucket in front of the tamest cow, the one she was most familiar with, she watched as he took his position on one of the small stools that were used.

"Ready, set, go," she said and grabbed the udder to milk as fast as possible.

Hearing the steady rhythm of the milk as it flowed into the metal container, she smiled broadly several minutes later and told him, "Finished."

"Already?" he asked in amazement.

"Yes. I believe I won hands down this time."

"You're right," he told her as he sprayed a stream of milk toward her, hitting her in her face.

Startled, she yelped as she jumped back, falling off the small stool and knocking her bucket over in the process. Two cats quickly appeared to lap up the spilled milk.

Standing to his feet, his face held an apologetic look as he said, "I'm sorry, Rachel. I didn't mean to make you fall."

Giggling, she let him help her to her feet. The touch of his hand in hers sent shivers through her, and she quickly looked away to hide the warmth in her face.

"It's all right. I would have done it to you if I had thought of it first," she said as she brushed away the loose straw on her skirt.

Quietness remained for a moment before she asked, "Want to play hooky?"

"What do you mean?" he inquired with a puzzled look.

"Instead of you going back to work on your house, why don't we go fishing? There's this big guy in the pond that I've had my eye on for three weeks and I haven't been able to catch him."

Needing no encouragement to spend time with her, he replied, "Your wish is my command. Let's go."

After gathering fishing poles and the worms she had dug up a few days ago, the two strolled slowly to the water.

"Isn't it gorgeous weather?" she asked as she sat on the bank where it was fairly steep.

"Yes. Is this where you've seen him? It's gonna be tough to pull him in if you actually catch him," he said with uncertainty in his voice.

"I know, but it's where he stays, under the fallen tree." Reaching over, she placed her pole on the ground and pulled off her shoes and then turned slightly to remove her stockings. Grinning at the look on his face, she said, "I have to be ready in case I hook him."

"I'll let you do the hauling in then. I don't want to get wet," he replied. "I've got my boots on, and they don't need to be water-logged, despite how hot it is."

As she expertly baited her hook, she lightly tossed it into the water near the submerged branch. Turning to face him, she saw that he had rested back on the ground with his hands behind his head and was smiling.

"What's so amusing?" she asked.

"You. I was just trying to picture Laura sitting here and putting her own worm on. She'd be squealing by now."

With an easy laugh, she told him, "Yes, she never did quite like all the tomboy activities, did she?"

Turning back to her pole, Matthew continued to observe her profile and the concentration on her face as she waited patiently. He felt like he could lay here forever with Rachel by his side.

A few minutes later, he heard her squeal as she jumped to her feet. "I've got him!" she exclaimed.

Rising quickly, he watched as she tried to maneuver the fish closer.

"Oh, he's stuck on the branches. Here," she told him as she handed him the pole, "hold this and take my hand. I need to untangle him."

"Be careful," he warned. "That ground looks slippery."

"I will, but I'm not about to let him get away now that I've finally caught him."

Feeling the tension on the line, Matthew knew that she was right and that he must be a pretty good size.

Clinging tightly to his hand, she began to descend slowly down the embankment toward the base of the large tree. As her foot touched the tree, it gave way and, falling forward, she clung to Matthew's hand, plunging them both headlong into the cold water.

After they surfaced, sputtering water from their noses and mouths, she saw him climb on the tree and sit for a minute. Afraid to look into his face, she heard him say, "I should have taken my boots off too. Now they're soaked."

Hearing the amusement present, she glanced his way and saw him shaking his head with a smile. He held his hand out to her, assisting her out of the water. He had to pull her strongly because the weight of her wet dress held her down. After resting a moment on the log, he heard her say with disappointment, "And he was such a fine fellow too."

Unable to stop himself, laughter vibrated through him. Reaching out his arm, he grabbed the pole that had wedged between the branches. Feeling the tension still remaining, he handed it to her.

Without thought, as if it was the most natural thing in the world, she leaned over and kissed his cheek before taking the object from him.

Pulling the line to her, she slipped her hand beneath the surface and pulled the fish out of the water by his gaping mouth and turned to smile. Matthew, still in shock over the kiss, couldn't say a word.

"Isn't he a beauty?" Rachel said as she held him up to examine him. "I'll bet he weighs close to three pounds."

Finally gaining his thoughts, Matthew said, "He'll be good in a frying pan, that's for sure."

Swiftly facing him, she said in astonishment, "The frying pan! No, I'm letting him go."

"What!" he exclaimed. "After getting us soaked, you're letting him go?"

She erupted in giggles, and soon he joined her merriment. "Yep, he's too fine to eat for supper. I'll let him live another day."

Without a word, he pulled her to him and hugged her quickly. *Will I ever cease to be amazed by this woman?* he asked himself.

After she set the fish free, he told her, "We'd better start back. The sun is starting to set."

Nodding, she watched as he deftly climbed around various branches and stood on the shoreline, extending his hand for her to grab. Matthew held her pole and the worms while he waited for her to put her socks and shoes on once again.

Walking back toward her house, she said, "Thank you for not getting mad about me pulling you in."

"Nah, a little water never hurt anybody. I still can't believe you released him."

"It's just the thrill of the catch that is the challenge. Wasn't it fun?" she asked impishly.

"Yes, it was fun," *but then everything is fun when I'm with you,* his thoughts reminded him.

Reaching the front steps, she turned to face him.

"Thank you for doing the chores and for the fishing. I enjoyed it."

"You're welcome. I'll be back tomorrow morning if D.J. needs me."

"He did say something about not getting finished in the fields."

"I'll just plan on coming over then. Goodbye."

"Goodbye."

As he turned to leave, he heard her say, "Next time I go fishing, I'll let you know."

"Yes, please do. I need to bring a set of dry clothes with me."

"Oh, and Matthew?"

Turning once again to face her, he replied, "Yes."

"I just thought it would be fair to tell you that I always milk Daisy. She's the easiest and doesn't give as much milk as Dinah."

Seeing her eyes sparkle, he knew whoever married her would be fortunate indeed.

Hearing her chuckle as she went inside, his step felt light despite the heaviness of the wet clothes and water-laden boots he was wearing.

Entering the house, Rachel leaned up against the door and felt her heart beating swiftly as she remembered kissing his cheek. Embarrassment flooded through her as she recalled his shocked expression. *What made me kiss him?* she asked herself. *And why did it feel so right?*

Anticipation filled Matthew as he entered the Parkers' barn the next afternoon.

"Rachel, you up there?" he asked, hoping to hear her voice.

"Yep, I'm here. Why, you want help again today?" she teased him.

"Sure. D.J. is out watering the livestock in the fields. I saw him a few minutes ago."

Climbing with nimbleness down the ladder, she turned and smiled. "Okay, what do you want me to do?"

"If you want to take some hay down to your pa's horse and check on her, that would help. He wants me to keep an eye on her because she's due to have that colt of hers any day."

Nodding, she set off to gather some hay while he went to feed the pigs outside the barn.

A few moments later, he heard her call his name. Climbing over the wooden fence, he saw her run to his side.

"It's the mare. She's down and I think she's in trouble."

Not saying a word, he lightly took her arm and the two moved toward the stall.

Opening the door, Matthew quickly went to the horse's side and bent down, speaking in a soothing tone while feeling her stomach.

"Yes, she's in labor."

"What do we do?"

"They usually have them in the middle of the night, so this is a bit unusual. We'll watch her for a little while and then see if she needs help."

Glad that he was there and seemingly knew what to do in this situation, Rachel walked to the corner after shutting the stall door and sat on the new straw.

After observing for several minutes, he told her, "She's having trouble. I'm going to have to see what's wrong."

Rising to his feet, he asked, "Can you get me some old rags while I fill a bucket with some water?"

"Yes, I'll be right back."

After returning a short time later, she saw that he had rolled up one sleeve on his shirt and went to stand behind the animal.

"Can you sit by her head and talk to her? Stroke her neck to help keep her calm."

Nodding, she went to sit by her father's horse and talked softly to her, rubbing her lightly, all the while observing what Matthew was doing.

He placed his hand inside the horse and was feeling for the position of the colt. He had a look of concentration on his face.

"The foal is just turned the wrong way. I'll have to see if I can grab a hoof and help a bit."

Rachel thought she might feel embarrassed at what he was doing, but she only watched with pride as he helped the animal.

"There, that should do it," he said as a contraction flowed through his arm. Grimacing slightly, he said, "That hurts me, it has to hurt her even more."

"I imagine it does. Having never experienced it myself, I can't say for sure though."

"Someday you will, Rachel," he told her as he washed and dried his arm "And your husband will be beaming with pride as you give him his child."

Hearing him say these words somehow brought pleasure to her instead of embarrassment.

"I hope so," she said quietly.

"I know so," he returned, gazing into her eyes and winking.

Seeing the mare strain once more, Rachel stood to her feet and came to stand near him as they watched a little filly appear. She was brown with white leggings and a patch of white on her face.

"She's beautiful," she whispered as she felt a tear fall down.

Noticing the tear, he said, "Yes, birth is a miracle."

Feeling strong emotion himself, but not because of the birth, he took her arm and led her from the stall.

"We'll let mama and her baby have some time alone now and watch from out here."

Realizing that he still held her arm and neither moving, the two stood and marveled at the wonder before them.

Later, after he had finished chores, Rachel told him, "Thank you for helping Papa's horse."

"You're welcome. I am just glad I was here."

"I am too."

Standing and looking at one another for a second, he cleared his throat before saying, "I'll be back tomorrow after I get a few things done around our place. Goodbye."

"Goodbye."

"Oh, Rachel, I almost forgot. Mark said to tell you he can't make it over tomorrow evening. Something has come up. It'll have to be the day after that."

Walking into the house, she wondered why his words did not bring joy in her heart like the anticipation of his visits used to do.

Matthew, however, knew the exact reason why his words disturbed him; it was the thought of Rachel and Mark spending time together.

As Matthew rode his horse into the drive the next afternoon, he saw Rachel exit the house with a trail of smoke following her. She was coughing and swinging a rag around her face.

"What's the matter?" he asked in amusement.

"Lunch is done," she told him flippantly.

"Think I'll pass."

"Me too," she said as she giggled. "Now I know why Mama stays near the house when she's cooking. I guess I shouldn't have taken that stroll to the creek."

"Just what was lunch anyway?"

"It was supposed to be a pot roast. Well, it is, actually—a very well-done pot roast. Knowing D.J., he won't even notice. That boy eats anything and everything now."

Chuckling at her words, he said, "That sounds like John. He never gets filled up either."

Looking at the house, Rachel told him with disappointment, "Guess you'll have to do the chores by yourself today. I've got a mess to clean up."

"You can't go back in there with it so smoky now, can you?" he remarked slyly, as if making a point.

"No, you're right. I'm sure it'll take a little time to clear out. Probably about as long as it takes to do chores," she added thoughtfully.

"I'm sure of it."

"What do you want me to do?" she asked with excitement.

"The sows are getting ready to have their little ones. We need to separate them into their own pen away from the boars."

"Lead the way," she told him happily.

As they reached the muddy hog pen, Matthew glanced at her dress and said, "You'd better just watch this time. I wouldn't want you to get dirty."

"Nonsense," she told him as she began to remove her shoes and stockings and tucked her dress up, revealing the lower half of her legs. Matthew, trying not to stare, asked, "Is there anything you won't do?"

"I don't know, but I'm willing to try about anything."

Reaching down, she picked up her shoes and placed them near the gate for safekeeping and began to climb the fence.

"If you want to stand here, I'll open the door and see if we can't get one in at a time. Just kind of move them toward me. We'll start with this big one right here."

As she walked slowly, clapping her hands gently, the pregnant sow headed toward Matthew and into the awaiting area.

"That was easy," she told him with a grin.

"Too easy, I'm afraid," he replied in a warning tone.

The next went in with little problem, and they had only one more to go.

As Rachel walked toward the pig, it abruptly swiveled and ran in her direction, knocking her backwards in the mud. With a new resolve, she quickly stood up and took a step toward the beast, pushing it in Matthew's direction. He had not moved since her fall, trying his best to keep laughter from escaping. Her backside was covered with thick, brown mud and her face had a streak splashed across her cheek where she had tried to get a piece of hair out of her eyes. She was a mess and had never looked so delightful.

"You will not get the best of me," she told the large animal with determination.

Grabbing the pig's curly tail, she pulled and yanked until she had her headed Matthew's way. She had noticed the smile plastered on his face and felt one of her own begin to surface. As the pig trotted past him, Rachel's foot stuck in the deep mire and she plopped down once again, but this time she landed on her hands and knees. It was too much for Matthew, and he doubled over in laughter after closing the gate.

With a wicked grin, she asked innocently, "Aren't you going to help me up?"

Holding out a hand, she placed her mud-ridden one in his and tugged him toward her. Catching him off guard, he fell beside her.

As he felt his knees sink into the soft mire, he saw the smirk on her face, and laughter erupted from them both again.

"Things are never dull with you, are they?"

"I don't know what's gotten into me. I only seem to be accident prone when I'm with you," she said as she reached a filthy hand toward his cheek to remove a spot of dirt, only to leave a bigger mark.

"Maybe the house is cleared out enough now to get cleaned up."

"Somehow I think we'd better go to the barn for this job," he said as he helped her to her feet.

Getting buckets of water, they were trying to clean off as best as possible when they saw D.J. enter the barn.

"Don't even ask," Rachel warned him with a stern look.

"Looks like the pigs won," he told both with a silly smile, taking in the muck as he walked toward the house.

"Lunch is on the stove," Rachel told the parting figure with a sly grin.

Turning to face Matthew, the two burst out in laughter once more.

"I think I will bring extra clothes next time. My boots still feel wet from the fishing trip."

"And now they are filled with slop from the pigs," she added.

"Yep," he said, and then asked more seriously, "Can you tell me one thing?"

"If I can."

"What do I need to be prepared for tomorrow?"

"I like to be a woman of mystery, so I guess you won't know until then," she told him lightly as she turned toward the house and awaiting pot roast.

And I can't wait, he told himself as he trudged home to remove his filthy clothes. *Mama is gonna kill me when she sees these.*

Rachel watched anxiously for Matthew the next day after school and was disappointed to see John riding his horse down the lane. Meeting him as he walked up the steps, he said, "Matthew is helping Pa in the woods today and asked me to come help D.J. with the chores."

Trying to hide her disappointment, she went inside to finish the housework and begin their evening meal. The day seemed to pass in an overly long fashion to the young woman. Turning her thoughts to Mark and his visit later that day, she told herself that she was thinking far too much of the wrong brother.

A few minutes after supper, Mark appeared at her door.

"Hello," she told him with a smile as she stood to let him enter.

"Hello, yourself. I'm sorry I've been wrapped up in the evenings and haven't been able to get over to visit."

"That's all right. I have been busy myself cleaning house and making meals as well as doing lessons. I will be glad when Mama gets back," she told him with a sigh.

"What about when you have your own home to take care of?"

"That will be different. At least I think it will."

"Yes, it will be, especially with a husband and family of your own to take care of," he told her as he pulled her to himself and hugged her tightly.

"I've missed you."

"You have, have you?" she asked him, wondering in her mind why she had not missed him as she usually did.

"What did you fix to eat tonight? You don't have any leftovers by chance, do you? I haven't been home yet."

"Yes, I saved some for you. It's just ham and fresh bread. Will that do?"

"That sounds great," he said as he stepped toward the basin to wash his hands.

It was an enjoyable evening. They played checkers and laughed at various stories of the past few days. Mark leaned back in his chair and startled to chuckle to himself when there was a slight pause in conversation.

"Now you have to tell me what is so funny," she told him, a grin appearing on her own face.

"I got called yesterday afternoon to a place far out in the country. It took me over an hour to get there. It was a good thing I took my horse and not the buggy," he said as he remembered the winding trails he'd taken to get to his destination.

"The husband retrieved me saying that his wife was having terrible bouts of indigestion and needed my help."

He paused again as he recalled the moaning and groaning of the woman when he had reached the somewhat rundown house. Kids of various ages were playing in the yard, and their disheveled appearances spoke of their impoverished state.

"Come on now," she chided him gently. "You have to tell me what happened."

"I counted ten kids outside running around when I arrived. I could tell they were poor, but I didn't have much time to check things out further because the husband beckoned me inside to look at his wife. She was lying on her bed in a small room and writhing in agony."

With another chuckle, he continued, "After a quick examination, I found her to be in labor with another child."

"What!" Rachel exclaimed. "And she didn't know it?"

"No, she was a rather stout woman to begin with, and I guess she thought she was going through the change. I know she argued with me for a few minutes, telling me that she had birthed ten babies already and would certainly know if she were birthing another. She told me it was probably the turnip greens she'd eaten last night for supper and all she needed was some medicine. It wasn't until another contraction hit did she realize that I was right. A large male was delivered shortly after to a very contrite, embarrassed new mother. She profusely apologized while I cleaned her up and kept muttering and asking herself how she could have missed it."

"The poor woman. Is the baby healthy?" she asked in sympathy.

"Yes, but somehow I don't think Papa is over the shock," he told her, hearing her laugh with him as they both thought about the situation. "He kept mumbling, 'Another youngin,' to himself."

"That's what makes your job so interesting—not knowing what you will have to deal with from case to case."

"True, it is never dull. Well, I'd better go now. I have to be in Cheyenne for the next week or so. A doctor is going to teach us some new methods for childbirth."

"Sounds like something you'll be able to use frequently."

"Yes, sometimes just a little more knowledge or a new technique can save a life."

Standing to his feet, he followed her to the door. Bending down, he brushed his lips against her forehead and told her, "Bye for now. Thanks for supper."

"Goodbye, be careful."

"Oh, one more thing. Mama told me to tell you that she had a terrible time getting the mud out of Matthew's clothes. What did she mean?"

"It's a long story," she said with laughter, her eyes twinkling.

"When I have the time, I'd like to hear it."

"All right, you'll have to remind me though. It's not something I want to think about too often, especially seeing as how it was my fault."

Reaching up, he lightly stroked her cheek with his finger before turning to leave.

Later, after lying down in bed, the image of Matthew kept flitting through her brain instead of the man who had just left her.

The following day was Saturday, and Rachel had an agenda for the morning. She had just finished hanging clean clothes on the line outside when she heard whistling from a distance. Recognizing the tune, she watched as Matthew came around the bend.

"You doing chores again?" she asked him, hands on her hips and a grin on her face.

"Yep."

With a slight frown on her face, she told him, "I guess you'll have to be on your own while you feed now. I have one more load of clothes to get hung out, and I need to sweep the floors. For some reason," she told him with a snicker, "there seems to be some extra mud on them."

"Now I wonder where that came from?" he asked with a light tone.

Glancing at one of her dresses hanging on the line, she saw smudges of mud that could not be removed and began to laugh. Noticing her look toward the garment, he started to chuckle.

"I'll tell you what, if we get done at the same time, I'd probably let you talk me into riding over to see your house. I've never been there," she told him in a hinting voice.

"Sure. It shouldn't take me too long to finish. I want to check on the mare and her foal and may even let them out in the side lot this morning."

"They are doing great. I've already looked in on them." Turning, she began to walk toward the house and said, "Come get me when you are through."

As Matthew finished milking the last cow, he grabbed the buckets laden with milk and set off toward the house. As he climbed the steps, he heard Rachel singing quietly to herself. She had a sweet, soft voice that would be easy to listen to. He let his mind wander a moment, thinking how one day she would sing to her own children. Mentally shaking his head, he knocked lightly before he entered. He saw her standing with a broom in one hand and a mop in the other.

"I keep finding chunks of mud everywhere. Just when I think I've got them all, another appears," she told him with a grin as she strode toward the pantry to put the items away. "All finished with chores?"

"I am, and you?" he asked.

"Yes, let me grab something from the kitchen and I'll be ready to leave."

Seeing her return with a picnic basket, he raised his eyebrows.

"I thought maybe we could have lunch by the stream on the way to your place since it's about that time."

"That sounds nice. As long as it's not leftover pot roast," he told her with a chuckle.

"Nope, D.J. cleaned the rest of that up two days ago. I told you he'd eat anything. He just trimmed the burnt off, doused it in gravy, and ate it like it was done to perfection."

Following her as she headed toward the door, she quickly stopped and turned, causing him to bump into her from behind. Feeling his warm hands on her arms sent a quickening to her heart.

"I'm sorry," she said as she stepped around him, "I forgot the quilt." Grabbing the item, which had been placed on a nearby chair, she handed it to him and said, "Okay, all ready now."

"Do you want to walk or ride?"

"Since you've got your horse, why don't we fasten the quilt and basket on him and walk. It is a beautiful day out."

After securing both items on his animal, he had to stop himself from taking her hand as they strolled toward the creek to find a place to eat.

"So, what are we having for lunch?"

"Just leftovers. I hope you don't mind. I cooked a ham yesterday and made some potato salad and bread."

"Sounds great. Breakfast seems like it was a long time ago now."

As they reached the creek, they found a small clearing. Rachel spread the quilt while Matthew tied the horse to a tree and carried the basket.

Working in unison, they soon had everything arranged before them. After saying grace, they laughed and ate until almost everything she had packed was gone.

"That was terrific," he told her as he patted his stomach. "Why does food always seem to taste better out in the open?"

"Maybe it wasn't the food so much as you being hungry," she teased.

Or possibly the company, he thought before saying, "Nope, your husband will be a lucky fellow if you cook like this for him every night."

Rachel would continue to wonder why her thoughts turned to the man at her side instead of Mark many times over the days ahead.

Cleaning up and putting things back in the basket, they began to walk toward the house he had been working on.

The long lane brought back many memories for Rachel. With a snicker, she said, "This reminds me of the time after school that we chased the Smiths' cow."

"I'd forgotten that. I know we were all skinned up by the time we finally caught her."

"Yes, she took us through that wild raspberry patch and the thorns really scratched us up."

Reminiscing about the incident caused them both to chuckle at one another before she concluded, "And Mr. Smith wasn't too pleased that we brought home the cow and put her in the field with the others."

"No," he said with a smirk, "especially since it wasn't one of his cows."

The two could still recall the look on the man's face as he checked out his returned cow. He had stood still for a moment and then said, "Why, that's the Sheffields' cow, ain't mine a 'tall."

"He sure could move pretty well for an old man," Rachel added as an afterthought.

"You're right. I've never seen someone get so mad at an animal before as we chased her around the field."

"And I've never seen an animal not want to be caught as bad before," she told him with a smile.

Walking a short distance farther, she began to chuckle again.

"Now what are you thinking about?"

"How about the time we took one of the pumpkins from the Millers' place?"

"Oh, that was bad. Mark and I got a good tanning for doing that."

"We only wanted one, and besides, how did we know that the owner was working in the field then? Papa scolded me over that one too."

"You only got a scolding?" he asked in unbelief.

"Yes, he said that since I had been honest and told him about it, he wouldn't spank me."

"But did you have to tell him that we were there too?" he inquired in a teasing tone.

"Of course. He asked me if I was alone, and I couldn't lie to him. I still can't to this day."

"We did have good times growing up, didn't we?"

"Yes, I hope we all will always be good friends."

No, Rachel, I want to be more than just a good friend to you.

As they turned the corner and the woods opened up, the two-story-frame building stood before them.

"Oh, Matthew, this is beautiful." Her words brought pleasure to him as he watched her eyes take in every detail of the house. "Why haven't I been over here before?"

Because you've been too busy with Mark.

"I love the big porch, and look at all the windows. It will be light and airy, and you'll get a great southern breeze in the spring and fall."

"Yes, I hope so. I purposely put the largest bedroom on that side so that the view could be seen."

Turning, she saw what he meant as the valley stretched before her. The soft, rolling hillside gave her a warm, welcoming feeling, as if this were indeed home.

"It's perfect, absolutely perfect," she beamed at him. "Hurry, I can't wait to see the inside."

Grabbing his hand without thought, she began to drag him in anxiousness to see inside. As they reached the front, he reluctantly released her hand to tie his horse to the small post.

He held the door open while she entered, blue eyes large as she admired his handiwork. He was working on the wood flooring at the moment. The handrail had not been set for the staircase, nor had any of the cabinets been made for the kitchen. The house had an open floor plan, and several rooms were visible as they stood in the foyer.

Watching her walk around, he grinned as she headed toward the fireplace and gently ran her hand admiringly across the oak mantle.

"That fellow gave me fits. I had to sand it many times to get it as smooth as it is."

"It's lovely, well worth your effort now, I'm sure. Imagine sitting here in front of a blazing fire while the snow is falling outside."

Strolling slowly through the house, she remained quiet, in awe of the fine workmanship he had put into the new structure. As he opened the bedroom door, which would one day serve as the main bedroom, he heard her gasp as she walked swiftly to the large window that enhanced the view of the countryside below.

"This is spectacular," she whispered. "One day your wife will be sitting here in a rocking chair holding your baby." Letting her eyes roam across the fields before her, Matthew had to force himself to keep from walking to her side and pulling her close to him.

Turning around to face him, her eyes sparkled as she said, "You thought of everything. You should be very proud of your accomplishment."

"Thank you. I've still got a long way to go."

"And here I tempted you with a picnic when you could have been working. I know you must be eager to live here. I know I would be if it were my home," she replied with sincerity.

Afraid to reply to her last remark, he mentally shook himself before he told her, "Believe me, I need a break every once in awhile. The picnic was a nice diversion." He wanted to add that anytime with her was time well spent, but refrained.

"Let's go downstairs. I want you to tell me where all the cabinets will be placed in the kitchen. I can just imagine where everything should go."

"Maybe you should tell me then. I'm the man here, remember? I think I need a woman's advice on these things."

"I'm sure your mother is more than willing to give her opinions."

"Actually, all she says is, 'It's your house, son. Put them where you like.'"

"I can hear her saying that. We are both fortunate to have such wonderful parents."

"Yes, you're right. Okay, come on. Let's go downstairs and you can tell me what you think."

Following her down the stairs, he watched her move in deep thought for several moments, surveying the large kitchen. Her brow wrinkled, she began to disclose where she would arrange things. Shaking his head from side to side, she chuckled and said, "I guess you don't agree."

"It's remarkable. You've placed things just as I had imagined them to be."

"Really? Then we both can't be wrong," she said with a bright grin. "I love all the wood you have throughout. Those beams on the sides of the doorway in the living area add a touch of elegance."

"I don't know if I'd go so far as to say elegant, but I do like wood, especially oak."

"It fits in with the style and the setting here. You, Matthew O'Malley, have done a terrific job."

"Thank you, Miss Parker," he replied with a smile, glad that she approved.

"Well, I've kept you long enough, so I guess we should go. I want to hitch up the wagon and take Hannah for a ride in a little while. I thought I'd take her to the lake and let her wade to release some of that energy. It will also give your parents a little break."

Throughout the remainder of the day, all Rachel could think about was Matthew's house, wondering who would sit on that swing by him and hold his child one day.

Matthew, his mind frequently recalling what she had said, prayed in his heart that it would be her who would adorn his house with her presence.

Mark and Rachel were on their way to town. He had asked her to dinner at the local restaurant on this particular Saturday evening.

"Have you heard from your parents yet?" he asked.

"Yes, they will be home in a few days and Mama said she'd tell us all about it then. She said her uncle had passed away but God had been so good in ways she never imagined. She said she'd explain in detail when they got back home. I have missed them."

"I can't imagine someone wanting to go back to face a man who had abused them."

"No, me either. But Mama insists that God wants her there. I'm just glad that Papa is with her. I don't worry so much with him by her side."

Pulling into the small town, Mark parked the team next to the establishment and assisted her down.

"I haven't been here in a long time," she said, taking in the hustle and bustle of the quaint restaurant.

"I eat here almost every day," he told her with a grin.

She believed it when a young, attractive waitress came to take their order, telling him, "Hi, Doc. What will it be today?"

Knowing that she should be jealous of the welcoming greeting, Rachel wondered why it bothered her so little.

"I think I'll try the meatloaf today. How about you, Rachel?" he asked.

"Yes, that sounds fine to me," she replied, watching the young woman place a hand on his shoulder in an overly friendly fashion before saying, "That's what you order about three times a week."

"I like it," he said as he watched her walk away.

"She's friendly," Rachel stated flatly as he turned his smiling face her way.

"Yes, that's Lisa. She's been working here for about a month now," he told her in a nonchalant voice. "So, tell me, how you are making out without your folks?" he asked.

"Fine. Hannah is missing them. I asked your mama if she needed to come home yet, and she told me no. I hope she's being honest with me."

"Whenever I see them, they are doing little projects together. Mama is thoroughly enjoying having a little girl around again. She said that Hannah reminds her of Laura when she was young."

"I've never thought about it, but she's right. They both have inquisitive minds and would rather stay inside than outside. I pop over every day to spend some time with her, but she's not in any hurry to come back and stay with us. I think she is smitten with one of the puppies and has hopes of bringing it home with her."

"Yes, she has taken a fancy to one of them and has even talked Mama into letting it come in the house for short periods of time."

"She's gonna be spoiled rotten by the time my parents return home."

"Probably," he added with a smile that lit his already handsome face.

After the meal, they took a leisurely ride around the lake. The moon was bright and the reflection off the water made for a romantic setting. Feeling him place his arm around her shoulders, she leaned her head against him, relishing the clean smell of soap.

"This is nice," he told her as he placed a kiss on the top of her head.

"Yes, it is. It seems like we never get to do things like this anymore."

"I know. I'm sorry. But now that I'm the assistant, I get most, if not all, of the house calls."

"I understand. So we'll just enjoy the moments as we get them."

On the way home, Rachel's mind kept returning to the brother of the man near her, wondering what he was doing at the moment. Realizing that she thought far too much of him, she snuggled up closer to Mark and felt him squeeze her shoulder as he hugged her tightly.

Chapter Five

The three adults climbed aboard the train in a somewhat frazzled frame of mind. It had been an extremely hectic time back in Pinebluff and all were tired, not only emotionally, but physically.

"I don't know about you two," Tucker's mother offered as they sat in the seats, "but I do believe I will be able to sleep for several hours, despite sitting straight up and the noise that surrounds us."

Smiling at his mother, Tucker told her, "That does sound pretty tempting. Maybe I should sit in the middle so you can use me as a pillow."

"No, that won't be necessary. That's why I brought an extra blanket with me, so that I can cuddle up and rest. You hold your sweet wife in your arms. That is as it should be," she told them with a smile directed toward McKenna.

Placing a hand on the older woman's arm, McKenna told her, "I have missed you and am so happy you are coming back."

"Me, too, honey. I don't know why I waited so long now."

"We have been praying for quite a few years, Mama," Tucker told her, "but like you said, God's timing is not always ours."

Turning to look out the window as the train began its motion, his mother watched with a small measure of sadness, knowing that she was leaving a part of her past behind her. With a prayer in her heart and peace in her mind, she knew that she was doing what God wanted her to do. She also knew that He would bless her because of the step of faith she was taking. She was not a person who liked change but was ready for one in her life now; especially since she'd be close to her family once again.

Feeling the gentle lull as mile after mile passed, the threesome all felt the busyness catch up with them and tried to get as comfortable as possible to try and sleep.

Waking up later, Tucker grinned as he watched his wife and mother sleeping. Trying to adjust his arm to relieve the tingling in it, memories from the past filtered through his mind as he recalled their long wagon trip out west and how McKenna had frequently fallen asleep on him. He could still see it as if it were yesterday. How bashful and uncertain McKenna was of him during their early days on the trail. Both were afraid of love for different reasons; he, because he didn't want to betray his first wife by being attracted to someone else; McKenna because of the mistrust from her abusive past. He'd slowly gained her trust and soon love followed.

As McKenna lay unconscious from falling and hitting her head and her eventual kidnapping, the hardships of the long trip caused the couple to rely on one another, and their love blossomed. He was indeed a lucky man to have her by his side.

The object of his thoughts opened her eyes and smiled at him.

"Hello," he whispered.

"Hello. Did I sleep too long?"

"No, only about an hour. We still have a long way to go."

"Good," she told him as she closed her eyes once again and burrowed her cheek against his shoulder. Tucker leaned over and planted a kiss on the top of her head, resting it lightly there for a moment.

The next day, as the train pulled into the small station at Cheyenne, the three were startled to see all of the family waiting eagerly for their return. Not only the children, but all of the O'Malleys were there to greet them.

After hugs and welcome backs, Genie told them, "I know you are tired from the trip. Go home and rest and come to our house for supper this evening."

On the way to their home to unpack, McKenna smiled a motherly smile as she thought about Mark standing with his arm around Rachel. She couldn't wait to find out the latest development concerning the couple. From the looks of things before they'd left, she figured there might be a wedding in the near future.

"Mama," Tucker asked his mother in shock, "how can you want to stay in the soddy when you can live here with us?"

"I want to live by myself. I know you need to be alone as a family. I am a very independent woman and not accustomed to having others around. I will enjoy every moment in the quaint, little place."

"All except the dirt floors," McKenna added with amusement.

"I am going to start building you a house next to ours this fall as soon as the cattle are branded and rounded up to be sold," her son told her in a no-nonsense voice.

"All right, if you insist. But I'm really in no hurry," she said as she began to carry her bags in the direction of the small home built in the side of the hill. The rest of her belongings were to be shipped within the next week.

"Let me get you some clean linens for the bed at least," McKenna told the somewhat persistent woman as she went inside.

"Thank you, dear, that would be nice," Mrs. Parker replied with a grateful smile.

Rachel and Mark were taking a leisurely stroll near the stream. The weather would be turning cooler, so they had decided they'd better get in another day of fishing. With school under way, Rachel was busy during the weekdays.

Holding his arm lightly, Rachel chuckled as she thought of her first fishing experience with her father.

"He knew I would be disappointed if I didn't catch anything, so he put one of his fish on my hook while my mother called my attention to something else," she told him with a smile.

"We are lucky. We have terrific parents. They are firm in their convictions for God, and we've all been blessed because of it. We are very fortunate in the upbringing we've had. I am more aware of that now than ever when I make house calls. Many do not have God in their lives, and it is very evident. Godly parents are very important."

"You're right, although Mama had a rough time for several years after her mother died.

"Yes, but God took something bad and brought something good from it."

"Yes, just like the verse in Romans 8:28 tells us, 'And we know that all things work together for good to those that love God, to them who are called according to His purpose.'"

"And I sure am glad He does that."

"Me too," Rachel stated softly, dwelling for a moment on the things her mama had told her about her earlier life with her uncle.

As they spent the next few moments searching for a place to fish, she asked," "Isn't Mrs. Connor expecting a baby soon?"

"Yes, in the next week or so. Why?"

"I was wondering if you'd let me watch you deliver it? The way Papa talks, there wasn't much time when Mama went into labor with Hannah, and I would like to have an idea of what to do if I'm there alone."

Wrinkling his brow, he told her, "I don't see why not. It is her fourth baby, and she's had no problems in the past. When I see her again, I'll ask her if it would be all right."

"Thank you," she told him.

Wrapping his own hand over hers, he said, "You're welcome. It might come in handy in the future anyway; especially when we have our own."

Feeling the redness creep up into her cheeks, she was glad that he had returned his attention to putting the worm on his hook.

The following Saturday, Rachel answered the door and found Mark standing outside with a smile.

"Are you ready?" he asked lightly.

"Ready for what?" she returned.

"To see a baby born, of course. The Connors' son just came and told me his mama is in 'pain something awful,' I believe were his exact words."

"Yes, let me tell Mama," she told him, excitement flowing through her.

As he helped her into the wagon, she asked, "Are you sure Mrs. Connor doesn't mind?"

"No, she said it would be fine. She did laugh and tell me that if it had been Matthew or John wanting to be there, she'd have to reconsider."

Warmth quickly spread into her at the thought of a man watching her give birth.

Noticing her discomfort, he smiled and asked, "Did I embarrass you?"

"Yes, I was just imagining another man watching me during that private time in my life."

"What about me assisting?" he asked in seriousness.

"Mmm…I don't know," not quite knowing how to reply to his question.

"I am a doctor, you know. I'd like to be more than just your doctor helping you though," he told her in a hinting tone.

"And what other capacity might that be?" she asked with bated breath, almost afraid of the answer for some reason.

"I'd like to be your husband."

Turning to face her, he told her quietly, "I was going to wait and say something later, but since the subject came up on its own, would you consider being my wife?"

I knew it was only a matter of time before the topic arose. Shouldn't my heart be racing at the prospect of getting married? Should I be excited, joyous? Shouldn't I not be able to wait to become united with the love of my life? Maybe that is a make-believe world, and this is the real world. Is this all there is to receiving a marriage proposal?

"Well…" he prompted.

"I think I've always loved you," she returned softly.

Satisfied with her answer, he placed an arm around her and hugged her. "And I think I've always loved you." Leaning over, he kissed her cheek tenderly.

Both were wrapped up in their own thoughts as they pulled into the Connor residence a few minutes later.

Mr. Connor opened the door to greet them, telling them anxiously, "She's a-wailin' in the bedroom. Don't think it's gonna be too much longer now the way she's a-carryin' on."

Hiding the disappointment she was feeling from the man's lack of sympathy for his hurting wife, Rachel followed Mark into the house and entered the bedroom.

"Oh, Doctor," the laboring woman spoke to him as she saw him near the bed, "the pains are something fierce. I'm glad you are here."

"This is Rachel," he introduced her quickly, moving to the basin to wash his hands. "Let's just see how far along you are."

As Rachel observed, her face flaming red, she saw Mark stand near the woman's feet and examine her in a professional manner.

"I can see the baby's head now, so you're getting close. Do you feel like you should be pushing?"

"No, not yet, but I feel some pressure something awful."

"That's good. You tell me when you feel the urge to push, and we'll get this little one delivered."

When another contraction began, the woman did indeed do as her husband had told them—she wailed. In fact, Rachel had never heard anyone yell and carry on in such a pitiful manner and with such force.

"I need to push now," she told him a short time later.

"All right, when you feel the next pain, you bear down and push until I tell you to stop."

Rachel was relieved to note that instead of wailing, Mrs. Connor concentrated on delivering the baby. She watched in amazement as a small head appeared, and then shoulders, and finally little legs slid out from the woman's body. She felt tears run down her cheeks at the miracle she had witnessed. Watching Mark clean the baby's mouth and nose, she listened as the newborn started to wail just like his mother, and she smiled to herself. She saw Mark clamp and cut the cord and then hand the infant to his mother. She was so overcome with emotion that she could not have spoken a word.

Mark, noticing her quietness, looked with understanding toward her before whispering, "It's incredible, isn't it?"

Nodding her head, the tears continued to gather and fall as she watched the little one turn his face to listen to his mother's voice.

While Mark cleaned up Mrs. Connor, she stood by the woman and watched as she bonded with the new little boy, touching his cheek gently with her fingers.

"Soon you'll be having one of your own, dearie," she told Rachel.

"Oh, but I'm not even married yet."

"Somehow I don't think it will be long though, will it?" the astute woman asked as she looked in Mark's direction.

"No, I guess not," she replied quietly.

On the ride home, Mark broke the silence by asking, "What did you think of your first birthing?"

"I think it's the most wonderful, glorious, frightening experience I've ever witnessed."

"That about says it all, I'd say," he said with a grin.

"I'm sorry I was so emotional, but it is indeed a gift from God."

"Yes, I'm not the crying kind, and it's a good thing or I'd be wailing with the mothers at each birth."

"Speaking of wailing, her husband was right, she did," she told him with amusement.

"At least it was quick this time. With the last baby, Dr. Hill warned me that he had to listen to that for over two hours."

Hearing his words brought laughter from her lips.

"You enjoy it though, don't you?"

"I love it. I can actually help people and improve their quality of life. And when a new baby is delivered safely, it is an added bonus."

"Yes, it's definitely your calling."

"And what is your calling, Miss Parker?" he asked with a smile.

"I guess to be a wife and a mother," she returned as she wrapped her arm snuggly into his.

"Fine choice, I think," he told her as he placed a kiss on the top of her head.

"The annual dance is Saturday evening at the school. I don't suppose you'd want to go with me, would you?"

"I might, if you ask me nice," she teased him.

"Just pray that I don't get any calls that evening. I'm afraid that's what happens when being courted by a doctor."

"Yes, I have noticed that we tend to miss quite a few things, but I don't mind," she told him quickly.

"Great, I'll pick you up around six o'clock or so."

As he walked her to the door, he thought about kissing her on her lips, but she seemed shy all of a sudden and he resisted the temptation.

"Thank you for taking me today."

"You're welcome. Any time you want to go with me, just ask. I kind of like the company, especially when it's my fiancée."

"Oh, that's right," she replied.

"I'll come early Saturday and ask your father for your hand, if it's all right with you."

"Yes," she told him, uncertainty filling her mind, "that will be fine."

"Goodbye until then."

"Goodbye."

Entering her room a few minutes later, she sat on the bed and thought about the day's events. Although she had wanted to die in shame while watching such an intimate occurrence, she couldn't tear her eyes away from the actual birth. *Someday,* she thought, *I will be sharing that with Mark, and he'll be delivering our own child.* As she sat there for a moment, she wondered again why this didn't bring her happiness and excitement. She did love him. They had grown up together and were best friends. Why, then, did she have such emptiness inside her?

Shaking her head to clear her mind, she washed her face and hands in the small basin that stood on her dresser and walked to the kitchen to assist her mama with supper.

"What can I do to help?" she asked as she stood near her mother at the table.

"You can peel potatoes, if you'd like," McKenna told her daughter.

After several minutes of silence, Rachel asked her mother, "Mama, how did you know that you wanted to marry Papa?"

"It was different for us than most couples," she returned with a smile. "I really didn't have much choice. I had asked God to provide a way, and your papa was that way."

"Did you love him right away?"

"It didn't take long for me to know that I wanted to spend the rest of my life with him."

Watching the seriousness on her daughter's face, doubts began to rise in McKenna's mind about her relationship with Mark. There was no glow or excitement about her, only a look of uncertainty.

Maybe we pushed them together, and they are doing what they think we all expect. I need to pray about them more often, that their eyes might be opened to what You want for them, Father.

Saturday arrived, and Rachel waited anxiously for Mark to retrieve her for the dance. It was held twice a year for the younger folks and was a great time of fellowship and entertainment. Pressing her hands down the length of her dress to make sure there were no wrinkles, she smiled as she let them linger a moment to feel the softness of the material. Her Mama had made her a new outfit to wear, and the royal blue color highlighted the blonde, curling hair and blue eyes. She had left her hair down, only pulling back a small section to one side. Hearing a knock a moment later, she walked to the front door. Opening it, she saw appreciation on the young doctor's face as he took in her appearance.

"You will be the most beautiful girl there tonight," he told her as he emitted a soft whistle.

"Why, thank you, Doctor O'Malley," she told him with a grin. "Do you like my dress? Mama just finished it this afternoon."

"Definitely, you look terrific. Is your father around?" he asked with a knowing grin.

"Yes, I think he's in the pantry."

"Good, I'll be right back."

Seeing the questioning look on her mother's face as he passed by her, she pulled Rachel into the closest bedroom and shut the door.

"Is Mark going to talk to your father for any particular reason?"

"Now, Mama, you know what he's asking."

"And this is what you want?" she prodded.

Seeing her daughter's slight hesitation filled her mother with doubt. Finally, she heard her say, "Yes, it is."

"Make sure, Rachel, that he is the right one for you."

Hearing her mother say those words brought a flush to her face. How could she know about her own reservations concerning the engagement?

Hearing her name called, she swiftly turned and opened the door to the man she was going to one day marry.

"Are you ready?" he asked with a smile.

Nodding her head, she told him, "Whenever you are." As she turned around to tell her mother goodbye, she couldn't help but notice the questioning look present on her face.

As Mark assisted her into the wagon, he felt himself lucky to be with her.

"Did everything go all right with Papa?"

"Yes, he said he'd been waiting for a visit."

They both knew that their families had anticipated such an announcement for quite some time and would not be surprised when it came.

"What did you do today?" she asked as he turned the buggy around to start down the road.

"No house calls; only a few minor check-ups at the clinic. You know, sniffles and such."

"So it was an easy day for you. That's good."

"Yes, it gave me a chance to go through our inventory and order the things we are low on."

"I'll keep my fingers crossed that tonight will be as slow."

"It would be nice for a change to be able to stay until an event is over."

Chuckling at a past memory, he asked, "Do you remember the first time we danced together?"

"How could I ever forget that? I distinctly recall having hit a growth spurt that summer and was several inches taller than you."

"My father made me ask you. I didn't even know how to dance."

"I know. You were all over my feet."

Shaking her head as she thought about the event, she told him, "I do hope you've improved since then."

"If I haven't, just pretend that I have. My pride might suffer a blow if you tell me I'm still as bad."

"All right. I won't say a word. But if you see me grimace while we're dancing, you'll know things haven't changed," she told him.

"At least I'll be the taller one this time."

"True," she told him, thinking of the several inches that separated them now.

As they pulled up in front of the school, several wagons and horses were already present. Helping her from the buggy, he tied the horse to a nearby hitching post, and the couple made their way inside the festive atmosphere.

Spotting the table on the side that was already adorned with food of various kinds, Mark told her, "I'm glad the parents supplied us with something to eat. I haven't had anything since breakfast and am starving."

"We'd better make that our top priority then," she returned as she took his hand and led him in the direction of the food.

After eating and dancing several dances, the room began to fill up with couples of all ages. Amidst the laughter and music, the noise was beginning to give Rachel a headache.

"Do you think we could take a quick break and get a breath of fresh air for a minute?"

"Of course," he told her as he led her toward the doors.

Just as they reached the doors, a small boy entered and grabbed Mark's arm.

"Doc!" he exclaimed in an urgent tone. "Papa's cut himself and is bleeding like a stuffed pig all over the place. He's a holdin' a rag over it to stop the blood, but Mama thinks he needs some stitching."

Turning to look with an apologetic face, she asked, "Do you want me to come with you?"

"My word, no. I wouldn't want that new dress spoiled, and besides, I don't know how long it will take." With a thoughtful look on his face, he continued, "Wait right here. I've got an idea."

Entering the crowded room, he walked toward his oldest brother and pulled him aside.

"I need you to do me a favor. The McRoy boy just came to get me. Seems his papa cut himself. I just need you to stay with Rachel and dance a few dances with her and then take her home."

"I can't. I rode my horse here," Matthew told him, knowing in his heart that being near her was making things worse for him.

"That's no problem. I'll take your horse on my call, and you take the buggy."

Without further talk, Mark told him thanks over his shoulder and moved toward where Rachel was standing.

"Matthew is going to stay and keep you company and then take you home."

"There's no need of that. He doesn't want to have to entertain me," she told him. She was unaware that the object of the discussion was standing behind her until she heard, "It's all right, Rachel. I really don't mind and wasn't planning on staying very much longer anyway."

"Well… she hesitated slightly before Mark said, "Terrific. Thanks, Matthew."

Leaning over to kiss her cheek, he told them both goodbye and ran to get his bag out of the buggy before hurrying to Matthew's horse.

"I'm sorry," her new date told her.

"For what? It's not your fault that he's been called away. I'm the one who is sorry you have to be with me when you could be in there with your date."

"I didn't bring anyone, so it's no problem."

"Oh," she replied, wondering why his words seemed to make her feel better.

"Do you want to dance some more or for me to just take you home?"

"I really don't want to go back in there. All the noise has given me a headache."

Her words gave him a quick moment of relief. He didn't know if he was strong enough to hold her in his arms and then let her go.

"How 'bout we take the long way back to your place and see if the night air will help you feel better?"

"That does sound nice," she told him in thankfulness.

Walking down the steps, she felt his light touch against her bare arm and it sent a small shiver up to her heart.

Lord, she asked herself, *what was that all about? This is my fiancé's brother.*

Matthew, lifting her up quickly into the buggy, smelled the fresh scent of lilac as he placed her in the seat.

Keep your head now, he reminded himself.

After climbing in to sit beside her, she glanced at his profile to remind herself who she was sitting next to. Instead of helping her relax, she noticed the strong, firm jaw and the blonde lashes that curled up to enhance his sky blue eyes. His hair shone from the moon above and gave it a warm, honey color.

Feeling her gaze upon him, he shifted to stare into her face. He wasn't sure what she was seeing, but he definitely saw a very enticing woman; a woman with whom he was having difficulty keeping his hands off at the moment.

Clearing his throat, he quickly turned his attention to the horse. He had almost leaned over to kiss her, and he knew that was not acceptable.

"Do you want to drive past the lake or by the orchard?"

"Can we go by the lake?" she asked. "It's such a warm night out, and with the moon shining so brightly, it must be breathtaking."

"The lake it is then," he told her as he lightly slapped the reins against the horse to head in that direction.

Words seemed unnecessary to the couple; there was a comfortable silence that permeated through both of them, a feeling of oneness that neither could explain.

As they came to the edge of the lake, Matthew stopped the horse and pulled back on the brake to hold the buggy in place.

"Want to take a walk?" he asked invitingly, his heart telling him one thing while his mind told him another.

"Can we?"

"Sure, don't see why not."

Coming around to her side, he lifted her out of the wagon, smelling the wonderful, clean fragrance of her hair. He wanted to run his fingers through the long, silky tresses and had to fight the urge to stop himself.

Rachel, grasping his shoulders, could only think of the rippling muscles that could be felt through his shirt.

"Isn't this gorgeous," she said to cover her discomfort as she turned to gaze at the beautiful scene before them.

"Yes, God's creation."

"I don't suppose you'd want to be a kid again, would you?" he asked suggestively.

"What did you have in mind?"

"Let's take our shoes and socks off and wade in the shallow part."

Without hesitation, he saw her run toward the lake, laughter filling the air. Watching her long hair bouncing on her shoulders and hearing her contagious giggle, he thought, *Maybe this wasn't such a great idea after all.*

Walking closer, he saw her slip her shoes off and turn her back to him before rolling down her stockings. Sitting down beside her, he began to do the same.

"Come on, hurry," she told him as she pulled up her dress to reveal shapely legs before stepping into the cold water.

"I'm right behind you."

They talked and reminisced for over an hour before Rachel said, "I think it's time to get out. I can't feel my toes anymore."

"You're right. But it has been fun."

It was wonderful, almost slipped out before she caught herself.

"Yes, it has. Better than a dance, that's for sure."

As they made their way to where their shoes and socks were, he told her, "We'd better dry off a bit before we put them on," hoping to have the night last a little longer.

"Yes, that's probably a good idea."

Sitting side by side on the bank, their shoulders touched. Both were aware and neither wanted to move.

"Thank you for the evening," she told him softly.

"You're welcome. The pleasure has been all mine. Did it help your headache?"

Frowning slightly to see if the pain was still there, she turned a beaming face to him and said, "Yes, it's gone. I guess when you act like a child, there's no place for aches and pains."

Sitting beside one another in a comfortable silence, a warm, cozy feeling passed through Rachel. Realizing that she could stay next to him forever, knowing it was wrong, she hastily began putting her stockings back on. Sensing her change in mood, Matthew did the same.

Standing quickly to her feet, she walked to the buggy and began to climb in. Suddenly, she felt two strong arms around her as he lifted her easily onto the seat.

"Thank you," she told him in slight embarrassment.

"You're welcome, for everything."

The ride to her house was quiet. Matthew was having an extremely difficult time keeping his arm from pulling her closer to him.

As they reached her house, he climbed down quickly and came to her side. Reaching for her once again, he set her slowly to the ground, keeping his arms around her. Bending down, he kissed her gently on her cheek.

"Matthew, you mustn't," her mouth told him while her eyes seemed to encourage him. Spotting the bewildered look on his face, she continued, "You need to know that Mark and I became engaged this week."

Taking a step back, he looked into her eyes and felt the cold blow of her words pierce his heart and shatter his dreams.

"I'm sorry," he whispered. "I hadn't heard."

"No one knows. He asked my father tonight for my hand."

"Congratulations then, to you both," he told her stiffly. "I'd better be going now, it's getting late."

"Yes, all right. Thank you for the visit to the lake and the ride home," she told him quietly, feeling a sudden tightening in her chest.

"You're welcome. Goodbye, Rachel."

"Goodbye," she replied, feeling as if the world had suddenly changed.

The ride home was a long, bleak one for Matthew. He had been so certain that she was beginning to return his feelings tonight that he had felt a surge of happiness for the first time in many years. Her parting words, however, dashed any hope of a life together. There would be no days of sitting by the fire while it snowed or of rocking his child in their room. She now belonged to another man…and that man happened to be his brother.

How could I be so wrong, Lord? he would ask himself repeatedly for many days to come.

As Rachel tossed and turned throughout the night, thoughts of her impending marriage kept surfacing in her mind. *I do love Mark*, she told herself repeatedly. *I have committed myself to him and will go through with this marriage. After all, Mama and Papa began as friends and grew to love each other. And he is such a good man. He will make me a fine husband. I wouldn't hurt him for the world.*

With new resolve, she punched her pillow lightly and nestled down deeper into it. She would talk to her mama tomorrow about wedding plans and think no more of Matthew O'Malley. Her future was with Mark, and that was where it would remain. She would not break a promise made no matter what her wayward heart was telling her. She would not dishonor the Parker name in any way, even though she knew deep within her that she was in love with Matthew O'Malley. A kind of love she had always dreamed she would have someday; the kind that seemingly was not to be. Rachel had always loved discovering new things as a child. This discovery, however, was one that she had not counted on, nor enjoyed.

Rachel approached her mother with a small smile.

"What is on your mind?" McKenna asked as her daughter sat next to her at the kitchen table.

"Will you make my wedding dress?" she asked.

"I was wondering when we were going to get started on it. Actually, I already have the material and want to show it to you to see what you think."

Rising to their feet, the two women went into the bedroom and walked toward the small chest in the corner. Opening it up, Rachel fell in love with the beautiful satin material immediately. Reaching over to touch it tentatively, she said, "This is so beautiful. When did you get it?"

"I found it in Pinebluff, and it was such a good price that I couldn't resist."

Watching her daughter lift the lovely piece from the chest, she asked, "Do you have a particular style in mind?"

"Yes, let me get a piece of paper and try to draw it so you can see what I'd like."

"I'm just an average seamstress, remember? Don't get too fancy."

"No, Mama. It's a simple style, similar to the dress you made me for the dance."

"That's a relief. Now that pattern I can do."

As the two women discussed not only the dress, they decided on a small reception to follow the ceremony. Rachel felt a hollowness in her heart but was determined to fill it with the love of her future husband.

I've just been spending far too much time with Matthew. From now on, I will be by Mark's side.

Chapter Six

School was in full swing, and Rachel was getting to know her students and their individual needs. She did love teaching them. The drawback was that several of the older boys seemed to be a little difficult at times; especially one by the name of Jimmy Richardson. He was large for his fifteen years of age. His gaze seemed to travel everywhere she went. When she would glance up from her lesson, she would lock her eyes with his and he would smile a small, somewhat leering smile. She felt very uncomfortable but, as of yet, had not said anything about it to anyone. She would often remind herself that he was only a child, almost the same age as her brother.

Following recess later that afternoon, she returned from the outhouse to find him sitting nearby on a large rock. He never said a word, but she could feel his eyes on her as she walked rather swiftly to the school.

The hair on the back of her neck stood up and her palms became sweaty from nervousness. She was going to have to tell someone about him soon. Something was not right about the way the boy watched her constantly.

All through supper that next evening, McKenna stole glances at her daughter and future son-in-law as they conversed amongst themselves. They did make an attractive couple. Halfway through their meal, a loud knock echoed at the door and Tucker went to answer it. Standing before him was the Tyler boy, who spoke in a jumbled fashion. "It's Pa," he told them as they tried to calm him down so they could understand. "He fell on the plow in the barn and he 'bout cut his arm off."

Hearing these words, Mark rose abruptly and turned to face Rachel as he said, "I know you don't like blood, but could you come with me to help?"

Fear rising inside her, she nodded her head in a somewhat numb state and stood to follow him.

"I don't know how long we'll be. Please pray," he beseeched her family as they left.

Pulling the wagon to a standstill in front of the small log cabin, Rachel felt like a cold hand had been placed on her spine as she heard the agonizing moans coming from inside. Not knowing what to expect, she prayed that God would be with Mark and herself to help the poor man.

Stepping inside, Mark felt his heart sink when he saw how bad it was.

"Get me clean rags and some cold water, quickly," he told the wife, who seemed unable to move as she watched her husband writhing in pain. Walking swiftly toward the bed, he saw that the man's arm was severed almost completely off. Thankfully the object he had fallen on had somehow sealed off the blood flow that could have cost him his life very swiftly. Having the woman clear off the table, he assisted the man onto it. He saw her slip into a bedroom, her hand to her mouth in distress.

Rachel, feeling the vile taste of acid in her throat, tried to swallow several times. Mark beckoned her to the side of the room and told her quietly, "I'll have to amputate his arm. I have no other option if he is to survive."

Nodding in understanding, he continued, "I need you to help if you can. I'll put some chloroform on a rag, and you try to keep him comfortable without putting him completely under. Can you do this, Rachel?"

"I'll try," she whispered with anxiety in her voice.

Watching him roll up his sleeves as he walked toward the basin to wash his hands, he then reached for his bag. With a grim face, he began the task at hand.

Rachel tried to look elsewhere while he worked, but she felt her eyes drawn to the surgery. At one point she quickly covered her mouth and rushed outside, returning a few moments later to assist again. After more than an hour of intense suturing and cutting, Mark straightened up and moved his head from side to side with his eyes closed, flexing weary muscles. He was getting tired, but things were proceeding well.

After he was finished, he looked to Rachel and smiled slightly, telling her, "You did wonderfully."

"Are you through?" she asked, hoping that he was.

"Yes, we'll need to watch him closely for a while though."

Nodding her head, she felt a yawn break through and heard Mark say, "Let's see if there is somewhere you can rest." Walking in the direction of one of the bedrooms, he knocked and watched as the wife's worried face appeared.

"It's over, Mrs. Tyler, and your husband is resting. Is there somewhere that Rachel can lie down?"

"It will have to be with the two little ones," she told him as she led her to a small room at the side of the kitchen.

Rachel followed wearily, not caring where she would be. Seeing the bed in the corner and the two sleeping children, she watched as the mother gently moved them closer to one another and stood back for Rachel to climb in. Feeling the somewhat lumpy bedding beneath her, she shifted and closed her eyes, only to vividly recall the past few hours. With her mind turned to God, she began to pray and drifted off to sleep, her prayers being sent heavenward.

A hand shook her gently, and she opened her eyes. Seeing the smiling face of Mark standing above her, she recalled where she was and why.

"Is Mr. Tyler all right?"

"At the moment, yes. I will take you home and then come back. Your family is probably wondering what has happened."

Shifting her feet out from under the quilt, she rose and stretched. Glancing out the window, she saw that it was just beginning to become light outside.

Mark, watching the woman in front of him, thought, *She is truly remarkable, God. Thank You for bringing her into my life. She will be a help meet to me in all areas.*

"Are you tired?" he asked with concern.

"No, I'm not. How long did you stay up with Mr. Tyler?"

"I dozed off in the chair as I sat next to him. I had to give him something for pain several times. At least the bleeding has stopped, and he's awake this morning."

"Did you tell him what you did?" she asked quietly.

"Yes, he's still in shock, though, and probably won't fully realize what's been done until later. That's why I need to be here to help his family."

"You are a good person, Dr. O'Malley," she told him proudly.

"So are you, Miss Parker," he replied as he led her from the small room.

Several weeks later, long after the Parkers had turned in for the night, sounds could be heard echoing over the valley.

The church bells were ringing. Tucker, waking up to the sound, sat up in bed quickly. As he reached for his clothes, McKenna asked sleepily, "What is it?"

"I hear the bells."

Understanding that this meant someone was in some sort of trouble, she began to rise with him.

"No, love. You stay here. I'll get D.J. and Rachel to go with me. I don't want to take any chances with you now," he told her as he reached a hand out and lightly touched the small swell of her stomach.

Watching him dress, she saw him head toward their children's respective rooms. After the length of several minutes, the three exited the house to help those in need. Grabbing a light shawl, McKenna slipped it around her shoulders and climbed out of bed herself. If she couldn't help physically, she could pray. Walking toward the rocking chair near the cold fireplace, she beseeched God for His protection and guidance for whoever needed it. Little did she know that she was praying for her own daughter.

The smoke and bright yellow glow could be seen in the distance as it reached upward into the sky. Worry clouded Tucker's face as he realized what had happened. They had been in a drought lately and the fields were extremely dry. A small spark could cause a fire very easily.

"It looks like the Smiths' house is on fire. I want you both to promise to stay near me. I don't want to have to worry about either one of you while we work."

Nodding in understanding, both sets of eyes were large as they pulled into the homestead of their neighbors. Few remains of the smoldering house were left. The barn was engulfed, and men and women were at work trying to stop the flames from spreading to the open fields, where their own lands and homes would be threatened.

Blankets were handed out and all available got as close as possible to the hot, burning blaze that seemed to have a mind of its own. As Rachel and D.J. worked, beating continuously to ebb the evil monster before them, Rachel felt the intense heat against her face. Pounding over and over again, all tried desperately to douse the inferno that was as strong willed as they were.

After more than a half hour of arm-wrenching thrashing, Rachel heard the soft neighing of a small colt. Looking in the pasture where the fire was headed, she saw the mare and her foal pacing back and forth in fear. Without thought, she began to run toward them to release them from their captivity. As she reached the gate and opened it, she realized her folly too late. She had trapped herself as the fire raged a circle around her. The thickening smoke became evident, and she felt panic rise inside her. Calling for her papa, she fell to her knees as the air surrounding her became heavy, causing breathing to become difficult. Trying to stand to her feet, she could feel the searing fire as it became closer. Coughing violently to clear her lungs, she prayed to God that He would help her. Her sobbing became cries for help as she saw the hem of her skirt become laced with small flames. Bending down, she slapped fearfully to distinguish them rapidly. As she brushed the hair out of her eyes with a soot-covered hand, she felt herself lifted in strong arms.

"Put the blanket over your head," the familiar voice told her. "We have to try and get to the lake. It's our only chance."

Doing as she was told, the heat became suffocating as her rescuer carried her swiftly through the blaze that had enclosed them. After what seemed like an eternity, Rachel felt the frosty water as they plunged into the lake. Tears began to stream down her cheeks, and she clung securely to the strong body that had saved her, holding tightly and sobbing in relief.

"Shh…" the comforting voice told her as he gently moved several strands of hair from her face. "You're safe now."

"We could have died," she whispered in anguish as the reality of the situation settled in. The intense heat could be felt on their faces even from the distance. She began to shiver uncontrollably and was grateful for the security she now felt. Only when she began to gain control over emotions did she pull herself back enough to look into the eyes of Matthew O'Malley.

"How can I ever repay you for saving me?" she asked as tears began to fall again. Realizing that she was still in his arms, she felt him pull her to him closely.

"You don't have to thank me. I'm just glad I heard you cry out." Thinking briefly, *Even if I can't have you for myself, in no way would I want you harmed. I care too deeply for you.*

Enjoying the comfort and solace he offered, Rachel could only dwell about how right the moment felt to her, as if this was where she truly belonged. She needed to feel the strength he offered. Snuggling up closely to him, the warmth from his body began to flow through her, and she didn't want to move as strong arms held her safely. She could feel the strong, steady beat of his heart beneath her hand and knew that it matched her own. Their fright of the situation had quickened both heart rates.

Matthew, never wanting to let go, held securely to the woman in his arms. Never before had he felt such fear as when he heard her cry out.

I could have lost you tonight. No, he reminded himself, *you are not mine to lose.*

How long the two embraced one another, neither could be sure. Time seemed to have no place while the fire danced its angry steps before them.

Rachel, remembering that she was promised to be married to his brother, began to squirm until she felt him release her to stand beside him.

Making himself turn from her, he let his eyes roam the land before him. "It looks like it's stopping now. Thank God the lake was here for us," he whispered quietly.

"Yes, and I thank God for you also," she said as their eyes locked again.

Knowing how weak he was around her, he broke their gaze and watched as the smoldering embers of the fire began to die down.

"We may have to wait a bit until it's not so hot."

"Yes. Did you get hurt?" she asked as an afterthought.

"I'm all right," he told her with a shrug. Rachel, not sure she believed him, asked again, "Please, tell me, did you get burned?"

Shrugging his shoulders, he smiled for the first time since their ordeal. "Nothing that some of Mama's good liniment won't cure."

Shaking her head at his answer, noticing the lopsided, boyish grin on his face, she could only smile back.

Hearing shouts from the distance, the couple saw the faces of concerned men heading their way. Rachel, spotting her papa, picked her water-laden dress up to her knees and began to trudge toward his waiting arms.

"Rachel!" he exclaimed. "You're safe. Thank God."

"Yes, thank God and Matthew. He's the one that who brought me to the lake."

Turning to face the younger man, the words became choked in Tucker's throat as he told him, "Thank you for saving my little girl."

"You're welcome, sir."

Feeling the wetness of her clothes seep through his own, Tucker told her, "Let's get you home and into some dry things."

Watching the two walk off, Matthew was praising God for His faithfulness in protecting the woman he loved, even if she was never to belong to him.

On the ride back to their house, Tucker told Rachel and D.J. with sorrow, "I'm afraid that Mr. and Mrs. Smith did not survive the fire. Their only daughter, Sarah, discovered the smoke and was able to get out safely. The poor little tyke does not understand that her mama and papa are gone. She kept asking for them."

Rachel began to weep softly as she remembered their quiet neighbors. They had been godly people and hard workers. It would have broken their hearts to know that their precious child was left in the world without parents or someone to care for her and the heartache she would suffer because of this night.

While Rachel was teaching school the next day, talk of the fire and her rescue seemed to be on everyone's mind. Only when Tommy Tucker's voice broke through the story did she listen attentively.

"And I heard that Matthew O'Malley got burned on his feet pretty bad. Pa said he's got blisters and can't even walk."

Sadness flooded through her, and she knew it was because of her that this had happened. She wished she could find a little corner away from everyone and relieve the emotions she felt. Praying that the day would pass quickly so that she could head to the O'Malleys' and check on him herself, she anxiously watched the clock on the wall.

At precisely three o'clock, she dismissed the children and gathered her things. She asked D.J. to drive the wagon and drop her off at the O'Malleys' place before taking Hannah home. She knew that Mark would bring her home later.

Striding quickly to the door, she knocked and was rewarded with Genie's welcoming smile.

"Hello, Rachel. Come on in."

Entering, she heard her ask, "Are you feeling all right after your adventure last night?"

"I'm wonderful, thanks to your son. How is he doing?" she asked fearfully.

"He'll be fine. Mark bandaged his feet and said that as soon as the blisters heal in about a week, he'll be able to get around again."

"Can I see him?" she asked with sorrow.

"Yes, and Rachel, it wasn't your fault. Matthew is not blaming you."

"But it is my fault," she whispered to Genie as she walked toward his bedroom.

Seeing him sitting on his bed, both feet heavily bandaged, Rachel walked toward him and sat down on the chair nearby.

"I'm so sorry," she said as she felt a tear slip down her cheek.

Resisting the urge to wipe the tear away, he told her, "Don't blame yourself. I'll be back to myself in no time. I'm just thankful that this is all that happened."

Looking deeply into his eyes, she saw that he meant every word, but it didn't relieve the guilt she felt.

"You wouldn't be burned if it weren't for my impulsiveness."

"Your impulsiveness saved that horse and her colt."

"Did it?" she asked as she thought of them.

"Yes, I would have done the same thing given the chance."

"You're not just telling me that, are you?"

"No, I'm not."

As she let her eyes roam to his feet, staring at the bandages that were wrapped securely, she asked, "Does it hurt much?"

"No, I'm fine," he replied in a nonchalant voice.

Shaking her head, she knew he wouldn't tell her if he was in pain or not. Silence filled the room for a moment as both of them recalled what had happened. Rachel remembered vividly his muscular arms around her and the safety she had felt in them. Matthew was thinking about how her body molded itself perfectly into his arms and her softness against him.

Glancing up, he knew she was thinking of the same thing when he saw her face flush slightly.

"How was school today?" he asked, averting her uneasiness.

"Pretty good," she answered, not being able to remember anything about it after discovering that he had been hurt.

"How are the kids this year?" Seeing her hesitation, he asked, "Is there a problem?"

"Well," she began and stopped. She had not told anyone about the situation at the school yet, not even her parents.

"Well, what?" he asked her with a serious note.

"It's just that Jimmy Richardson is giving me some trouble."

Matthew, letting his mind think about the Richardsons' boy, felt an uneasiness enter him. He was fifteen or sixteen years old and a large boy for his age. He tended to be very spoiled, and his parents had to keep a tight rein on him. His father was a prominent bank owner in Cheyenne, and they had moved to their small community, in hopes that by getting the boy out of the city and away from his unruly friends, he would change. His name was linked to several robberies in the town, although there was nothing to prove it. He was not someone to take lightly.

"What's going on, Rachel? Tell me, please."

"It's just that he watches me all the time. Every time I glance at him, he has a grin on his face and a certain look in his eye. It just gives me an uncomfortable feeling."

"You need to be careful around him. You promise me you will go home and tell your father tonight."

As she stared into his eyes, she saw worry there. For some reason, she wanted to sit beside him and have him pull her closely to feel safe again.

"All right, I promise," she replied softly.

Hearing the bedroom door open, Mark walked into the room with a smile.

"Rachel, what a pleasant surprise. How are you feeling after last night?"

"I'm fine. I was worried about Matthew and thought I'd stop by."

"He's doing great. Next week by this time, he'll be as right as rain."

Glancing his direction, she saw the injured man smile and say, "I told you."

Standing to her feet, she watched as Mark held out his hand for her to take and asked, "Can you stay to supper now that you're here? I'll take you home later."

"Yes, I think that will be all right."

Watching the two leave hand in hand caused Matthew an ache in his heart that was worse than his burning, blistered feet.

On the way home, Mark was in no hurry to part with Rachel's company. With an arm wrapped firmly around her to keep her warm from the night air, he said, "You know, we haven't even discussed a date for the wedding yet."

Knowing that he was right, she told him, "I guess we've both been too busy to think about it."

"Can you think about it now?" he asked with a boyish grin.

"Let's see, this is October. Mama is due to have the baby in November. How about the middle of December? That will give her time to get back on her feet."

"That sounds great. I'm looking into renting a home in town near the practice until something else opens up."

"Oh, I guess we will be living in town, won't we?" she asked. She had always thought she would live near her parents. Seeing how silly this was, she continued, "I guess it would be wise to be closer to the practice for you."

"Yes," he agreed.

"I do love you, Rachel. I don't know what I would do without you," he told her as he pulled her closer.

"I know. We will have a good marriage, of that I'm certain," she said aloud, trying to convince her heart of the same thing.

"And God will bless our home and any children He gives us. Plus, I'll be by your side to help you deliver them and also help them when they are sick," he told her with a chuckle. "You'll see that having a doctor around can become pretty handy at times."

This intimate remark about children made her flush brightly. She was glad that he could not see her red cheeks.

"Mama has actually started on my dress. She picked up some material when she was taking care of her uncle. It's a beautiful white satin."

"You will be lovely no matter what you wear," he told her softly.

"Thank you," she replied back. "We are planning on having a small reception at the house afterwards, if that is all right with you."

"That will be fine. It sounds like you have been giving this some thought."

"Yes," she said quietly, and added to herself, *I have given much thought to certain things lately.*

"Soon, Rachel, we will not have to say goodbye in the evenings," he told her as he walked her to her door.

Leaning over, she felt him kiss her cheek before turning to leave for his own home.

"Papa, can I speak with you for a moment?"

"Of course," he said as he patted the chair next to him.

As she sat down, the warmth of the small fire warmed her body, although the heaviness within her caused her heart to feel chilled.

Seeing the thoughtful expression on her face, he asked, "What is it, Rachel?"

"I'm having a little trouble with one of the boys in the class."

"Tell me about it. Maybe I can help."

"It's Jimmy Richardson," she whispered, shivering slightly as she remembered the leering way he studied her.

"The Richardson boy? What is he doing?" her papa asked, appre-hension rising inside him at the mention of the young man.

"It's not so much what he is doing; it's just that he watches me all the time. I feel uncomfortable around him."

Hearing her daughter's words, McKenna felt fear in her heart as she glanced toward her husband.

"Rachel, in no way are you to be alone with that boy. You make sure there are others around you all the time."

McKenna, who had risen to her feet, sat awkwardly on the hearth beside her.

"Rachel, God gives us these feelings to help us protect ourselves. This is not just your imagination working overtime. You need to listen to your instincts and be on your guard continually. I will mention this to D.J. and make sure that he stays by you also. Please, sweetheart," she said as pain from her own past resurfaced into her heart, "do not ever be alone with him or place yourself in a situation where others are not around."

"I won't, Mama. He frightens me."

"Fear can be a good thing. It makes us aware of our surroundings."

"I will see what I can do about the situation tomorrow," her father told her. "We need to pray about it right now."

Bowing their heads, they heard him enter the portals of glory.

"Father, we ask You to protect Rachel, to wrap Your arms around her. Keep her encircled in Your love and guide her steps. Give her wisdom on what to say and do in the days ahead. We know You love her more than we do and want what is best for her, so we place her in Your loving hands, for it's in Jesus' name we pray, Amen."

McKenna wrapped her arms tightly around the young girl, and both parents watched with heaviness in their hearts as she walked toward her bedroom.

"I don't like this," Tucker heard his wife say. "Rachel is in danger. I feel it."

"I do too. I will make sure that she is not alone and will tell D.J. to be on guard at the schoolhouse. I'll also tell the O'Malley boys to keep their eyes open."

"I don't know what I would do if she had to suffer at the hands of someone cruel," McKenna whispered as tears began to fall. "I know my uncle did not sexually assault me, but even the physical side never leaves me. It seems to be buried in the deep recesses of my heart, and Satan gladly brings it out when I am weak."

Pulling her into his lap, Tucker said, "I can't say that I know what you have been through, because I don't. I do know that when you hurt, I do too. I would take all your past pain from you if I could."

Smiling through her tears, she said, "I know you would. Actually, things are better now since I had to take care of Uncle Hilton. His coming to the Lord has definitely helped. Every once in a while, memories of long ago still arise unannounced."

"Because they are a part of your life. Those things made you the person that you are today; a wonderful, caring mother, a thoughtful, loving wife, and a godly woman. They have also afforded you to have empathy with others who have suffered such as yourself," he told her, both thinking of the Henderson woman whose husband had beaten her. McKenna had been able to grieve with her and help her through her pain after her husband had died.

"Yes, I just pray that it wasn't to prepare me to help our own daughter through such an event," she whispered in an agonizing voice.

A few days later, Genie lay awake next to her husband. Listening to his even breathing, she knew that he was asleep. Tossing and turning for quite some time, she heard him ask, "Genie, me darlin,' whatever is the matter with ya'?"

"Oh, Ian, I'm so glad you are awake. We need to talk."

"Aye, must be something mighty important for ya' to keep a movin' about the way ya' have been," he told her as he sat up.

"Yes," she replied quietly.

Hearing her serious tone, he reached over and drew her close to him.

"Whatever it may be, we'll face it together, lassie."

"The Lord has placed something on my heart, and I don't know what you'll think of it."

"My lovely lady, if the good Lord has given ya' something, who am I to say anything aginst?"

"You remember the little Smith girl who lost her parents in the fire the other night?"

"Aye, I do at that. Seems Tucker said she has no other kin to raise her."

"Can we?" she asked suddenly.

"Can we what, me darlin'?"

"Can we raise her? We could legally adopt her. She's all I've been able to think about lately, and I know that God has placed this on my heart."

Trying to wake up enough to make sense of her words, he dwelt on what she had said. Genie felt like she was waiting an eternity before he finally answered.

"And this is what our Father is tellin' ya', me love?"

"Yes, He is," she replied with certainty.

With a nod of his head, he said, "We'll go first thing in the mornin' and see what we need to be doin' for that wee one."

Throwing her arms around her husband, Genie shrieked with thankfulness.

"I do love you Ian O'Malley."

"And for that I'm grateful," he replied, "'cuz my love for you is something fierce, Mrs. O'Malley."

The following morning, the couple rode in their wagon to the small law firm that had been set up a few months ago. Entering through the doors, they saw a young man stand with a smile, extending his hand.

"Ian O'Malley is the name, son, and this here is me wife, Genie."

"I am Tom Reilly. Nice to meet you. Is there something I can help you with?" he inquired.

"We sure hope so, laddie."

Looking toward his wife, he saw the eagerness on her face as she began to tell him, "Mr. Reilly, my husband and I would like to find out if it is possible for us to adopt the little Smith girl whose parents were killed in the fire the other evening. Our children are grown, and we would be able to provide a good home and, more importantly, love for the child."

Leaning back in his chair, a smile appeared on his face before he said, "Are you Christians by chance?"

"Aye, that we are, sir," Ian replied.

"You, my dear folks, are an answer to our prayers. Little Sarah Smith has been placed in the care of my wife and myself. We would be glad to take her, but we already have three little ones to provide for, and my wife is expecting our fourth any day now. We have been praying, asking God to bring someone forward that would give her a loving, godly home."

With a beaming smile, Ian told the man, "Then we are indeed your answers to that prayer."

"She is the sweetest little girl. Of course, she does not understand fully why her parents are not here with her. It will take time for her to heal."

"Yes, and we are more than willing to be patient with her," Genie told him.

The lawyer, looking deeply into both their eyes, knew that she spoke the truth.

"I will need to draw up the papers. I can do that this afternoon. Why don't you come over after supper this evening and meet her. Let her get to know you a little before you take her home."

"Fine idea," Ian told the man. Standing to his feet, he placed an arm around his wife and told her, "You were right, darlin'. God did want us to have this wee babe."

As the man watched the husband and wife leave, he said a prayer of thanks to his heavenly father for answering their prayers so swiftly.

As the O'Malley family gathered around the table that evening, Ian cleared his throat for a second before he began,

"Me fine, strappin' boys, your mama and I have a little surprise for each of ya'."

He then turned to his wife, encouraging her to continue.

"Do you remember the little Smith girl who lost her parents in the fire the other night? God has spoken to me, and your father and I are going to adopt her. She has no other relatives and nowhere to go. She is only four years old."

Having said the words, both parents looked into the stunned faces of their three sons.

"I think that is terrific," Matthew told them, breaking the silence. "I remember Rachel saying what a well behaved little girl she is.

Besides," he continued sadly, "I'm sure she is grieving from the loss of her parents and will need lots of love in the days ahead."

Seeing their other two sons nod in agreement, they sighed with relief.

"Yes," Mark spoke next, "and Mama, somehow I think you need someone else around here. After Hannah left, you were a little low for quite a while."

"I know. I couldn't figure out what was wrong until I saw her in church the week after she left. I missed her terribly."

"Well, John, me son," Ian began as he turned to face his youngest, "and what might ya' be thinkin' 'bout this here arrangement? We have already discussed it with your sister, and she thinks it's a grand idea."

"It's fine with me, I miss having Laura around to tease anyway."

"Wonderful," their mother said with a radiant smile. "I think we have the best children in the whole world, my husband."

"And we're about to add one more to the clan," he said with amusement. "We are indeed blessed, Mama."

After several visits to let Sarah feel more comfortable with them, the older couple felt they were beginning to gain the little girl's trust. They had decided to take her on a picnic near the lake today for their first outing alone with her. After watching her play for more than an hour, the three sat under the large oak tree before eating.

"Sarah, honey, sit with me a while," she said as she pulled the little girl on to her lap. As the child's eyes met her own, Genie felt tears form and hugged her closely before continuing. The little girl looked like an angel; she had large, dark eyes and almost black, curly hair that graced her little pixie face. Her complexion was fair, which seemed to emphasize her rosy cheeks. Genie felt like she could hold her forever.

"How would you like to come and live with us?" she asked, almost fearful of the answer.

"You mean to stay forever and ever?"

"Yes, darling, forever and ever."

"But what about Mama and Papa, won't they be sad?"

"Ach," Ian piped in, "of course they were sad that they had to leave their sweet baby behind, but they had God send us to ya' to love and take care of their wee one."

They could see her dwelling on these words a few moments before she asked, "Do you think Mama and Papa can see us in heaven?"

"I don't know, darling," Genie told her quietly. "But I do know that they would be glad someone is taking care of their precious baby girl."

Watching the small, rounded cheeks widen with a smile, the child placed arms tightly around the woman who held her. Genie, overcome with emotion, saw her husband wipe the tears from his own eyes. God had given them another child to love.

Sarah had been with the O'Malleys for almost two weeks. During most days, the little girl was fine. She asked frequent questions about her parents, and Genie noticed that she was extremely quiet at times, a faraway look on her face, as though she was thinking of the past. It was during the night that her new parents' hearts were broken. She would begin in her own room each evening, only to waken them both crying out for her mama and papa. She was reliving the fire through her dreams. Only after gathering her up into their loving arms and carrying her back to bed with them did the sobbing cease.

One particular evening after John had stoked the fire, Sarah, noticing the brightly burning flames, quietly began to cry and ran to her room. After consoling and assuring her that the fire would not hurt her, she slowly entered the room to watch with uncertainty.

Ian and Genie knew that in time, with God's help, Sarah would begin to heal. And both knew they would be patient and wait as long as it took to help the little girl through her difficult days. She had lost the only people she had loved and depended on, and in the eyes of a four-year-old, that was everything.

Chapter Seven

As Rachel sat in the loft to prepare her lessons for school the next day, she opened her bag and reached for the papers inside. Seeing the familiar note, she felt panic rise as she began to read. The handwriting was that of a younger person, and she knew who that person was. It stated simply:

> *Teacher,*
> *You are the prettiest girl I have ever laid eyes on. I like watching you and know that you are secretly watching me too. Soon we will be together.*

With shaking hands, she slowly climbed down from the loft. It was the third such letter she had received in two weeks, and it was time to show her parents.

Entering the house, her mother turned to her with a smile, which quickly faded as she saw the distress on her daughter's face.

"What's wrong, Rachel?" she asked, afraid to find out the truth.

Handing the letter to her mother, she watched her read it and place a hand over her mouth. Her face paled at the words on the paper.

"We have to show this to your papa. It's time for something to be done."

After supper, the women showed him the note and watched as fury clouded his face. Only once before had she seen her husband as angry as he was after reading the letter.

"Tomorrow, the Richardson family will receive a visit from me. We will put an end to this before it gets out of hand," he said. "Rachel, under no circumstances are you to be alone. I will remind D.J. of this. Promise me you will be careful," he begged.

"Yes, Papa, I promise," she answered as she left for her room.

The following morning after breakfast, Tucker set off for town. He would pay Mr. Richardson a visit at the bank.

As he opened the doors to the building, he saw the man standing before him and approached with a grim look.

"May I speak to you in private?" Tucker asked without a cordial greeting.

"Of course. Come to my office," the business man replied as he led him to a smaller area at the back.

After closing the door, Tucker held the note out for the man to read.

"And what are you implying, Mr. Parker?" the banker asked in a defensive tone.

"This is from your son. My daughter, Rachel, is afraid of him, and I'd like for you to talk to him about this."

With a sneer on his face, he said, "This is preposterous. This note could have been written by any of the young men your daughter teaches. How dare you come in here and accuse my son of something like this."

Shocked by the man's words, Tucker asked, "So this means you will do nothing?"

"Absolutely nothing. Even if it were from Jimmy, we both know how young boys can be infatuated with their teachers." Poking him lightly in the ribs, he added, "Especially when they are as comely as Rachel."

Offended by the tone of the banker's suggestive voice, Tucker grabbed the man by the front of his shirt and told him warningly, "If your son touches my daughter, you and he will pay dearly."

"Come, come now, Mr. Parker. Don't become distraught over a teenage crush."

With a shake of his head, Tucker left the room, slamming the door behind him.

School had just been dismissed, and Rachel was gathering her supplies to take home to study later. D.J. was outside talking to his friends, waiting for her by the wagon. Hannah had been invited to a friend's birthday party and had left earlier.

Facing the side door, she saw Jimmy enter with a leering smile on his face.

"School is over. You may go home now," she told him, trying to keep her voice as normal as possible.

"I know," he said as he took a step closer.

Rachel turned to look toward the double doors at the front and noticed they both were firmly shut. Feeling her heart begin to race, the stocky teenager stood directly in front of her. Without a word, he reached over and touched a tendril of her hair with his finger, twirling for a moment. Leaning over, he inhaled the clean scent of it and said, "I always wondered what it smelled like."

Looking into her eyes and seeing the fear present gave the young man a new boldness, a feeling of power. He had been bragging to the older boys that he would be with the pretty schoolteacher soon and be the first to kiss her.

"Please leave, Jimmy," she whispered. "D.J. will be coming in at any moment."

"Nah, he's too busy talking about fishin' with his friends," he told her, a gleam in his eyes and a jeering smile on his face.

Backing up slowly, she felt the desk against her backside. Taking a step toward her, he grabbed her and pulled her against his body, his lips pressing roughly against her own. Feeling her struggle in his arms only increased his enjoyment.

Stomping on his foot as hard as possible, he jumped back and yelled in alarm.

With a hand on her tender mouth, she watched rage appear as he said, "This is not the last you will see me. This is only the beginning. You'll not make a fool out of me." With an evil grin, he left as quickly as he had come.

Standing in a daze, tears formed in her eyes, and she stood for several moments trying to think of what to do. Running quickly toward the front door, she opened it and saw D.J. turn to stare at her. Seeing her face, he took the stairs two at a time and asked, "What's wrong, Rachel?" Noticing the concerned looks of his friends, she tugged him inside and explained what had taken place. Rage crossed his young face as he thought of someone hurting his sister. Holding her arm in a tender manner, he said, "Come on. Let's go tell Pa. He'll know what to do."

Traveling in silence, they began down the lane through the woods toward their home. Just before reaching the clearing, a loud thump was heard in the back of the wagon. Turning quickly to see what had happened, Rachel saw Jimmy lift his hand and strike D.J. in the back of his head with an object. She screamed as she saw her brother slump forward. Reaching for the reins, she stopped the horse quickly while holding onto her brother before she felt strong arms enclose her from behind. Jimmie lifted her roughly over the back of the seat and tossed her over his shoulder.

"I told ya' we'd be together soon, didn't I?" he said with a deep-throated laugh.

As she began to kick and scream, he threw her to the ground, slapped her across the face and told her, "You'd best shut up if you know what's good for you."

With a small cry, she felt the blood from her broken lip run down her chin.

Reaching down brusquely, he picked her up again and set off to an area where his horse was stowed away.

"Please," she pleaded, "let me check on D.J. and make sure he is all right."

"He'll be fine," he told her with a sneer. "He'll just have a whopping headache later, that's all."

Tossing her up onto his horse, he scrambled up behind her, firmly wrapping his arms around her to make sure she didn't try to get down.

"Why are you doing this?" she asked in despair.

"Because I always get what I want, and I want you."

As they rounded a bend in the lane, fear spread through Rachel. She remembered the small, empty cabin deep in the woods and knew that was where they were headed.

Tucker had finished his chores and was beginning to worry about his children. They should have already been home. Without bothering to saddle his horse, he put the bridle on quickly and jumped on the animal's back. Urging his horse into a brisk cantor, he set off toward the school. When he entered the woods, his feelings of concern became a reality when he spotted the wagon. As he drew up closer, he saw D.J. just beginning to open his eyes, rubbing the back of his head.

Jumping down swiftly, Tucker ran to his son's side and asked, "Are you all right?"

Nodding, the boy said, "He's got Rachel."

Needing no other words, he mounted his gelding and kicked him in the ribs, encouraging him to go as rapidly as possible down the winding lane as he called out his daughter's name in a panic-stricken voice.

Rachel, as they were almost to the cabin, heard her papa's voice and screamed for him. Jimmy, knowing that he was about to be confronted by her father, abruptly pushed her from the horse to the thick brush that covered the ground.

"The next time you won't be so lucky," he told her before galloping away.

Feeling the twigs and thorns tear at her flesh, she stood to her feet and began to run toward her rescuer. Seeing her, Tucker jumped from the horse and hurried to gather her into his arms.

"Oh, Rachel," he said as he felt tears sting his eyes. "Did he hurt you?"

Only able to shake her head, she felt him pick her up in his arms and carry her back to where his horse stood.

"Let's go home," he whispered tenderly to his child, who was trembling in his arms.

Assisting her on his horse's back, he noticed the angry welts and swollen, blood-tinged lip and grimaced. He was thankful that was all that had happened.

"How is D.J.?" she asked, worried about her brother.

"I think he is fine. He was coming to when I found him."

Having said those words, they noticed the wagon appear, with the face of their loved one before them. Hopping from the wagon, he ran to the horse's side.

"Did he hurt you, Rachel?" he asked in anxiousness.

"No, other than some scrapes and cuts, I'm fine. How about you?"

Reaching up to touch the tender area at the back of his head, he told her with a small grin, "I think I'm gonna have a headache from this. I've already got a beaut of a knot."

Laughing at his words, words that she knew were said to lessen the seriousness of what had happened, only made her love her brother more, if that were possible.

McKenna had watched her husband rush away on his horse and was pacing back and forth in the yard. She had not known what to pray for, but she beseeched Christ to intercede on her behalf.

Seeing the wagon in the distance with both of her children in it, as well as her husband riding beside them, relief flowed through her. Only as the three drew closer did her face fill with concern. With a sickened heart, she looked first at Rachel and then her husband, who only nodded his head, confirming what she had feared.

Before D.J. could stop the wagon completely, Rachel bounded out and threw herself into her mother's waiting arms, sobbing softly as the events of the past hour were recalled.

With arms entwined around one another, the two women entered the house in a solemn mood. Leading her to her bedroom, McKenna gently took her daughter's hand and led her to sit next to her on the bed.

"Tell me what happened," her mama said tenderly.

As she sat and listened to her story, McKenna sobbed with her daughter. Tucker, who was standing nearby in the hall, thanked God over and over for saving his little girl. Without a word, he turned and moved toward the door. It was time to pay a visit to the local authority and then he would collect Hannah from her party. He needed to know his family was safely in his care.

After hearing Rachel's entire story, McKenna stood and told Rachel, "Let's get you cleaned up and take care of those cuts. You look like you might need something cold on your lip for the swelling. I know," she continued, "why don't we get the tub in and you can soak for a little while. You may be sore from all that's happened."

"That does sound good," Rachel replied, inspecting the lip that was purple, a small cut evident. "I think by tomorrow I am going to be a sight."

McKenna quickly hugged the young woman and told her, "God kept you safe, just like He did me so many years ago."

Spotting her son in the kitchen, she saw him place a rag on the back of his head.

"Here," she told him, "let me see how bad you are." Leading him to a chair, she separated his hair and noticed the swelling at the back of his head. She placed her face against his cheek and whispered, "Thank you for watching over your sister."

With a slight chuckle, he told his mama, "I can't say that I really watched over her. One minute she was sitting by me, and the next I was seeing stars."

"I do love you," McKenna told him with pride. "Can you do us a favor?"

"Sure, as long as it doesn't require wearing a hat," he replied in a somewhat serious tone. He had a dry sense of humor, which made him endearing.

"Can you get the tub in and put it in your sister's room? I think she's gonna need to soak some of the soreness from her body. I'll start carrying water and get you some ice from the ice house to put on your head."

"No, Mama," her son told her. "You are not going to carry water now."

Knowing that he was referring to her pregnancy, she leaned down and kissed his cheek.

"You will make some girl a wonderful husband someday," she told him, watching as his face turned red at her words.

Tucker entered the sheriff's office with a serious look on his face. The older lawman stood to his feet and held out his hand toward him.

"Howdy, what brings you here today?" he asked, noticing the grim look on the man's face.

After taking a seat, Tucker proceeded to tell him of everything that had happened. Stroking his beard in thoughtfulness, he frowned before saying, "I'm sorry this had to happen to Rachel." He had two daughters himself, and he didn't know if he would be responsible for his actions should something similar happen to one of them.

"I have heard that the boy is trouble. I received word last week from Cheyenne, and they think he is involved with some of the thefts that have been happening there. Seems he is selling the goods to some peddlers. Since their family has moved to our little town, there has been a lot more crime." Standing to his feet, he reached for his weatherworn hat and continued, "It's time to do more than talk with the Richardson boy. Will Rachel testify against him if I bring him in?"

"Yes, I think so. And so will D.J. if he is needed."

The sheriff placed a hand on his friend's shoulder and said, "Again, I am so sorry this had to happen. Tell Rachel I wish for her a speedy recovery."

Knocking on the Richardson's door a short time later, the lawman saw the puzzled look of Mrs. Richardson as she stood before him.

"May I come in?" he asked.

"Of course, Sheriff," she replied, calling her husband's name before shutting the door.

Coming around the corner of the hall, the banker felt anger rise in him as he wondered what the man had to say.

"Please, take a seat," Mrs. Richardson told him as she led him to the sofa.

"What can we do for you, Sheriff?"

"Have you seen your son in the last few hours?"

"Jimmy? Why, no. Haven't seen him since he left for school this morning."

The sheriff proceeded to tell the couple what had transpired a short time ago. Listening in disbelief, the boy's father stood to his feet and yelled, "This is ridiculous. My son would never hurt a woman. This is all her fault. He's been telling me how she watches him constantly at school and has seemed to encourage him with her actions."

Listening to his words, the sheriff knew Rachel and her family well enough to realize that she would never do such a thing.

"What Rachel says is true, I'm afraid, whether you wish to believe it or not. As soon as I can find him, I will lock him up until the circuit judge comes to town."

"And I will have the finest lawyer from Cheyenne that I can get on his case," the fuming father told him.

"That's your choice, but the testimony of Rachel Parker will far outweigh your son's words."

"Why, that little tramp. Who would believe her?"

His wife, upon hearing her husband's words, looked at him in astonishment. She knew Rachel personally, and she was in no way that which he described her to be.

Standing to his feet, the sheriff placed his hat on his head and told them warningly, "If your son returns and you protect him, you also will be arrested for harboring a fugitive."

"And you, sir, need to leave before I throw you out," he told the man as he opened the door and stood back for the lawman to leave.

Slamming the door angrily, Mr. Richardson turned to his wife, who had not spoken during their interlude, and said, "The nerve of the man, accusing our son of such actions. He obviously does not know Jimmy, or he would never imply such charges against him."

Watching him set off to their bedroom angrily, the woman sat silently, recalling all the times her own son had struck her in the past few months. She knew what Jimmy was capable of and was sorry that Rachel had been hurt by him. She would pay the Parkers a visit as soon as possible and offer her apologies. For now, it was time her husband knew the truth about his son, and she had that proof from the bruises on her arms from just the day before.

When she entered the room, she saw her spouse standing near the window, staring absently outside. The stiffness of his back spoke of the fury he felt.

"Dear, will you listen to me? I have something to tell you." she asked her husband in a quiet voice as she walked closer.

"Can you believe the audacity of our sheriff to imply what he did against Jimmy?"

Waiting for a reply, none came, and he turned to look into the sorrowful features of his wife of many years.

He saw the serious expression on her face and watched as she rolled up her sleeves to reveal angry bruises that were present.

As Mr. Richardson reached out to observe them closer, he asked in startling revelation, "Did Jimmy do this to you?"

"Yes, he began hitting me over six months ago. I have hidden it from you, hoping that he would change. Things have gotten worse lately."

With grief written on his face, he whispered in misery, "What the sheriff said is true, isn't it?"

With only a nod of her head, too choked up for words, their tears fell freely as they clung to one another for comfort. Their hearts were breaking and further words were unnecessary.

Climbing back into the wagon, Tucker headed in the direction of the home of Hannah's friend. As he parked the team out front of the small house, he could hear the squeals of little girls and knew that his daughter was not going to be happy about leaving. Rapping on the front door, he watched as the father opened it and greeted him.

"Hello, Tucker," he said as extended his hand.

"Hi, Marshall. I've come to pick up Hannah. We've had a family mishap, and she needs to go home."

A frown appeared on the man's face as he asked, "I trust everything is all right."

"So do I," was Tucker's only reply.

Sensing that he did not want to talk about it, the father of the birthday girl headed through the house and opened the back door, calling to Hannah.

The little girl ran to the man, and saw her Pa standing beside him.

"Hannah, you need to come home with me now," he said in a serious voice.

"Papa, I want to stay and play," she began to plead.

"No, it is time to leave."

"Patty hasn't even opened up the present that I got her," she told him sadly.

"All right, give her your gift and then we must leave."

Watching her walk away, head down and dragging small feet, she went to the table to retrieve the small package and handed it to the child.

As Patty undid the brown paper, she saw that it contained several different hair bows. Holding them up for all to examine, she exclaimed, "Look, Mama, new ribbons!"

"How nice, dear. Tell Hannah thank you."

"Thank you," she replied, as ordered.

"I have to go now. Thank you for letting me come," Hannah told her friend.

"I'll see you at school tomorrow. Bye."

"Bye."

As she walked back to her papa, he picked her up and hugged her.

"Thank you for obeying me, sweetheart."

Shifting in his arms, she looked into his eyes and asked, "Why do I have to come home now?"

Sifting through what had happened, he decided it would be best to tell her the truth for he knew she would hear of it at school the following day anyway.

"Because Rachel and D.J. got hurt."

"Got hurt?"

"Yes, Jimmy from your school hurt them."

"Why would Jimmy do that?" she asked in innocence.

"I don't know, little one. Sometimes people do things that are mean."

"I hope somebody beats ole' Jimmy Richardson up then."

Feeling the same attitude toward the boy, but knowing it was wrong, her papa quickly told her, "No, Hannah. That is for God to do, not us. We'll let Him take care of Jimmy."

"Then I'm gonna ask God to do it," she replied with fierceness.

Tucker, unable to reply, couldn't help but agree with his small daughter. He knew he was going to have to pray for his heavenly father to remove the bitterness and anger from him, for at the moment he was incapable of doing it himself. He feared what his reaction might be should he cross paths with the boy.

After supper that evening, there was a knock at the door. McKenna opened it to see Mark standing on the other side.

"Come in," she told him, understanding his visit.

"How is she?" he asked, getting straight to the point.

"Other than being shaken emotionally, plus some bumps and bruises, she is fine."

"Can I see her?"

"Of course," she replied. "She's in her room."

Walking down the hall to Rachel's room, he knocked softly and heard her say, "Come in."

Opening the door, she saw Mark's concerned face appear.

"What are you doing here?" she asked, as if nothing were wrong.

Walking closer, he saw the bruised and swollen lip where she had been hit. Taking a step to the edge of the bed, he placed a finger tenderly on the area and asked, "Are you all right? I just heard a short time ago from the sheriff what happened."

As her tears gathered again, she felt the bed shift and then his arms gathered her close. He let her sob quietly for a few moments, and then she began to tell him in broken sentences what had happened. She could feel his body stiffen with anger at her words.

"Where is the boy now?" he asked, thinking that she was not going back to school as long as he was free.

"I don't know. Papa talked to the sheriff, who was going to see the Richardson family himself."

"Oh, Rachel," he said as he held her tightly. "I am so sorry." Pulling back to look into her eyes, he asked fearfully, "He didn't assault you, did he?"

Feeling embarrassment flood through her, she shook her head no.

"Where are you hurt? Let me check you over and see for myself that you are all right."

"Really, I am fine. Other than my lip and a few scratches from the branches when I fell, I am not hurt. You had better look D.J.'s head over though. He took an awful wallop and has a good-sized bump."

"I will, but first I just need to hold you for a minute and make sure that you truly are fine."

Feeling the warmth that his body offered, she relaxed for the first time since the incident.

Matthew had just entered his parents' house and saw his mother sitting in the rocking chair with tears in her eyes.

"What's wrong?" he asked as he came to stand next to her, leaning down to look into her eyes.

"It's Rachel," she told him, which struck fear in his heart. "She's been attacked by the Richardson boy. D.J. was hurt also. Mark went over a short time ago to make sure they are all right. I haven't heard how bad it is, so I am praying until I get word of their conditions."

Taking her hand in his, he squeezed briefly and rose to his feet. Genie watched as her son left the house again, and she knew exactly where he was going.

As the Parker residence came into view, he saw that Mark's horse was tethered near the front porch. Jumping down quickly, he tied his gelding near his brother's and dashed up the stairs. Before he could knock, the door opened, and Tucker nodded at him.

"Come on in, Matthew," he told him as he stood back to let the man enter.

McKenna, spotting the oldest O'Malley boy, saw him walk toward D.J. and ask, "Are you all right?"

Turning his head away from him, the young boy held his hand up and pointed to the place where he had been hit.

"Yeah, got a headache though," he told him with a slight grin.

"And your sister," he asked quietly, "is she okay too?"

"She's got a fat lip and some cuts," he replied, not noticing the anxiety on Matthew's face as he voiced the question.

Hearing the sound of approaching footsteps, Matthew shifted and saw Rachel and Mark enter together. There was a smile on her face, and he saw that she did indeed have a fat lip as her brother had stated.

"Matthew," she said in wonder, "what brings you here?"

"I had to come and see for myself that you are both all right."

Coming to stand near her little brother, Rachel put her arm around him and hugged him before saying, "D.J. and Papa were my rescuers."

"Not me, I slept through everything," the young boy told them with frankness, causing the adults to laugh aloud.

Stepping to his side, Mark lightly grasped his head and began to examine the knot.

"I'd say you are gonna have a good ache for a day or two, little buddy. Did it bleed at all?" he asked as he continued to search for cuts.

"No, it was swollen by the time I woke up."

"Keep a cold cloth on it tonight."

Straightening up, Mark looked into McKenna's eyes and said, "He should be woken up frequently during the night to make sure he is all right, probably every few hours."

"That will be no problem," she said with a laugh. Placing her hand on her swollen abdomen, she added, "This little one has me awake visiting the outhouse several times during the night."

Matthew, seeing that Rachel was not harmed, began to calm down and knew that he should leave. Mark was with Rachel, and that was all she needed or wanted. Excusing himself, he left with thankfulness to God for protecting the woman who was wrapped so firmly around his heart.

McKenna went to tuck her youngest daughter into bed for the night after the emotional day. As the little girl got down on her knees, she began her prayers.

"God bless Mama and Papa and Rachel and D.J. and all my friends at school. And God, please beat up Jimmy Richardson real good for hurting my brother and my sister. Amen."

Astonishment flooded through her mother as she watched her daughter climb into bed and snuggle beneath the covers.

"Hannah, why did you ask God to beat up Jimmy?"

"Because Papa said that we shouldn't do it but that God would take care of him."

She was filled with understanding, and almost laughed aloud at the serious expression on the child's face

"Maybe we should pray that Jimmy will ask God into his heart," she suggested thoughtfully. "Then he would be changed and be a better person."

Watching Hannah frown, obviously deep in thought from her mama's words, she finally asked, "But if he doesn't ask Jesus into heart soon, can I pray again that God will hit him?"

"How about we pray and leave it in God's hands? Don't you think He knows best?"

"I guess He does."

Leaning down, she wrapped her arms snuggly around the cuddly little one and hugged her tightly.

"Goodnight, sweetheart. Sweet dreams."

"Night, Mama."

Oh, to be like a child again, she thought as she walked through the door. Things were either black or white and so much simpler through the eyes of the young. With a smile lingering on her face, she moved to the kitchen to share with her husband. He would get a chuckle out of it.

Chapter Eight

The Richardsons watched in sadness as they saw their son pacing back and forth in the kitchen.

"I should have killed her," he told them with a frightening fierceness in his tone. "And if I get the chance again, I will. She won't testify against me. She'll die first."

"Son," his mother began but was quickly brought to a halt as he raised his hand to her in a warning movement. His father, seeing for the first time what his child had become, felt shame course through him.

"I'm leaving this place," he said as he briskly moved toward his room.

"What can we do?" Mrs. Richardson asked her husband after hearing the bedroom door slam.

"We have no choice but to turn him in before he hurts someone worse than he hurt the Parker children."

Walking toward Jimmy's room, he heard the shuffling of furniture and cracked the door open to see what was happening inside. The boy had placed the dresser under the attic door and was pushing it aside. Pulling himself into the small opening, he watched as Jimmy began throwing objects onto the bed. Jewelry, silver, even a family Bible was tossed with little thought. Hopelessness filled the father as he realized that he had helped his son become the person he was. Shoving the door open, he waited as Jimmy lowered himself to the floor to stand beside him.

In astonishment, he asked his father, "Did you really think I didn't take these things, or that I couldn't hurt someone if I wanted to?"

His father, his own anger surfacing, grabbed the boy's arm roughly and said, "You will turn yourself into the sheriff if I have to drag you there myself."

With a swift motion, he lashed out and struck his father in the face, knocking him down on the bed. Quickly grasping the quilt on the chair by his bed, he placed it on the floor and began to throw the stolen items onto it.

His mother, who had heard the commotion, waited in her own room until he was gone before going to the assistance of her spouse. He was sitting on the edge of the bed and held his head in his hands, sobbing.

Wrapping her arms around him, he asked in despair, "Where did we go wrong?"

"I don't know," she whispered back as she rocked him gently back and forth. Her prideful, arrogant husband was now a broken man. It was the second time she had ever seen him shed a tear. Only when his own mother had died had he wept.

Shifting to face her, he said, "Maybe I should have let you take him to church with you when you went. Maybe I was wrong by not going myself."

"Yes, I fear that only God can help our boy now. We must pray and ask Him to love him and change his heart."

"I don't know how to talk to God," he admitted in a hoarse voice. "I've never needed Him before."

"Yes, you have," she told him softly. "You just didn't know it."

Staring into his moist eyes, she continued, "Ask Christ to come into your heart. He can make you a brand new person and give you what you need to deal with this situation. We must trust Him."

Knowing that his wife was right and that he had nowhere to look but up, he bowed his head. He asked God to forgive him for his sins and to come and live in his heart. With a wave of unexplainable peace flowing through him, he knew he was not alone. God would be with him during the days ahead. If he but knew what was to take place, he would have been exceedingly grateful that he had prayed that prayer and asked for the heavenly father's comforting hand, for what lay ahead in the future, he could not have bore alone.

Jimmy Richardson made his way straight toward the Parkers' place. If given the chance, he would take care of his teacher and make sure that she would not be able to testify against him. As he tied his horse to a tree in the woods, he ran down the lane. Edging himself near a window, he peered inside to see not only the Parker family, but the O'Malley boys inside. Realizing it would be futile to try anything at the time, he set off once again to mount his horse. He would make the long ride to Cheyenne and stay with one of his friends, whom he hadn't seen in quite some time. They would be happy to see what he had been able to steal since moving into the small, boring community.

Later, when the Parkers had relaxed, he would come back and take care of Rachel, and there would be no mistakes or surprises.

As he slid off of his horse in front of his best friend's house, he led the animal into the barn. He would stow the goods there in the hay. Putting the mare in the open stall, he removed the saddle and bridle and latched the stall door shut. Climbing the ladder wasn't easy with the cumbersome quilt, but he made it into the loft and buried it beneath the soft hay. After making his way to the house, he rapped swiftly on the front door. Hearing footsteps, he saw Joe's face appear.

"Hey, Jimmy, what ya' doing here?" he asked in surprise.

"I need a place to stay for a few days."

"Sure, Ma won't care if ya' bunk down with us."

Letting him enter, he shut the door quickly; the two set off toward the boy's small room at the back of the house.

"I got me some loot for us to sell," Jimmy told Joe when they were by themselves. "I also been thinking about something and got a plan to make more money."

"Count me in," his friend told him with a grin.

"When your folks go to bed, let's go to the barn and I'll show ya' what I got."

Waiting for another hour, the two heard Joe's parents' door close. Watching for the darkness that followed, they opened the bedroom window and crawled out quietly. When they reached the barn, Jimmy and Joe climbed the ladder and walked over to the loose hay and dug underneath, pulling out the quilt. As Jimmy spread it on the floor, Joe whistled under his breath as he touched the items.

"Nice haul," he told his friend. "Especially the silver. We'll be able to get a good price for that."

"Let's hide it again until morning, and then we'll set off to town and see what we can get for them. I want to tell you my plan. I think you'll like it."

After they had returned to the room, Jimmy sat on the bed and grinned with satisfaction.

"I know how we can get some *easy* money."

"How's that?"

"We're gonna rob my Pa's bank," he told him smugly.

"What!" his friend exclaimed. "Have you gone plum crazy?"

"Nope, he'll give us the money without a fight. I know my old man. He wouldn't dare lay a hand on me. And besides, with this, he won't say a word," he told him, pulling a small gun from his pocket.

"Where'd ya' get that?" Joe asked as he reached for the weapon to look it over.

"Stole it from a neighbor, that's where."

"But we'll have to stay on the run after that. They'll know who we are."

"Don't matter to me. I was planning on getting out of here anyway."

"Just when you wanting to do this?"

"I figure on Friday morning. Thursday night old man Farley makes a deposit from his mercantile, and we'll be rich."

"Sounds like you been thinking 'bout this for a while."

"I have. Well, what ya' think?"

With a flashing grin, Joe told his friend, "Let's do it. Your pa ain't man enough to shoot us."

Hearing these words brought a fleeting moment of wanting to defend his pa, but Jimmy pushed the thought into the recesses of his mind and began to think about how they would spend the stolen money they'd soon have.

Friday morning, both boys arose early. They had watched the bank closely the day before and saw when the best time would be to make their move. With masks made from a torn piece of cloth, the gun snuggly in Jimmy's pocket, the two crept around to the back of the building. After an elderly couple left, they checked out the empty street and ran into the bank. Spotting his father, his back to him, Jimmy yelled, "Everybody down, this is a hold up!"

Hearing the familiar voice, Mr. Richardson remained standing and turned to look into the bold eyes of his son.

"Give us your money and no one gets hurt," he yelled at the woman behind the counter and his pa, waving the gun at them.

"Son, what are you doing?" his father asked in disbelief.

"Pa, give us the money and we'll leave." Pointing the gun at his father, his hand shook slightly.

"Jimmy, what're ya' doing?" his friend asked. "Ya' can't shoot your pa."

In anger at being told what he could not do, the young boy pulled the trigger and watched in panic as a loud sound echoed through the building and his father tumbled to the floor.

In the jail next to the bank, the sheriff jumped to his feet and ran through the door, heading straight for the gunfire. He arrived in time to see the two masked men in the middle of their crime. One had a gun pointed at the woman while the other stuffed money into a bag. The lawman fired his own gun, sending one robber sprawling swiftly to the floor. The other masked man, watching his friend drop before him, threw up his arms and yelled, "Don't shoot!"

Hearing footsteps behind him, the sheriff saw Mark and Dr. Hill enter the small bank. Spotting the injured man on the floor, they dashed over and turned him over on his back to assess his wound. As they removed his mask, stun flooded through them when they saw that their patient was none other than Jimmy Richardson. Mark, knowing that this was who had attacked Rachel and D.J., rose to his feet, trying to get his emotions under control. Dr. Hill, knowing the feelings of the young man, nodded his head in understanding.

"I'll handle this one son," he told him quietly.

Joe, who stood silently, watching all that was happening, said, "Jimmy shot his Pa," pointing to behind the counter. Mark rushed back to find the man trying to sit up and holding his shoulder where the bullet had struck him. Blood was coursing down his expensive suit. It wasn't the injury that worried the young doctor; it was the look of hopelessness on the man's face.

"My son," he asked, "how is he?"

Dr. Hill rose to stand before him, shaking his head sadly as wrenching sobs poured from the banker.

"We need to take care of you, Mr. Richardson," the old doctor told the man, assisting him to his feet.

Walking past the dead body of his young son, the father knelt down and placed his bloody hand upon his only son's face, whispering softly, "I loved you, Jimmy. I gave you everything you ever wanted, thinking that I was helping you. Now I realize that I ruined you. I'm so sorry."

As he rose slowly to his feet, his heart felt like it had been wretched from his body. Never before had he felt such agony.

God, where are you now? his heart cried as they moved toward the clinic. Hearing his heavenly father speak to him as clearly as possible, he listened to the words.

I am right here with you, my son. I will carry you when you cannot walk; I will give you hope when all you feel is hopelessness, and I will give you comfort whenever you need it. I am all you need.

The funeral took place the next afternoon. The rain had begun early that morning. The boy's parents found it fitting that the weather should reflect their own moods. As they listened to the pastor tell about their son and his short life, they knew they would never see him again, that it was too late for him to receive Christ. Mr. Richardson, with stark revelation, became committed at that point to share his savior with whoever would listen. If he had anything to do with it, anyone he came in contact with would know for certain that Christ had died for them, and they did not have to be condemned to an eternal hell—a hell that now held his own son captive.

Chapter Nine

Little Sarah was finally beginning to sleep through the night without the terrifying nightmares. She was adjusting well to life at the O'Malley house, and Genie was positively glowing over her new daughter. As they sat at the table and practiced writing Sarah's name, she looked toward the woman beside her with a question in her dark eyes.

"Mrs. O'Malley," she began shyly.

"Yes, honey," Genie said as she brushed a stray piece of hair from her face.

"Would my real Mama be mad if I called you Mama now?"

Hearing her words, Genie did all she could do to stop from pulling the child into her arms and hugging her closely.

"I don't think so, why?"

"'Cause I want to," she replied in a serious tone.

Unable to stop herself, she gathered the little girl up into a loving embrace.

"You are one special person, do you know that?"

"What's that mean?"

"It means that we all love you dearly and are glad that God allowed us to be a part of your life."

Hugging her new mama tightly, Genie rocked the little one back and forth, humming softly. Supper and lessons could wait; Sarah needed reassurance that she was where God and her parents wanted her, and Genie was more than willing to offer it.

Ian walked through the door a few minutes later and, with tenderness on his face, walked over to them. Placing a hand on the child's head, he asked, "And how are my two lovely lassies this fine day?"

Shifting in Genie's arms, the little girl lifted her arms to be held by the man. Surprise covered his face when he heard her say, "We're fine, Papa."

Looking toward his wife, he saw her dab at her eyes and winked at her, whispering, "Aye, God is good, isn't He?"

At supper that evening, Matthew sensed a change in the attitude around the table. After hearing Sarah call his parents Mama and Papa, he smiled to himself. He knew what had happened.

"Sarah, how about if I pick you up after school tomorrow and we go looking for mushrooms in the woods?" Matthew asked with thoughtfulness.

"What's a *mushroon*?" the little girl asked to the pleasure of the adults, enjoying the mispronunciation of the word.

"It's a funny-looking thing that Mama will clean and cook for us for supper."

Nodding her head, dark eyes shone as she looked toward her new parents to make sure it was all right.

"That does sound like fun now. And maybe you can talk John into going with you so we'll have a batch to cook."

Hearing his name, John looked at his mother and smiled before telling them, "Well, if I can have a kiss, right here," he told the little girl, pointing to his cheek, "I might consider it."

With a small giggle erupting from the child, she climbed off her chair and ran to place a kiss on the young man's face. Grabbing her before she could leave, he tickled her until more giggles erupted.

"Okay, you two," Genie interrupted with a tender smile, "time to finish the lovely fried chicken the two of us worked so hard to fix."

As the little girl climbed up into her chair once more, Genie let her eyes linger on her two sons, thanking them with her eyes. She watched their latest addition with pride. In the short time Sarah had been with them, she had indeed worked her way into their hearts, every single member of the family. Even Laura, who had popped over for a short visit a few days ago, had been enamored with her new sister. Sarah needed them as much as they needed her.

"Hannah, are you almost ready?" her mother called to the young girl who now was bounding down the stairs.

"Yes, Mama," she answered with a giggle.

Watching as she passed, McKenna reached out and pulled her close for a hug.

"I love you, my little sunshine," she said as she felt the little girl touch her growing abdomen.

"I think it's a girl," she replied, distracted easily as the baby kicked her small hand.

"Do you, now? And what if it is a boy?"

Wrinkling up her brow, she told her mother in a serious voice, "Can we send him back for a girl?"

Laughter erupted from McKenna, and she said, "No, Hannah. God will give us the perfect baby, just for us. It won't matter if it is a girl or a boy, you will love being a big sister to the new little one."

Thinking on her mama's words, the girl brightly asked her, "Will I get to boss it around like D.J. does me?"

"I think D.J. is very patient with you. It's just that you can't go with him everywhere he goes."

Rachel, who was standing in the background, heard the exchange and smiled. She and Laura had always followed the O'Malley boys around. She knew they must have been pests to them, but the brothers never said a word about it. They were indeed special. Thinking about them, Matthew's face quickly appeared in her mind, and she felt a piercing in her heart.

Lord, please take these thoughts and feelings from me. It's not right now that I am engaged.

Shaking herself mentally, she saw her mama and Hannah head for the wagon to begin their journey to church.

"What do you think of Pastor Keller?" Tucker asked his mother on the way.

"He is a good preacher. He seems very nice."

"He is. He's a kind, godly man."

"Yes," McKenna chimed in, "he helps me deliver things to those in need when Tucker can't. He's the first one there whenever someone needs him. I've seen him stay awake all night on a Saturday with a family and still arrive at church to preach the next morning."

"It's hard to find good men like that," Mrs. Parker replied thoughtfully, recalling the distinguished older gentleman she had seen only a few times.

As they drove in front of the church, Tucker assisted the girls down from the wagon, and they entered the small building. Taking their usual seat in the middle, Mrs. Parker felt her eyes travel to the man they had been discussing. He was of average build and had salt and pepper hair and deep gray eyes. He was smiling, and the smile lit up his entire face.

I wonder what it would be like being married to such a man, she thought to herself. She noticed the woman sitting on the front row watching him intently.

It must be his wife, she thought with a flickering of disappointment. *What has gotten into you, woman?* she scolded herself. *Thinking about a married man in such a fashion, and a preacher no less.*

In somewhat of a daze throughout the sermon and singing, she felt the presence of someone behind her at its conclusion. She turned to see the woman from the front row.

"Hello, my name is Cora Keller. It's nice to meet you."

"Hello, I am Susan Parker."

"Yes, I heard that Tucker's mother was here to live. I hope you like our little community."

"I'm sure I will in time. It is wonderful to be near my family again, I must say."

Out of the corner of her eye, she saw Pastor Keller come to stand at their side.

"It's nice to have you with us again, Mrs. Parker. I hope you are adjusting to our area."

"Yes, I was just telling Mrs. Keller that things are going fine. It seems as though I've been here much longer than a month. I do love being around my loved ones again."

"Nothing like friends and family being near," he told her with a smile.

Grasping the woman's arm lightly, he told her, "Are you ready, Cora? I've got a family I need to stop by and visit and we must hurry."

"Of course, William."

Turning to face her again, the reverend said, "I hope to see you soon for a visit, Mrs. Parker. Would that be all right?"

"Yes, any time is fine. Goodbye now."

Watching the couple walk away, Tucker's mother felt a stirring that she hadn't felt since James's death. She was beginning to desire the need for male companionship.

God, You have been my husband since the death of James. Why am I feeling these things now? I have my family and grandchildren near, and You are always close. I thought that was enough.

All the way home, similar thoughts ran through the older woman's mind. She would pray and study God's Word to see if He was indeed trying to prepare her for something more in the days ahead.

A few days later, she heard a knock outside her door. Expecting to see one of her grandchildren, who had become frequent guests, she opened it up with a beaming smile. The smile quickly faded as she saw Pastor Keller standing before her.

"I'm sorry," he told her, noticing the look of surprise on her face. "Did I come at a bad time?"

"Oh no. I was just expecting one of the children. They usually stop by about this time. Come in," she told him as she held the door ajar.

"I'm afraid you'll have to excuse my living arrangements for now. Tucker insisted on my staying with them, but I know how a young family needs their privacy." With a small laugh, she said, "Besides, I think I've become a little independent over the years and fear that I may need my own privacy as much."

Hearing her honesty, the man chuckled and agreed. "I know exactly what you mean. Since my wife's death six years ago, I tend to like doing things my way now also."

Shock flooded her face, and she quickly tried to gain composure before asking without thought, "I assumed that Cora was your wife."

"Cora?" he answered in astonishment. "Heavens no. She was my eldest brother's wife. He passed away a little over two years ago, and I pick her up for church and occasionally help her around her house. We are just friends."

"Oh," she answered, unable to think of a single thing to say.

Glancing around, he admired the small soddy before telling her, "I have never lived in one of these types of homes, but I have to admit, it is rather cozy in here, isn't it?"

A flush appeared quickly on her face from the innocent remark, and before she could look into his warm gray eyes, she asked, "Would you care for some coffee? I just made some for myself."

"Yes, that does sound nice."

Pulling out a chair, the preacher sat at the table and placed his Bible in front of him.

"How long have you been in the ministry?"

"Almost thirty years now. And I can honestly say there is no other place I would rather be than doing what I have been called to do—serve God."

"I can tell. It shows when you are speaking."

Setting his coffee in front of him, she turned to retrieve her own cup before sitting opposite him. The pastor watched with interest as the woman walked the few short steps. She was an attractive woman, and her light step did not hint of her age.

The conversation flowed easily for the couple, and time flew. He shared some Scripture with her that had meant something to him through the years and also gave a bit of his testimony. Mrs. Parker had revealed far more than she had intended about her past life. He was so easy to talk to and had a real empathy for her when he offered condolences over the loss of her husbands. As she looked into his eyes, she knew intuitively that he was genuine. He did indeed have a heart for God.

Peering out the window much later, the pastor rose and told her apologetically, "Mrs. Parker, please forgive me. I feel I have over-stayed my welcome."

Rising to her feet, she smiled and, "I've enjoyed it immensely. Please come again any time you would like," she said, realizing that maybe she had spoken too much.

"I will. I wish all my visits were as pleasant." Turning to face her, he offered her his hand to shake. Feeling his warm one in hers, she averted her eyes to the floor.

"Will you be in church Sunday?" he asked quietly, reluctantly releasing her hand.

"Yes."

"I'll look forward to seeing you then. Thank you for your hospitality."

"You're welcome. Goodbye."

"Goodbye," he told her as he left the small place.

Watching him shut the door, she felt the warmth of her cheeks and grinned, knowing that it had nothing to do with the hot liquid she had been drinking.

Sunday morning arrived, and Susan Parker was ready early. She hoped it was not her imagination at how well the pastor and she had gotten along. She had heard him preach for several weeks. Not only had she talked with him briefly before the day of the visit but recognized the small fluttering of attraction to the handsome man. Walking to the mirror on her bureau, she examined her own appearance. She was a little on the plump side, and her once-dark hair had streaks of gray liberally sprinkled throughout. Her light brown eyes twinkled merrily as she began to recall the pastor's looks.

Does he find me as attractive as I find him? she wondered.

The ride to the church passed in a blur as she waited eagerly for sight of the building to appear. Taking Tucker's hand, he assisted her out of the buggy, and she waited while the rest of the family entered before her. She didn't want to appear overly anxious.

Taking their normal seats in the middle, she sat down and let her eyes search the front of the church. Pastor Keller was speaking to a young mother, and she watched as he leaned down to say something to the child in her lap with a smile on his face. Nodding his head at the child's words, he turned to leave and sat in the chair near the podium. Opening his Bible, he read for a few minutes and suddenly raised his eyes to look directly into her eyes. A small smile appeared on both of their faces, and he nodded before once again returning to study his sermon.

No, she thought to herself with relief, *it isn't just me who had these thoughts. Now what do we do, Lord?* she asked silently. Trying to recall how long ago she had experienced a similar feeling, she suddenly felt like a young school girl with her first crush instead of the fifty-nine-year-old woman that she really was.

Trying hard to concentrate, but hearing very little, her eyes seldom left the man's face in the front. She saw things about him that she had not seen before. His hair had a tendency to curl slightly at the nape of his neck, and darker streaks were evident of earlier years. His gray eyes twinkled when he smiled, and he obviously had a sense of humor as he related about several of his visits over the years. His voice had a soft, melodious quality that was easy to listen to, and when she was able to focus, she realized that he knew God's Word well. He often quoted verses without using his Bible. Her admiration was growing by leaps and bounds from just one very attentive hour in church.

After the service, she felt a hand on the back of her arm and knew intuitively that it was the man in her thoughts. Turning to face him, she saw him smile and heard him ask, "Could I speak to you for a moment, please, Mrs. Parker?"

"Of course," she returned and took the few steps to give them a little privacy.

"I know this may be somewhat forward, but would you mind if I asked you to supper tonight?" Seeing his hesitation, she heard him continue, "That is, if you don't mind my attentions."

Feeling warmth creep into her neck, she answered, "I think that would be fine. What time would you like for me to come?"

"Now what kind of a man would I be if I didn't retrieve you myself?" he asked her with a grin. "Somewhere around five o'clock would be perfect."

As their eyes locked, she whispered, "I'll be waiting. And Pastor," she added, "the name is Susan."

"And mine is William," he told her as he left her side to greet others.

Feeling the presence of her son next to her, he leaned down and asked, "Somehow I don't get the feeling that Pastor Keller was wishing you a good day."

Seeing the look in her eyes at his statement, she asked, "Is it silly for an old woman to go courting again?"

Realizing that she was very serious, he told her, "No, if that is who God has brought into your life, then there is nothing silly about it."

As they walked to the wagon, he knew his mother would be praying that afternoon about the new development. As for himself, he smiled. He couldn't be more thrilled with the prospect. Maybe he wouldn't build that house after all.

Over the next few weeks, the pastor and Tucker's mother seemed to be courting officially. Following lunch one day at the restaurant in Cheyenne, the couple drove near the lake. After assisting her down from the wagon, they headed toward a small grassy area and sat down to admire God's handiwork.

"It's beautiful, isn't it?" Susan asked as the sun's reflection shone off the gently moving water sparkling before them.

"Yes, it is at times like this that I wish I could paint or draw."

"I know just what you mean, but somehow I don't know if a portrait would do this justice."

After a moment of silence, Susan felt him take her hand in his and clear his throat before he began to say, "I think you know that I am coming to care for you."

"Yes," she answered as she peered into his eyes.

"I feel, however, with my position as pastor in the community, that we must take things slow."

Nodding in agreement, she said, "I would in no way want to interfere with your reputation as a leader of the flock."

"I am relieved to hear you say that. There are several people who would love nothing more than to spread rumors about us, and I would not want to jeopardize you in any way."

Feeling the warmth of his hand in her own for the first time, she felt her eyes travel in that direction.

With a small chuckle, he said, "I want you to know that it will not be easy going slowly. I suddenly feel like a lovesick teenager and want to shout it to the whole world."

With eyes that lit up her entire face, she exclaimed in understanding, "That's exactly what I thought a few days ago!"

"You know, my dear, after Martha's death, I didn't think I would even remotely entertain the possibility of getting married again. And until I met you, I didn't. Do you understand what I am saying?"

"Yes, I do. My husband James has been gone many years, and I thought I was happy by myself. Now, however…"

Placing her hand against his lips for a moment, he rose to his feet and assisted her up also.

"We'd better get going before someone sees us down here and lets their imagination wander."

"I am thankful that you don't want to harm your position," she told him sincerely as he helped her back into the wagon.

Before walking to the other side, he looked directly into her eyes and said, "It's you I am thinking about, not myself, Susan."

Long after William had left, his words dwelled in her mind.

Do men like this really exist, God? Is this where my future lies? Am I rounding a new bend in the road? Guide us and give us wisdom, Father.

With a smile of contentment on her face, she continued, *And Lord, I did say that if You told me I was to marry again, I would. I guess that's what You are saying, and I guess I'll have to be obedient.* She knew in her heart that this time obeying was going to be easy.

Chapter Ten

Two days later, Susan Parker heard a knock at the door and was surprised at who stood before her.

"Mrs. Parker," Cora Keller greeted her in a somewhat stiff manner. "May I come in?"

"Of course, Mrs. Keller," she returned as she stepped aside to let the woman enter.

After shutting the door, she shifted and looked into the very upset face of the woman.

"I don't think you realize what you are doing," she stated in a no-nonsense voice.

"What do you mean?" Susan asked.

"William and I had planned on getting married this fall. It has been an unspoken arrangement for quite some time. We have become very close, and he wanted to give me time to heal from the grief of losing my husband. Now that you are here, you have begun to place ideas in his head, and he is unsure how to handle this situation with you."

Not knowing how to reply to her words, Susan stood in astonishment.

"I didn't know," she whispered in shock.

"I felt I had to tell you before this little thing of yours begins to change. William has already told me that he said things to you in a weak moment and regrets his words. He is unsure of how to tell you of his mistake and asked me to speak with you."

Feeling the words penetrate and cut her heart in two, Susan listened in shock as the woman concluded.

"I ask you for the sake of our love and impending marriage, please tell him that you wish to end your friendship. I really don't think you want to humiliate either yourself or him by continuing. He is a man of honor and does not wish to hurt you."

Knowing that the woman spoke the truth about the pastor, she watched in disbelief as Cora walked to the door.

"I know you are to see him tonight. Would you like for me to take a note back to him, telling him you have had a change of heart? It's the least I can do to help ease a somewhat embarrassing situation."

Moving to the small desk against one wall in a daze, Susan took out a piece of paper and a pencil to write an apology to the man who had somehow found his way into the regions of her lonely heart. She stated briefly that she no longer wished him to call and that she had changed her mind. Handing it to a smiling Cora, she stood in the doorway for several moments, feeling a wave of sorrow flood through her.

How could I have been so blind? she asked herself as she felt tears gather in her eyes. Walking in automation, she sat in the rocker.

Her heart felt as empty and cold as the black coffee cup that sat on the table.

Cora knocked on William's door and waited with a smile of satisfaction until she saw him open it.

"Cora, this is a surprise," he told the woman.

"I just happened to run into Tucker Parker, and he asked if I would give this to you. I told him I would be happy to drop it off on my way home."

Taking the letter from her outstretched hand, he said, "Thank you for bringing it by. I hope it's not bad news."

Not for me, she thought as she watched him open the door enough to allow her to pass.

"I've just baked some fresh bread. Would you care for a piece?" the kind man asked his sister-in-law.

"That sounds marvelous, William," she replied as she placed a hand over his own and entered to stand near him, not bothering to withdraw her own hand.

Feeling slightly uncomfortable with her action, the pastor cleared his throat and walked toward the cooling bread near the sink, breaking the contact.

"Take a chair. I'll cut you a piece and pour you a nice, cold glass of milk."

Susan Parker sat for some time in a foggy haze. Something did not feel right about the entire situation. She couldn't believe that William would not have told her of his plans with his sister-in-law. Standing to her feet, face set in determination, she headed to get the old wagon to hitch up the horse and go talk to him herself.

Working as quickly as possible, she climbed up and set off in the direction of William's house. Words from the woman kept running through her mind. And her smile before she left, it almost looked as though it were a triumphant one.

As she rounded the bend before his house, she noticed a small buggy out front. Drawing closer, she could see the distinct silhouette of a woman through the window.

"Cora!" she said aloud. With a sickening realization that she had told the truth, she turned the wagon around and began to return to her small house.

Tears fell unchecked and she wept silently. How would she ever go to church and face the couple again, knowing that they knew her feelings? She had made a fool of herself by encouraging the attention of the pastor—a man who was already spoken for.

Maybe instead of a house next to Tucker and McKenna, she would move to Cheyenne. She knew that she would not be able to show her face in the small church again.

Help me make the right decisions, God, she cried in aching her heart.

William had not had time to read the letter sitting on the mantle. His sister-in-law had stayed for the better of two hours. Although he enjoyed her company, her strong personality could become tedious after any lengthy time spent in her presence.

Reaching for the letter, he walked to the rocking chair to read its contents. In disbelief, he read it twice. Leaning his head back against the chair, he felt hurt permeate his soul. He thought he had known Susan Parker; he was wrong. He had obviously made a fool of himself, and she had toyed with his affections. A wall of bitterness grew around his heart. They had seemed so right together. She understood him. He had told her things he had not shared with anyone since his wife's death, and she had betrayed him.

Rising to his feet in a stupor, he moved toward the bedroom.

How am I to face her in church? he asked himself as he readied for bed. *And how am I to get over this pain in my heart?*

Sunday morning dawned bright and sunny, and as the Parker family gathered to climb into the wagon for church, Tucker told them, "I'll go and get Mama. She's a little late today."

Walking briskly toward the small soddy, he knocked lightly and entered. Seeing his mother sitting at the table with her Bible before her, he asked, "Aren't you going to church this morning?"

"No, I'm not feeling well today," she answered quietly, her eyes not meeting his.

"Are you sick? Does one of us need to stay with you?"

"It is nothing to worry about. I'm sure it will pass with time," she told him in a soft voice, not daring to look into his eyes.

"Can I get you something before we leave?"

"I will be fine. Please, son," she said as she brought her brown eyes to look into his own blue ones. "Take your family and don't worry about me."

Sensing there was more than just a sickness, he asked with concern, "Did something happen between you and Pastor Keller? I haven't seen him around the past few days."

"We have decided that we were not right for one another. I don't wish to embarrass him by attending for a few weeks."

Thoughts filtered through his brain, and he knew that something was definitely wrong. He intended to talk to the man himself if given the chance.

"All right, if you are sure."

"I'm positive. I'll see you when you get back."

"Goodbye," he told her as he shut the door and stood beside it for a moment. He knew his mother well, and one thing was for sure, she was heartbroken.

Hearing the door shut, Susan Parker laid her head down on her arms on the table and wept. She was wrong when she had told him that she would be all right in a few weeks. The hurt went too deep to heal in that short period of time. With weariness washing through her, she stood to her feet and moved in slow motion toward the bed. She had not been sleeping well since Cora's visit and thought that if she rested a little while, she might feel better. Removing her shoes, she climbed under the quilt, and sleep soon claimed her fatigued body.

"Pastor," Tucker called to the man walking toward the front of the church after the service.

Hearing his voice, the older man smiled and asked, "Yes, Tucker, what can I do for you?"

"If you don't mind my asking, is there something wrong between my mother and yourself?"

The abrupt statement caught him off guard for a second before he said casually, "It seems your mother has changed her mind, that's all. It's perfectly all right."

"Did something happen?"

"I really don't know. That's what puzzles me."

"Are you going to talk to her about it?" her son asked frankly.

"No, she wrote me a note and asked me not to call anymore. I will honor her wishes."

Shaking his head, the younger man was unsure of what to say. "I'm sorry," were the only words he could think of.

"Thank you, I am sorry too. More than you'll ever know," the pastor replied in sadness.

As he shook the reverend's hand, there was one thing Tucker was certain of—the man had the same hurt and bewilderment on his face that his mother had. He just didn't know what he could do to help.

The next few weeks were miserable for the older couple. Neither was aware of the scheme at work by Cora Keller. She had asked William over for the evening with every intention of trying to catch him on the rebound.

Hearing his wagon approach outside her door, she opened the door with a beaming smile on her face.

"Hello. You made it here on time," she told him.

"Yes, no calls to make on the way over, which helps."

As he stepped through the door, she reached over and gave him a quick hug, hoping to make him aware of her intentions.

"I hope you are hungry. Supper is ready."

"Yes, I am, and it smells wonderful."

"I made all of your favorites…just for you," she added.

After the meal, as they sat near the crackling fire, Cora spoke, "William, have you ever thought about marriage again?"

"Yes, lately I have," he told her honestly, his thoughts resting on Susan.

"I have also. I realize how much I need a good man around to care not only for the house, but for me."

Unsure of where she was going with her words, he waited patiently.

"What if we were to be married?" she asked abruptly.

Looking quickly at her to see if she was serious, he noted that she was.

"I would be a good wife for you and a good pastor's wife. I know the people in the community and am well respected." Turning to face him, she took one of his hands in her own and continued, "I think we would complement each other well."

Knowing she had surprised him, she asked quietly, "Don't you find me attractive?"

"Well, yes, Cora, you are a very attractive woman."

"What is the problem then? I find you handsome also, and we are friends already, which is always a good basis for a marriage."

Hearing her words, which seemed to make sense to him, he felt her lightly caress his hand as she told him, "I do love you, William. And I think in time, you would love me also."

Sensing that he was weakening, she continued, "We could be married a week from Saturday while the guest pastor is visiting."

Shock flooded through him. He was in love with Susan Parker, he knew it. But he also knew that there was no hope for the situation. Could he and Cora make a marriage work? Would he be able to love her also?

Without hesitating, lest he change his mind, he said, "Yes, we can."

Standing to her feet, she threw her arms around him and hugged him. As he hugged her back, he got the distinct impression that something did not feel right and perhaps he had just made the worst decision of his life.

"Wonderful. I'll take care of all the arrangements. We can be married late that morning."

As he sat and listened to her make plans, instead of feeling like a man in love about to be wed, he felt like he was getting prepared to preach a sermon at a funeral—*his*.

Walking toward the door a short time later, she asked, "Aren't you going to kiss me, William? After all, we are going to be man and wife."

Bending over, he brushed his lips against her forehead and heard her say, "I think you can do better than that," and stood on tiptoe to kiss him herself.

All the way home, he remembered her kiss and the coldness it made him feel inside.

The news of the upcoming marriage spread quickly through the small town. Tucker had heard it while picking up a part for a piece of his farm machinery. The postmistress had spotted him coming from the mercantile and told him of the news. With astonishment on his face, he listened as she told him the details of how the pastor and his sister-in-law would be married a week come Saturday.

On the way home, Tucker was deep in thought as to how he was going to tell his mother. He knew she was hurting already, and the news would just add to the ache. He and McKenna had talked about whether they should try to intercede, but hearing about the wedding took the matter out of their hands.

As he pulled into the long path that led to their house, he stopped the wagon in front of the soddy. Slowly and prayerfully, he walked to the door and knocked.

His mother, seeing the look on his face, asked, "What's wrong, son?"

"We need to talk. There's something I need to tell you, and I would rather you hear it from me than someone else."

Taking her arm, he led her to the small table and both sat down.

"Mama," he began looking into her questioning face, "I saw Mrs. Carter in town, and she told me that Pastor is to be married a week from Saturday to Cora Keller."

As she stared down at her hands folded on the table, Tucker saw her bottom lip quiver slightly before she said, "I have been expecting this news. It still doesn't make it any better actually hearing it though."

Grasping her hands in his, he whispered, "I am so sorry that you are hurting."

Glancing up to stare into his eyes, she smiled a small smile and said, "I know, son. God never promised us that life would be easy though, did He? My heart will heal in time. Just keep praying for me please."

"We always do." Standing to his feet, he said, "Come to the house with me. You can help McKenna fix supper and listen to Hannah's endless chatter about school."

"I believe I will," she replied as she followed him toward the door. "There's no sense in sitting here and feeling sorry for myself when I can be with my loved ones." Having said these words, she thought once again of the man she had given her heart to, only to be given it back.

Chapter Eleven

One week later, Tucker burst through the house with D.J. in his arms.

"Quick, McKenna, get the bed ready. He's been bitten by a rattlesnake and I've got to get the poison out of him now."

Feeling her knees go weak at the sight of her son, who was sweating profusely, she ran to prepare his room. Thoughts of her father and his death from a similar bite made her sick inside. She could not see her own flesh and blood perish like her father had.

"Get Rachel in the barn and tell her to go for Mark," Tucker said over his shoulder as he held the blade of his knife over the open fire. "I'll need some clean rags and hot water."

Needing to be told nothing more, the pregnant woman ran as swiftly as possible for the barn.

"Rachel!" she cried as she entered.

"Yes, Mama?"

"Get the horse and find Mark. D.J. has been bitten by a snake and we need him. Please hurry," she urged with a voice that quivered.

"I will, Mama," she said as she climbed quickly from the loft and grabbed a nearby bridle.

McKenna, rushing back to the house, felt the fear of death grip her and prayed that her son would not suffer and die before their very eyes.

As she entered the house, she heard D.J. yell out. She knew that Tucker was cutting away the bitten area of skin and was piercing the wound to drain out as much poison as possible. Helplessness moved through her as she gathered clean rags and waited for the water to heat.

Mark arrived a short time later with a grim look on his face. He had dealt with snake bites before and knew that few survived. Heading to the wounded boy's bed, he removed the bandage and examined the red, angry-looking area on D.J.'s leg. Reaching for his bag, he grabbed the chloroform and a rag and some vile medicine. Dousing the rag, he stood near D.J. and told him, "I'm going to help you rest a little while so I can clean out the area."

With pain evident in his eyes, the boy only nodded, saying nothing.

When Mark felt that he was semiconscious, he moved to sit on the bed and opened the bottle. The foul odor filled the air. Holding the rag to the side of the wound, he liberally poured the liquid over it, watching as it festered up. Pouring until there was no more bubbling, he meticulously wrapped it tightly again.

As he looked into the eyes of his dear friends, he had difficulty forming words that could offer them comfort.

"We will just have to wait and see now how much poison went through his system. I see you've drained the wound, Mr. Parker; that should help. I would like to say that everything will be fine, but I honesty don't know. He is young and healthy, and that will work in his favor. We also have the power of prayer. The next few days will tell one way or another."

At his words, McKenna felt her knees begin to buckle beneath her and saw her husband rush to her side.

"Come on, love, you need to rest. You can pray for D.J. in our room."

Knowing that she did not want to leave her son's side, he continued, "Mark will be here with him, and so will I. Please, McKenna. We may need you later to sit with him."

Realizing that he was right, she let him lead her to their bedroom.

Sitting down on the bed and hugging the pillow, she felt tears pour down her face as she cried out to God in a silent prayer.

God, spare him. You gave him to us, and I know You love him more than we do, but Father, we need him. Please, if it be Your will, let him live. Remove this poison from him and touch him with Your healing hand.

Tucker checked in on her later and was relieved to see her asleep. He didn't wake her up, she needed the rest. From the words of Mark, it was going to be a rough few days ahead.

McKenna bathed her son's face over and over throughout the long night. D.J. moaned and reached for his leg repeatedly. Sweat poured from him, and Tucker had to change his wet clothing several times.

Mark had gone home and would return in the morning. He had said D.J. was in God's hands, and they had much more healing in them than he did.

Feeling the touch of her husband's hand on her shoulder, he said, "Please rest now. I will stay and keep him cool."

"No, I need to be with him," was all she said.

"Mama," D.J. whispered a few minutes later, "can I have some water?"

Watching Tucker head to retrieve his request, she told her son, "Yes, now listen to me, D.J. You fight with all your might. Don't you give up, you hear?"

"I am trying, Mama."

Tucker walked to the front of the bed and assisted his son with a few sips of the cool liquid.

Lying back against the damp bedclothes, they watched as he drifted off into a tormented sleep, crying out frequently for someone to help him.

The O'Malleys had been over and taken Hannah home with them. It had frightened the little girl to see her brother in so much pain.

Throughout the long night, parents took turns bathing their son and talking soothing words to him. Tucker had even read from the Bible several times and noticed the calming affect God's Word had on him.

Mark arrived early the next morning as the sun was rising. He didn't know why he had even bothered to go home, for he had slept so little worrying about the boy.

Opening the door, he walked swiftly to his young friend's room. His fears resurfaced as he saw D.J. tossing to and fro with obvious delirium, which was not a good sign. Walking to the bed, he sat down and placed his bag near him on the floor. Unwrapping the bandage, he saw that the wound was fiery red and had pus oozing from it. Reaching for his bottle of disinfectant and a rag, he poured it over the angry bite marks until it no longer festered. At least D.J. was not conscious enough to feel the pain of the strong disinfectant. With a clean bandage, he wrapped it lightly and placed the bottle in his bag. Standing to his feet, he had a disheartening look present on his face.

"He's not doing well," was all he said.

McKenna began to sob, and she felt Tucker pull her close.

"We can't give up our hope and faith in God now though. And we can't let D.J. either. Keep talking to him, encouraging him." Looking into the eyes of Tucker, he asked, "Can you get the tub in and put cold water in it? It may help reduce the fever that is consuming him."

Without further words, the man moved toward the door to retrieve the large tub. After filling it with cold water, the men removed D.J.'s long underwear and lowered him into the water.

After fifteen minutes or so, they both helped him back to bed, covering him with a light blanket. Exhaustion was evident on the youth's features, but he drifted off to a more peaceful sleep shortly after.

"When he wakes up, we need to try and get fluids in him to replace what he's lost," Mark told his parents.

The door opened at that point, and Mrs. Parker entered with worry on her face. She had been a frequent visitor and had helped them during their vigil in the night. Tucker had insisted she go home and rest before returning.

"Is he any better?" she asked in a hopeful voice.

"He is sleeping now," Mark told her.

"I have been praying constantly."

"That is what D.J. needs more than anything," the young doctor told her, knowing in his heart how truthful the words were.

A few minutes later, there was a soft knock on the door. McKenna, opening it, looked into the eyes of Pastor Keller.

"I just heard about D.J.," he told her with concern. "Is there something I can do to help?"

"Just pray," she whispered as tears coursed down her cheeks.

"I have been and will continue to do so until God touches his body with His healing hand," the kind man replied, not adding that His healing hand may be when D.J. was in heaven. Only the almighty God knew that for Himself.

"Please come in," McKenna added as an afterthought, feeling the presence of her husband at her side.

Stepping inside the house, Pastor Keller noticed for the first time that Susan stood near the fireplace. He knew her presence might be unavoidable, but until actually seeing her did he realize how much love he felt in his heart.

Nodding his head in greeting, he asked if he could pray over the boy. Leading him toward their son's room, McKenna and Tucker showed the pastor the way.

Susan felt moisture gather in her eyes and knew she had to be gone before William returned. Grabbing her shawl off the peg, she left through the door and walked swiftly toward the barn.

After a short visit, with assurances that D.J. would be in his prayers constantly, the dear pastor left. As he began to climb into the wagon, he heard what he thought was crying coming from the barn. Thinking that it might be Rachel in need of comfort, he walked in that direction. Crossing the threshold, he saw Susan with her back to him, sitting on a small bench, sobbing softly.

Clearing his throat to make her aware of his presence, he moved closer to her.

"I'm sorry this happened," he told her, thinking that she was crying for her grandson.

"Thank you," she returned, afraid to discover if he was talking about D.J. or their brief relationship.

"I've heard of your engagement to Cora. May I offer my congratulations," she said after a moment of awkward silence.

"Yes, we are to be married this Saturday."

Silence enfolded them, and only the moving of the animals could be heard.

"Can I ask you a question, Susan?" the pastor asked a second later, running his hand distractedly through his hair.

"Yes," she answered in almost a whisper.

"Why couldn't you tell me yourself of your change of heart instead of having Tucker give your note to Cora? I had thought you would have more respect for me than to do so in such a manner."

Hearing his declaration and not understanding what her son had to do with any of this, she paused before he continued.

"I thought you cared for me enough to tell me in person of your decision. I must admit that you disappointed me." *And you broke my heart*, he thought to himself.

"I don't understand," she replied in a confused voice. "I gave the note to Cora herself when she visited me that day. Tucker didn't know anything about it."

He walked over to sit next to her.

"I distinctly remember Cora telling me that she had seen Tucker earlier, and he had asked her to hand deliver it to me herself. She never mentioned that she had been to see you." Thinking of their earlier conversation, pieces began to fall into place. He had always known of the woman's jealousy concerning him. She had often hinted that they should get married. Could she have deceived them both into a lie?

"Why did Cora visit you?" he asked her, wanting to get to the bottom of the situation.

Turning to face him, her eyes were filled with unshed tears as she told him, "She said that she came because you had asked her to handle things between us. You changed your mind about your intentions and were embarrassed by my feelings. The two of you were to be wed soon."

With disbelief on his attractive face, he replied, "What! She actually told you that?"

Nodding her head, she watched his face as a smile began to appear.

"No, my dear Susan. Why would I desire to be with her when I am already in love with someone else?"

Seeing the smile, she asked, "But I came to your house right after she left and saw her buggy. I could see her through the window."

Trying to recall that particular day, he took one of her hands in his own and said, "She came to deliver your note. I had just made some bread, I believe, and asked if she cared to have some. There was nothing more to it than that. You do believe me, don't you?" he asked with a pleading look on his face.

"Why would she lie to us both?"

"I'm afraid I am somewhat to blame for that. She has made her intentions known for the last year, and although I never encouraged her, I never dissuaded her either."

"What of your upcoming marriage on Saturday?" she asked, still not daring to hope that things might be as they were before.

"It will still take place," he told her with a satisfying smile, "only it will be with a different woman. At least I hope so," he added with a twinkle in his gray eyes.

"Will you, Susan Parker, take this man, William Keller, to be your lawful, wedded husband?" he asked her as he bent down on one knee before her.

"Oh, William," was all she could say as she wrapped her arms around his neck and clung to him, making sure she wasn't dreaming.

"I will take that as a yes, Susan." Pulling away from her, he gazed into her eyes and told her, "I love you."

"And I love you," she whispered back.

"May I kiss you?"

Nodding her head, he grinned before he kissed her with their first kiss. The feeling of love swept through him, and he knew that she was the woman God wanted him to share the remainder of his life with.

"Do you think we should share the good news with your family now or wait?" he asked thoughtfully.

"Now would not be the right time. Not with D.J. so critical. You go home and come back tomorrow evening. Somehow I think that God has more in store for that boy than taking him home to glory."

"I will be back tomorrow. I may not have to drive. I think I'll be floating," he told her with a grin as he headed toward the wagon.

On the way home, his grin changed to a frown. He would stop by his sister-in-law's house and pay her a visit first. It was time to get things cleared up.

The next morning when Mark climbed the steps of the Parker residence, he was afraid of what he would find. D.J. had not had a good night. He had taken a turn for the worse. Although he was resting somewhat more comfortably by the time he had left around three o'clock this morning, he was still uncertain of his outcome.

Opening the door, relief flowed through him when he saw McKenna sitting at the table with a smile on her face. Surely she would not be happy if her son were worse.

"Oh, Mark," she told him as she rose somewhat awkwardly to her feet, "D.J.'s fever broke this morning, and he actually said he was hungry."

Laughter bubbled up, and he came to hug her in relief.

"That is the best thing I could possibly hear," he told her as he released her and headed for the bedroom.

Entering the room, he saw Tucker and Rachel standing near the bed. His sister was feeding him sips of broth. Sitting on the edge near his patient, he stated, "You had us worried there, D.J."

"I sure didn't feel very good. At times I hoped I would die," he told them truthfully.

"There were too many of us praying that you wouldn't. I think God has things for you to do before He takes you home with Him. And we are all very thankful indeed."

"Papa and Mama wouldn't let me go. Every time I felt like I could close my eyes and drift away, I would hear their voices encouraging me to fight."

"You have good parents," Mark told him as he looked admiringly toward the Parkers.

Unwrapping the bandage on his leg, Mark noticed that it didn't look quite as swollen or red.

"I need to put some more disinfectant on it, you know," he told him with a frown.

"I was sort of hoping that you could forget that part now," the young boy said, remembering the horrible burning it caused.

"Just a few more times and maybe that will be all."

After finishing his broth, the young boy clutched the sides of the bed and told Mark, "Better hurry before I change my mind."

Reaching for the bottle, he grabbed another rag and quickly poured the burning liquid over the open wound.

Even though the boy grimaced in pain, he never cried out or moved.

"You are more of a man than some of the biggest, most burly men I have taken care of, D.J.," Mark told him with a grin. "I have seen this bottle reduce some to blubbering babies."

Hearing his words, D.J. felt himself glow.

"I can't promise I won't yell out the next time," the young boy added with a soft chuckle.

"And I won't tell anyone," Mark told him with a grin as he stood to his feet.

He felt the presence of Rachel beside him as he moved toward the door.

"Do you mind if I steal this lovely woman to myself for a short while?" he asked her parents. "It seems we have been too busy to see much of one another lately."

"Of course," Tucker told the couple, remembering new love and how exciting it was. *Although, I'm in love now more than ever*, he thought, remembering his decidedly pregnant wife. Walking into the kitchen, he stood near McKenna and leaned down to kiss her on the top of her head. With a look of love on her face, she heard him say, "I love you."

"And I love you," she whispered as she sat up straighter in the chair in a quick fashion, placing a hand over her rounded abdomen.

"Busy today?" he asked, referring to the baby.

"Yes, and getting stronger everyday. I think my ribs must surely be bruised by now."

Pulling up a chair to sit near her, Tucker placed a hand on her stomach and, after only a few seconds, felt a strong kick against his palm.

"Has to be a boy," he said with a grin. "Or one strong girl."

"It's hard to say. Hannah certainly worked me over while I carried her."

"That's true. Not much longer and we'll meet this little one," he said as he felt another kick.

Both laughed as they continued to feel the active movements of their little one.

The following evening, a knock was heard at the door of the Parker family. They had just begun to gather for their meal. Susan, knowing who would be on the other side of the door, opened it with a bright smile.

"Hello," she told William as she reached for his hand. Entering, the couple noticed the bewildered faces of McKenna and Tucker.

"Hello," the pastor greeted the family warmly.

"What a surprise," McKenna said as she looked with a puzzled expression toward her mother-in-law. "We're just sitting down to eat. Let me get a plate for you to join us."

"I didn't come to eat," he told her with a grin. "But since you are offering, I won't refuse."

"And what did you come for?" Tucker asked with perception, his voice filled with amusement.

"To ask for your mother's hand in marriage, my dear boy."

Looking at the beaming woman, he saw her nod her head.

"If this is what you wish, how can I say no?" he told the couple as he extended his hand toward the older man.

"Well, it took us a little while to sort through some things, but I think we're on the right road now," Pastor Keller declared.

"Let's sit down, and we can hear the details," McKenna told them with anxiousness. "I do like a good love story."

D.J. was not strong enough to join them and had already finished his supper. Although tiring easily, he had begun to feel like his old self.

While they ate, the two told of what had transpired, much to the bewilderment and shock of McKenna and Tucker.

"And she did this on purpose?" McKenna asked in amazement.

"Yes, she admitted it when I confronted her. She broke down and told me she had always hoped I would grow to love her."

"What are her plans now?" Tucker asked.

"She is moving to her sister's home to a small town south of Cheyenne."

"Was she remorseful over her actions?" Susan asked.

"Not as much as I had hoped. That lies between her and God now."

Dwelling briefly on the woman's behavior, McKenna quickly averted the train of thought and asked, "Can I ask when the wedding is?"

"Saturday morning," they both replied in unison.

"What!" her daughter-in-law exclaimed. "Why, that's not enough time to get things done and get you a dress made."

"My dear McKenna," Susan told her with a smile, "I am fifty-nine years old and don't need a fancy dress. We can make a few things for a reception at William's house following the ceremony. That is all either of us desire."

Seeing the perplexity on the younger woman's face caused Susan to laugh.

"It will be fine, honey," she told her.

"Are you sure that's all you want?"

Turning to face the man at her side, she replied softly, "This is all I want."

Taking her hand in his, the pastor lifted it to his lips and placed a tender kiss on it before saying, "And you are all I want."

"I think I'm going to cry," McKenna stated as she stood to her feet.

Her husband chuckled before telling their guest, "You have to excuse her, Reverend, my wife tends to be a little more emotional now."

"Perfectly understandable, my boy. No need to explain."

Facing his mother with a knowing grin, Tucker stated, "I guess the little seed sprouted this time."

"Not only sprouted," she told him with a beaming smile, "it's in full bloom." Noticing the baffled look on her fiancé's face, she told him, "I will explain later."

Throughout the meal, Tucker, watching in amusement his mother and her future husband, felt joy spread through him. He never would have dreamt that his own parent could act like a young girl in love for the first time. The couple kept darting small glances at one another, and he saw Pastor Keller more than once reach under the table to hold her hand. He looked toward his wife to see if she had noticed, and by the expression on her face, she had.

Saturday dawned cold but bright. The sun even tried to peek through the gray clouds above. McKenna, knocking on the door to the soddy, watched as a beautiful bride-to-be stood before her.

"Does this outfit look all right?" Susan asked with a nervousness she had not felt for many years.

Studying the light blue dress with the lace around the neck, she told her in a reassuring tone, "It is lovely, just as you are. Besides, I don't think your groom will even notice what you are wearing."

"I probably won't see what he has on either," she told McKenna in frankness.

"Now, aren't you glad you decided to move out here?"

"If I had known what was waiting, I would have been here a lot sooner. Was William here when I was staying with you last summer? I don't recall having seen him at the church."

"No, he just came in the fall. He had filled in several times previously for our old pastor and was familiar with the area and people."

"I know it's a little late to ask, but you and Tucker do approve, don't you?"

Hugging the woman as closely as possible considering her growing abdomen, she told her, "We are thrilled. Does that mean that God told you he was the one?" she asked, recalling the woman's words from before.

"Yes, right from the very beginning. I was drawn to him."

"I know just what you mean. I have felt that way about your son from the first time I saw him. He's all I could think about."

"I know, honey, and he felt the same way about you. I knew that things would work out for you once you were married. God had His hand in your marriage and had ordained it for you to meet."

"Just like He had His in your marriage, Mama Parker. It is a union made in heaven."

"I do like that, honey. I will share it later with William."

Laughing, McKenna saw her mother-in-law blush for the first time when she told her, "Somehow I don't think you'll be telling him what I said when you are alone."

Without further words, smiles on their faces and in their hearts, both women exited to find Tucker and get to the church. It was time for a wedding.

The ceremony was simple and quiet with only family and a few friends from the church present. Vows were exchanged with love and commitment, and their sincerity touched those who were present. As Rachel watched her grandmother get married, she felt Mark reach over and take her hand. Soon, they, too, would be standing before others and God as they were wed and the thought did little to cheer her.

As the newlyweds entered William's home, Susan turned to face her husband and said, "I didn't think I would ever be married again. But now, I don't know how I could possibly return to being single. I need you by my side. There was a void present when we weren't seeing one another."

"I feel the same way, my dear. If someone had told me that, after Martha's death, I would be standing before my new bride with wedding night jitters, I would have laughed."

"Truly," she asked with wonder, "you are nervous because of me?"

Gazing into her warm brown eyes filled only with love, he replied, "No, maybe not," and led her to the room they would share as husband and wife.

McKenna had been correct; thoughts of the women's earlier conversation were never discussed.

Chapter Twelve

"Matthew, where are you?" Mark called out as he entered the house.

Hearing his name, the oldest sibling descended the steps two at a time and waited for him to tell him what he wanted.

"I need you to do me a big favor," he told his older brother.

"What's that?" he enquired.

"Tonight is the first ice skating party for the church, and I can't make it. Mr. Johnson has taken ill and I need to run over and keep an eye on him for a while."

"So what's the problem?" Matthew asked.

"I promised Rachel that I'd take her, and I can't disappoint her now. She loves to skate so much and has been looking forward to it all week. I'm afraid I haven't been able to do much with her lately and can't let her down again."

Feeling his heart plunge to his stomach, Matthew found he couldn't find the right words to say.

"You don't have to stay long. Just let her skate for a little while and then take her home."

"Can't she go with John?" he asked in a hopeful voice.

"No, he has a date with Marsha. It's his first and he's a little nervous."

"Well…" he began with uncertainty.

"Great!" Mark finished. "I really appreciate it," he said as he turned and hurried back out the door. "It starts at five o'clock, by the way. I told her I'd pick her up around four thirty. Thanks," he said as he shut the door.

Feeling as though a weight had suddenly been placed around his heart, Matthew proceeded up the stairs to get ready for the evening. He both dreaded and looked forward to spending time with Rachel. He would have to be careful around her so that his feelings wouldn't be made known to her, which was not something that would be easy to do.

An hour later, Rachel heard the soft knock on the door and opened it with a beaming smile on her face. The smile quickly changed when she saw Matthew standing before her.

"Is Mark all right?" she asked in a worried tone.

"Yes, he's fine. He just had something come up with a patient and had to leave rather abruptly. I'm afraid you'll have to put up with my company tonight."

Trying to gather her composure at seeing the handsome man before her, she told him, "Let me grab my things and we can be going."

Watching her walk around the room and collect various things, he felt his heart flip. His love was becoming like a demon inside of him. He knew he was weak where Rachel was concerned. Praying, he asked God to give him strength to get through the evening.

After retrieving items she would need, she turned to smile a large smile at him.

I wish you meant that smile, he told himself inwardly. She was lovely with a warm, red scarf tied around her face, emphasizing the white, creamy complexion and her deep blue eyes.

"Are you ready?"

"Yes," he told her. "I brought an extra blanket for you to keep warm on the ride there and back."

"Thank you."

He is always so kind and thoughtful, she told herself as they trudged through the snow toward the sleigh.

Not daring to lift her up this time, he took her arm to assist her. The fresh aroma of her hair sent small sparks to his heart as he helped her. After climbing in himself, he tucked the blanket snuggly around her to keep the coolness of the air from her legs.

This is a mistake, his mind told him. *I should never have agreed to this in the first place. My heart is too vulnerable to handle her presence.*

After riding for several moments in silence, he finally asked, "So, have you and that brother of mine set a date for the wedding?"

"Yes, I think we've decided on the middle of December."

"Do you know where you are going to live?" he asked, cringing inwardly at the thought of the two of them sharing a home.

"Mark is checking on several places in town. We're not sure yet though."

Silence surrounded them again before she placed a hand on his arm and laughed an endearing laugh.

"Do you remember when we all tried to skate on the pond behind your house?"

Snickering as he recalled the event, he said, "Yes, how could I forget that? That pond was so rough from the wind, and we were just learning. It was terrible. I think I was sore for a week from all the spills."

"I think we all were black and blue after that brilliant idea of Mark's."

"Yes, but you were the clever one to suggest going sledding instead."

"I had to. My backside could not take another fall."

An easy, lighthearted mood followed after that as the two reminisced of various things from their childhood. Laughter flowed frequently from them, and time passed swiftly. Soon, they were pulling the sled in front of the large pond where the party was taking place.

After putting their skates on, the couple set off toward the ice and began to skate near one another. Christy Martins, Rachel noticed, began skating closer and closer to Matthew. She watched as the young woman pretended to fall near him. As she landed somewhat ungracefully near him, he helped her to her feet in a gentlemanly manner. In an over friendly voice, she told him thank you and smiled her brightest smile. She was an attractive, dark-haired girl who loved to get a boy's attention and then head for greener grass and new conquests. It made Rachel angry to think that she had set her eyes on Matthew. He was much too nice a person to be treated that way. Before Christy could draw him away from her, she grabbed his arm and asked, "Why don't we take a break and get some hot chocolate?"

"Great," he replied with a smile, unaware of her thoughts.

As they skated off toward the refreshments, Christy could be seen standing in the spot they had left with a very unattractive scowl on her face.

After taking only a five-minute break, Matthew noticed that couples were skating together. Seeing Christy head in their direction, Rachel grabbed his arm and asked him, "Are you ready to go?"

"Sure," he replied.

Needing no further encouragement, he assisted her to the pond, and the two moved flawlessly together, making a very attractive couple.

They smiled with amusement as they watched John and his date try to skate together.

"I think that's the first time he has ever even skated with a girl—other than Laura or me, that is."

"I think he'd do better if he'd take his eyes off the girl and watch where he is going," he told her with laughter.

"You're right. I wondered why he couldn't remember which foot to put where all of a sudden."

I know exactly how he feels, the man at her side thought, *I'd love to just stare at you*. Shaking himself out of his thoughts, thoughts that lead to nowhere, he concentrated on what she was saying.

"Puppy love," she whispered almost under her breath.

"You talk as if you know about that," he said lightly.

"Of course. Every girl remembers her first crush." Peering over into his smiling face, she told him, "And don't you dare tell me that you didn't like someone when you were younger."

"Well, there was Jessica Thomas."

"Jessica Thomas!" she exclaimed in astonishment.

"She's married with three kids."

"She wasn't then," he told her in amusement.

"Oh, I guess not." Wrinkling up her brow, she said in somewhat of an agreement, "She is pretty, if you like her type."

"Her type?" he asked in wonder. "She was every boy's type in seventh grade."

Thinking about the lovely woman, Rachel could only agree with him.

"How about you? Who was your first love?"

"I'd have to say Morgan Williams."

"What?" he asked in surprise, recalling the shy, somewhat overweight boy who was presently a banker in Cheyenne.

"Oh, not so much for his looks, but he was always so sweet and helpful. I guess I felt sorry for him when the other kids teased him," she added sadly.

Glancing over at her, he knew the exact reason he was in love with the woman at his side. She was everything that he desired for a wife: sensitive, caring, a wonderful Christian, and had the beauty to go with it.

Not noticing where they were skating or that others had joined them, a small child dashed in front of them, causing Rachel to lose her balance. As she grasped tighter to Matthew's arm, he lost his balance and fell backwards, pulling her down on top of him, their faces only inches from one another. Feeling a stirring of something deep within her as she gazed into his eyes, eyes that seemed to penetrate to her very soul, she quickly scampered off and awkwardly began to stand up.

Matthew, forgetting for a moment that she was engaged to his brother, had almost leaned up to kiss her and was glad that she had moved. Rising to his feet, he took her arm and pulled her up to stand beside him.

With an extremely warm look on her face, she told him, "I think I'd like to sit for a moment, if you don't mind."

Leading her to a bench at the side of the ice, they sat down and watched as others skated in front of them. Both were quiet after what had happened, or *had* almost happened. After a few minutes, Christy appeared at their side and asked sweetly, "Matthew O'Malley, are you going to ask me to skate or not?"

Glancing toward Rachel with hesitation, he turned to the young woman before standing to his feet. He didn't want to skate with Christy but was too much of a gentleman to refuse.

"All right, let's give it a whirl," he told her with a smile.

Her attractive face lit up, making her stunning. The white fur hat emphasized the darkness of her eyes and features. Firmly wrapping an arm through his, the couple walked toward the ice.

Rachel, watching them, saw Christy slip and noticed Matthew hold her hand on his arm with his free hand. Waves of jealousy swept through her, and she knew in an instant that she was indeed in love with him—hopelessly and without doubt. This was not a fleeting type of love, but the ever after kind her parents had.

Lord, how can I have these feelings when I am to be another man's wife soon? Please take them away from me.

After watching the couple skate together for some time, Rachel felt the coldness begin to seep through her body—coldness that she felt in her heart. Rising to her feet, she, too, walked to the edge of the pond and began to skate to warm up.

Matthew, noticing her on the ice again, had to stop himself from rushing to her side to be near her. Realizing that he was not listening to the woman beside him, he once again tried to concentrate to her words.

"Would you like to come over for supper tomorrow night?" she asked, "Mama makes the most glorious fried chicken."

Knowing he had no reason to decline the invitation, he told her, "Yes, that would be fine."

Squeezing his arm, she squealed and said, "Wonderful! Around five o'clock should be perfect."

Noticing the lateness of the hour, he excused himself and skated toward Rachel.

"I think I'm ready to leave now," she said.

Nodding in understanding, he led her to where their boots were.

As they were turning the wagon toward the road, Christy's voice reached their ears, "See you tomorrow night, Matthew. Make sure you are hungry."

"I will," he told her in a solemn voice.

The ride home was rather quiet as each were wrapped in their own thoughts.

As he drew near her home, he swiftly got out and began to help her from the sled. Unable to stop himself, he grasped her by her trim waist, holding on to her a little longer than necessary before he heard her say, "Thank you for taking me."

"You're welcome."

Watching as she turned and walked away, he closed his eyes and knew that his heart could not take much more of this. Never before had he felt about anyone the way he was coming to love Rachel.

Lord, he prayed again on the way home, *please remove this love I have for his woman if it be Your will. Is it Christy you want me to love, Father? Is that why you brought her into my life tonight?* Turning his thoughts again to the woman he was to eat supper with the next evening, he let his mind dwell on her. She was certainly pretty enough, with dark hair and eyes that sparkled. She was easy to talk to, and he knew that she and her parents attended church in Cheyenne. He would do his best to turn his affections from Rachel to Christy if at all possible. At least she was available and seemed to be attracted to him.

Rachel entered her home and leaned against the door with a per-plexed look on her face.

What is wrong with me? I'm going to be married shortly, and I cer-tainly do not need to be feeling things for another man. I have promised myself to Mark.

Slowly and thoughtfully, she removed her outer clothing and set off for her bedroom. She would read from her Bible and pray until she felt peace about the situation and her marriage to Mark.

Matthew had been over to Christy's house several times. Tonight, he was picking her up and taking her to supper with his parents. He enjoyed being around her, and although he didn't feel the stirrings of love, the two were becoming friends. As he stopped the buggy in front of her home, he saw her exit with a bright smile lighting up her lovely face.

"Are you ready?" he asked as he assisted her into the wagon. A fleeting thought crossed his mind as he recalled that he had picked up Rachel each time to help her. He felt no inclination to do so with Christy yet. Maybe with time, his feeling would change. *After all*, he reminded himself, *Rachel and I grew up together, and I have only just become acquainted with Christy.*

"Yes, I do love a man who is on time," she told him as she snug-gled up close to his side.

"My mama taught us to always be on time for everything. She'd have our hide if we made her late."

An easy laughter flowed from her as she replied, "Mine too. We wouldn't dare be a minute behind for anything."

Glancing at the woman beside him, he realized how easy she was to talk to.

Maybe this is the beginning of something, he told himself as they continued their journey.

Matthew had promised Christy that he would show her his house. On the ride there, talk flowed easily, and they conversed about their past and hopes for the future.

As they pulled into the lane near the home, Christy squealed in delight and squeezed his arm in the familiar fashion.

"It's big," she told him in awe.

"Yes, I figured I'd do it right the first time and see if God would fill it up with children over the years."

Having said that, he felt guilt in his heart—almost as if he should not have spoken the words to anyone but Rachel. Shaking himself mentally, he listened attentively to what she was telling him.

"If that's an invitation, I accept," she told him quickly and in a rather bold fashion.

Not knowing how to reply, Matthew climbed down and helped her to the safety of the ground. Taking his arm again, the couple walked up the steps and into the spacious home.

After a brief tour, he felt awkward as he listened to her tell him where she would put different pieces of furniture and how she would decorate. Feeling as if he had betrayed Rachel, he tried as quickly as possible to leave.

This is a bad idea. It is too soon. He knew it would take time, but how much time he wasn't sure.

It was the night of the church hayride, and Matthew had asked Christy to attend. The weather had taken a turn for the better, and since it had been cancelled previously, the young folks decided to try and slip it in before the cold weather returned. Matthew kept wondering to himself as he went to pick her up when his feelings of friendship might turn into something more. Although lovely enough, there was something missing, and he found himself continually comparing her to Rachel.

On the way to the church, his date kept up a steady flow of conversation, and little was required of him other than a nod here and there.

Does she always talk this much? he asked himself as he listened to her. Most of the conversation seemed to center around her. He knew she was an only child and would more than likely be somewhat spoiled, and he thought he was willing to make allowances for it, but at moments such as these, he wasn't so sure.

Seeing all of the wagons that were in attendance, he felt a small measure of relief knowing that they would be surrounded by others.

As he assisted her down, they walked to the wagon that held his brother and Rachel. For some reason, his feet seemed to do what his heart told him not to.

"Hello, you two," Mark told his sibling with a grin.

"Hi," he replied. "Do you care if we join you?"

"Not at all," Rachel told them as she moved over to make room for Matthew's date, all the while taking in the appearance of the girl. She was dressed warmly in a light yellow hat and an obviously new coat of darker browns. The light color seemed to emphasize her complexion, and she felt a stab of envy run through her.

Throughout the ride, Christy remained nestled up closely to her date and smiled sweet smiles at Matthew.

"How's the house coming?" Mark asked him at one point.

Before he could answer, Christy piped in and replied, "It's beautiful. I've been over there and know exactly where I would put things if I were mistress."

Glancing at his brother's face, Mark could tell that she had caught him unaware with her words when he noticed the discomfort of Matthew.

"Really?" Mark asked in astonishment. After all, the couple had been courting only for a month or so.

"Oh, yes," she told them with a giggle. "We walked through it, and the layout is exactly as I would have wanted. Matthew told me he planned on making it big from the start to fill it up with all the little O'Malleys that may make an appearance in the future."

Now Matthew did feel uncomfortable. He shifted slightly and dared to glance at Rachel, who had not spoken a word throughout the interchange of words. He could swear that she had a pained look in her eyes and had to look away.

Why would Christy's words bother her? he would continue to ask himself in the days ahead.

A bonfire had been planned at the halfway point to help warm the chilled couples. As the wagons pulled in around the brightly burning fire, Mark helped Rachel down and Matthew assisted his date toward the make-shift wooden seats that had been placed strategically around the blaze, Christy suddenly fell to the ground, grabbing her foot. Matthew quickly bent down to see if she was hurt.

"It's my ankle," she told him in pain. "I seemed to have stepped in a hole or something and twisted it."

Mark, hearing her words, moved through the crowd of onlookers to examine it himself. Seeing that there was no swelling apparent, he asked if she could try and put weight on it.

"Yes, if someone will help me," she replied in a pitiful voice, turning her focus to Matthew. Taking hold of her arms gently, he helped her to a standing position before she tried to take a step.

Crying out in alarm, she said, "No, it hurts too much. I don't suppose you could carry me, could you?"

Hearing her words, Matthew picked her up firmly, aware of how she clung to him with her arms wrapped snuggly around his neck.

Rachel, watching the happenings, noticed the woman's triumphant smile as she was being placed near the fire, obviously savoring the nearness of Matthew.

"Thank you so much," she told him innocently.

"You're welcome," he replied, not feeling quite right about the situation. She had enjoyed being in his arms a little too much for his liking.

After being lifted to the wagons after singing and roasting marshmallows, Christy sat as close to her date as possible, her arm looped through his proudly.

Mark could only watch in fascination at how expertly she took every opportunity to be near his brother. And from the looks of Matthew, he didn't seem to mind too much.

Later, after carrying the hurting woman inside her home and depositing her on her feet, she gripped tightly to his arm as if still in pain and told him, "Thank you for helping me. My ankle hurts terribly, and I know I couldn't have walked on it by myself."

"That's all right. I hope it feels better soon."

"I'm sure it will," she told him as she waited for him to kiss her.

Seeing her obvious intention, Matthew leaned forward and brushed his lips lightly to her cheek. Turning away quickly to leave, he told the bemused girl goodbye.

On the ride home, all he could think about was her apparent ploy of feigning an injury. He wasn't comfortable playing games as such.

As he was unhooking the harness and putting the horse in the stall for the night, Mark joined him.

"How is Christy?" he asked with a half smile.

"Why?"

"You know there was nothing wrong with her ankle, don't you?" the younger brother asked.

Looking into his eyes, Matthew replied, "Yes, and I don't understand why someone would do something like that."

"Because she wanted to be as close as possible to you, that's why. I think she's quite smitten."

"I could never picture Rachel doing something like that to gain a man's attention," he told him in disgust.

"No, you're right. Our Rachel is made of finer stuff than that."

"Yes, she's a lady. There're not many around like her," the oldest brother said softly. Shaking his head with repulsion on his face, Mark watched his sibling walk toward the house. Maybe he was wrong; Matthew was not falling for Christy. He would have to watch over the next few weeks. Time would tell whether his brother had feelings for her or not. As he lay in bed later that night, he continued to muse over his brother's last statement to him in the barn. It wasn't so much the words he had said about Rachel, it was the way he said them.

Matthew had eaten supper at Christy's home again the next evening. Talk seemed to be centered around who was getting married or having children. Christy's mother kept darting small smiles toward her daughter, which made him feel very uncomfortable.

"I would like at least three children myself," the girl told them.

"Don't you think you need to get married first?" her mother asked, shooting another look Matthew's way.

"Oh, yes, Mama. Maybe that won't be too far in the future," she told them both with a giggle, reaching for his hand under the table and squeezing.

Her father, noticing the uneasiness of the man at his side, took pity on him and turned the talk to his work in Cheyenne. Only as he spoke about events that had happened lately did Matthew feel himself begin to relax.

Sitting on the sofa in the living area a short time later, Christy's parents had excused themselves, and Matthew rose to his feet to do the same.

Walking him to the door, she stood before him and asked, "Do you find me attractive?"

"Yes, of course," he replied in complete honesty.

"Why haven't you kissed me yet if you do?"

Realizing that Rachel would never ask for such an invitation, he hesitated a moment too long. She reached up and wrapped her arms around his neck and kissed him his first kiss soundly on his lips. Feeling her warm lips against his made him jump back slightly and he heard her ask, "Now, was that so bad?"

"Well," he began before she interjected. "You have kissed a girl before, haven't you?"

With evident astonishment on his face, she added, "If not, don't worry. I've kissed lots of boys and can teach you. I've been told that I can kiss well."

Excusing himself rather curtly, all Matthew could think about was that she was not the woman for him. He did not want an experienced person to share his life. Recalling her lips on his, he remembered the cold, impersonal feeling that had spread through him.

Surely when you kiss someone you love, you feel something different.

Mark had taken Rachel to town for a quick lunch. As they sat down and their food had been ordered, Mark told her, "You should see Matthew. He's been seeing Christy Martin on a steady basis now."

"Oh," Rachel asked but didn't really want to know. "Are they getting serious, do you think?"

"Yes, I would say so. Since the hayride, she's been to the house to eat, and the folks seem to like her." With a grin, he added, "And she sure is pretty enough."

"Really?" Rachel asked as she tilted her head to one side.

"In her own way, but I wouldn't trade my girl for a million Christys."

Knowing that his words should make her happy, thoughts of Matthew and his new friend kept crossing her mind throughout the meal. Mentally adjusting her train of thought, she reached for his hand and told him, "Soon, we will be man and wife."

"Yes, the time is going quickly."

Too quickly, Rachel thought to herself.

Rachel, Hannah, and D.J. had just arrived from school for the day. Chuckling, McKenna saw D.J. walk to the kitchen and grab several biscuits and cookies before leaving to help with chores. It would do no good to stop him, warning him of not being hungry for supper, for the boy ate all the time.

Seeing her mother working on her wedding dress, Rachel walked over and touched the material.

"It's beautiful, isn't it?" she asked in awe.

"We'll know that in a minute. I'm almost finished except for the hem. I want you to try it on so I can pin it."

Scooping up the dress, Rachel set off for her bedroom to put the lovely garment on. After removing her school dress, she slipped it over her head and moved closer to the small mirror in her room. Swiveling and turning to watch the dress flow gently with her movements, she smiled when she saw her mother enter.

"What do you think, honey?" she asked Rachel.

"I love it. It's just like I had hoped it would be." Hugging her mother, she once again stepped in front of the mirror to look.

"It fits you perfectly. I think that Mr. O'Malley will not be able to keep his eyes off his bride."

Listening to her words, Rachel fleetingly thought, *Yes; however, it is the wrong O'Malley brother.*

Seeing tears gather in her daughter's eyes and mistaking the reason for them, her mama told her, "I know how you feel. This is all so new. But soon you will be with the man you love and everything will be fine."

"Yes," she whispered, dabbing at the tears. "You're right, Mama."

"Come out into the living area and let me complete the pinning. Then we will be finished and can begin to plan out a menu for after the wedding."

Following her mother back into the room, wearing the lovely dress did little to lift Rachel's spirit.

Chapter Thirteen

As McKenna and Tucker prepared for the day, she said, "Rachel and I are going to make a quick trip over to the Rogers' place this morning. The weather seems to be changing, and I think we'll get snow again soon. Mr. Rogers has been sick for a few weeks, and I think their food supplies are getting low, so we are taking some extra things over. I know Matthew has been there and chopped the necessary firewood they will need for a little while longer."

Listening to her words, knowing how her heart ached for those in need, he asked quietly, "Do you think it's wise to go when the baby is due in less than two weeks? Both the others arrived early, if my memory serves me right."

"I'm fine. Besides, we're not staying long—just dropping things off and returning. I worry about them since they have no family around."

"All right, but I think this should be your last visit until the baby is born. I don't like to have to worry about you when I'm out in the fields, especially after seeing those clouds gathering in the west. I think we're in for a snowstorm."

"I saw them. We'll return as quickly as we can."

After a hasty breakfast, Rachel and McKenna, with the assistance of Tucker and D.J., loaded the wagon with everything they thought the elderly couple might need to see them through for a week or so. Tucker returned after feeding the livestock and told her with concern in his voice, "Don't stay and visit more than a few minutes. Those clouds are getting closer. I don't think D.J. and I will be out too long either."

Nodding in agreement, she replied, "We're about ready to go now. Grab a few extra blankets, Rachel, in case we do get caught in the snow. At least we'll be warm."

Hearing her mother's words, the young woman gathered up two warm quilts from the chest in the living room.

"I'm ready," she replied as both walked toward the team outside.

The trip to the Rogers' small farm took the women about forty-five minutes. The ruts in the road were getting worse, and they had to avoid as many as possible due to McKenna's condition. As they were pulling into the long drive, snow began to fall in large, billowing flakes all around them.

"We'd better get things unloaded quickly so we can get home before the storm hits," McKenna told her daughter.

The elderly couple greeted them warmly and insisted they drink a cup of warm tea before leaving into the brisk weather. McKenna kept letting her eyes glance out to the snow that had begun to come down in a rather heavy fashion.

Trying to finish their tea as swiftly as possible, she stood and told the couple, "We really need to get going now. I hope these things will help for a short while. We'll be back next week to check on you again."

"Everything is lovely, dear," the kind woman told her sincerely. "I don't know what Edgar or I would do without our wonderful neighbors. You'd best get back home now where it's nice and warm."

After quick hugs, the women walked briskly to the wagon. As McKenna climbed up to sit in the seat, she felt a gush of warmth flood down to her feet.

"Oh no," she cried in alarm.

"What, Mama?"

"Oh, Rachel. Your papa was right. I shouldn't have come today. My water just broke. I'm afraid this baby will be arriving shortly. You'll have to drive home now and be quick about it. Please, honey, hurry!" she said in an imploring voice, feeling a sharp, shooting pain through her stomach. McKenna didn't want to concern her daughter, but Hannah had arrived only an hour and a half after her water had broken before.

"Maybe we should stay here at the Rogers' house?" Rachel asked, hoping her Mama would agree.

"No. I want to be home with your papa to deliver this baby."

Rachel, turning to look into the worried face of her mother, pushed the team despite the swirling snow that was dropping from the sky. The wind had picked up, and drifts had already begun to form on the road before them. Rachel kept darting glances at her mother, noticing the concern present on her beautiful face. Her large brown eyes shut often, and she knew she was praying for their safety. About halfway home, she saw her mother cringe and grip tightly to the side board of the wagon. The pains were getting stronger.

Unable to see very far ahead due to the blinding snow, the wagon lurched forward as it drove through a large rut, causing both women to hold on tightly. They heard a loud cracking noise as they dipped at a right angle.

"The wheel!" McKenna cried in dismay. "It's broken, isn't it?"

Climbing over the side carefully, Rachel walked to stand near the front and grimaced. "Yes, whatever are we going to do now? I can't leave you here and go for help."

McKenna, feeling a contraction ripple through her stomach, coursing around to her back, knew time was of the essence. Waiting for the pain to subside, she answered, "Matthew's new house, we'll go there. I don't know if he'll be working now or not, but at least we'll be dry and out of the weather. Quick, honey, unhook the horse from the harness. We'll leave the wagon and ride there."

Doing as she was instructed, the young woman worked rapidly and brought the old plow horse to the side of the buckboard and assisted her mother onto his back. She wrapped the quilts around her legs and shoulders to help keep her dry.

"I'll lead him while you ride," Rachel said as she noticed her mother's face, praying silently that they would make it and that Matthew would be there.

Holding tightly to the reins, Rachel felt the heavy, wet snow soak through her clothes, making it increasingly difficult to walk. Her feet were damp as she trudged through the mounting snow, and the wind bit at her face as she tried to watch where they were going. She had started to shiver and was relieved when the house finally came into view.

A lone light shone in a room upstairs, and thankfulness flooded through her when she saw that Matthew was still at work inside.

After assisting her mother from the horse, the women tramped through the forming drifts and made their way to the front porch.

Matthew, who had just descended the stairs, heard the noise and opened the door to their anxious faces.

"Rachel, Mrs. Parker, what are you doing out in this? Hurry, come inside. I'll add more wood to the fireplace. I was just getting ready to leave."

As they walked through the door, Rachel said, "We got caught in the snowstorm. Mama is in labor. Can we stay?"

Hearing her jumbled words caused anxiety to rise inside him. He knew nothing about birthings, except for assisting animals.

"Of course, I'm afraid I don't have any furniture here yet—just a few blankets in the back room from when I've spent the night."

"That will be fine," McKenna told him as she doubled over with another contraction.

"Right this way," he said as he led them down a hallway.

"I'm so sorry for bringing you into this," she told the young people as they made a make shift bed for her and lit the lantern that stood on the wood floor in the corner.

"Don't worry about that now, Mama. I don't know what I need to do to help," she told her in a small, frightened voice. "I'm afraid I've only seen one birth and was so fascinated by the whole experience that I didn't pay a lot of attention."

"You sound like your Papa when he delivered Hannah. There's not a lot to it when things go smoothly, and I pray this one will. You'll do fine," she encouraged her with a small smile. "Can you heat up some water, Matthew, for after the birth? If you'll both give me a moment alone, I'll get myself ready for this little one's arrival."

Nodding, he quickly went in search of a container of some sort. As he left the room, he felt the presence of Rachel behind him. When they entered the living room, he saw her shiver. He wasn't sure if it was from the cold clothing she had on or the tension of what was about to happen.

Without a word, he pulled her to him and whispered, "You'll do wonderfully."

Placing her head on his shoulder seemed like such a natural thing to do that she did it without thought.

"I'm so frightened. What if something goes wrong?"

"Let's pray, all right?" he asked.

As she nodded, neither moved, and Matthew began to pray softly for God's help in a safe delivery of the baby and for wisdom and guidance for Rachel.

"Thank you," she told him as she shivered again.

Taking a step back, he said, "You are soaking wet. Why don't you take your outer garments off, and I'll hang them by the fire to dry while you help your mother."

Hesitating a fraction, he looked into her eyes and said in a teasing manner, "It's okay. I'll try not to look. Besides, I do have a sister, you know. Two now, actually."

Feeling the cold begin to seep through her, she nodded. "I'll go back in with my mother and hand you my clothes through the doorway."

She was so prim and proper that he almost laughed aloud.

"Fine. I'll put the water by the door. I need to get your horse out of the weather. I won't be long."

As she turned to head back to the bedroom, he held her lightly by the arm and said, "You will call me if you need me to do anything, won't you? I've never seen a child born, but I have helped with lots of animal births."

"Yes, please stay near, just in case I need you," she whispered gratefully.

I wish you did need me, Rachel, his heart cried, *the way I need you.* Reaching for his coat, he left the warmth of his home and untied the horse from the post to put him in the lean-to next to his own mare.

After laying out some hay for the animal, he walked as quickly as possible back toward the steps. The snow was blowing as it fell around him, and he sent a small prayer heavenward, thanking God for bringing the women safely. He beseeched Him for a safe delivery.

Over an hour had passed, and Matthew had been pacing back and forth continuously. Other than a moaning noise from Mrs. Parker and encouraging words from Rachel, there was no sound of a baby's cry yet.

As he walked to the window to peer into the snow that fell heavily outside, he heard a shriek, and Rachel cried out his name.

"Matthew!"

Running down the hall, he entered the room to find her holding the baby in her arms.

"She's not breathing! What do I do?" she asked in a panicked voice.

Without saying a word, he took the newborn from her, and with the edge of the blanket, he cleaned the mucous around her nose and started to rub her briskly in a stimulating fashion. Soon, the infant coughed and began to screech with all her might.

Grinning at her, Matthew said, "Guess I made her mad, didn't I?"

Finally able to catch her own breath, Rachel watched as he handed the squalling infant to her mother. McKenna spoke soothing words to her new daughter while planting feather-light kisses on her soft head and beamed with adoration.

The two stood watching in fascination at the strong bond between mother and child. Turning slightly, Matthew noticed Rachel's reaction with heaviness in his heart. He knew that one day she would share this joy with his brother, and it was tearing him up inside.

"I need the string and the scissors," she told him, seeing him retrieve them off the floor. "I do remember Mark cutting the cord, thank goodness."

Matthew watched in astonishment at how she tied the cord tightly in two places and cut in between the knots.

"That's right, honey," her mother encouraged her. "Give me a minute and the afterbirth should be expelled also."

Feeling no embarrassment at him standing near and assisting her, Rachel turned and smiled brightly at him. He was grinning as he watched the new little one try to focus. She had quieted down and was blinking her eyes as if she were surveying the new world she had entered. He had witnessed a miracle. To Matthew, it was only fitting that the woman he loved was by him when the wonderful occurrence had happened.

A moment later, he realized that Rachel was not properly dressed, standing only in her camisole and petticoat, and her mother needed her privacy, so Matthew quickly excused himself to check on her dress and stockings. Finding them dry, he knocked quietly on the door. Rachel, opening it slightly, grinned when she saw what he held in his arms.

"Thank you," she told him, her dimples appearing.

"You may want to leave the door open now to allow the heat from the fire to warm it," he told her in thoughtfulness.

"I will," she replied.

Nodding, he turned and walked back to the living room. Despite the wonder of the birth, he felt an aching that seemed to pierce his soul. He felt as though his heart was a wound, and each time he was around Rachel, it was opened, the pain beginning anew.

Tucker and D.J. had arrived home over an hour ago and knew that something was wrong. Tucker was grateful that Hannah was staying with a friend from school for the night. After they had changed into dry clothes and returned to saddle their horses, they began their search to find the women. When they found the wagon with the broken wheel, worry was evident on both of their faces. Unable to see very far in front of them, they only prayed that they had made it to the O'Malley boy's new house, which was the most likely place for them to head.

When they entered the drive, relief flowed through them when they spotted their horse standing in the lean-to. Quickly tying up their own animals next to him, they took the steps two at a time to find Rachel smiling. She was completely dressed except for her shoes and threw herself into her papa's arms, telling him, "Congratulations again."

Seeing the frown on his face, she continued, "It's another girl."

"What?" he exclaimed in disbelief as she took his hand and led him to his new daughter. Matthew, sensing that the new father needed to be alone for a few minutes with his wife and baby, lightly held D.J.'s arm, preventing the young boy from following.

"Why don't we give your papa a few minutes alone with your mama?" he asked him quietly.

Nodding in agreement, D.J. watched as his father went with his sister.

Leaving them to admire God's latest masterpiece, Rachel came to stand next to Matthew and her brother in the living room.

Tucker walked swiftly toward his wife and got down on his knees to be near her. With a tender gaze, McKenna pulled back the blanket to reveal their newborn little girl. Gazing in amazement at the new life, he felt emotion gather and had to clear his throat before he asked, "Are you all right?"

"I'm fine. Our little Abbie Grace decided to make a rather hasty appearance, I'm afraid. I had wanted you to be with me when I delivered," she said somewhat disappointedly.

"After Hannah, I'm rather relieved that Rachel was here this time. Although," he told her seriously, "I certainly would have been here if you had wanted me to. You didn't give me any warning though," he added with amusement.

"I know. I'm afraid I didn't have any warning either. Poor Rachel, I fear that she may never want to have a child of her own after this. Abbie wasn't breathing after she was born and she became frightened."

"What happened then?" Tucker asked with a frown.

"She called for Matthew, and he quickly cleaned out her mouth and nose and then rubbed her thoroughly. It was enough to upset our little lady, and she began to cry rather loudly. I'm afraid that Matthew saw a little more than he planned also. I'll need to apologize and thank him at the same time."

Shaking his head, he said, "I am glad that I missed that. I wouldn't have known what to do."

"Oh, I don't know," she stated with pride, "you seem to always be able to fix things, no matter what the problem."

"Fixing things and birthing children are two different matters, my love…especially for a man."

Shifting her eyes to the small bundle in her arms, McKenna held Abbie Grace out for her papa to take. Without hesitation, he removed his coat and reached for his little one, holding her snuggly to his chest. Seeing dark blue eyes flutter open, he smiled and stood to his feet, walking around the room and speaking words of welcome to the baby. McKenna, feeling her eyes become heavy, closed them, listening to the bonding taking place between father and daughter. With thankfulness in her heart, her mind drifted off into slumber.

Watching the door open wider a few minutes later, Tucker grinned as he saw D.J. enter and walk over to where he was standing.

"Say hello to your new sister," he told the boy, while his mama opened her eyes with a tender smile on her face.

Placing a finger against the baby's cheek, he turned to grin before saying, "She's so small."

"Yes, but she'll grow fast and soon be toddling around after you."

With a thoughtful look on his face, his eyes never leaving the infant, the tenderhearted boy replied, "I won't mind. Are you okay, Mama?"

"I couldn't be better, son," she told him, a radiant glow present.

Rachel walked over next to Matthew at the large window overlooking the valley.

"I don't know any words that can ever tell you thank you for what you did today," she said softly.

"I didn't do anything, Rachel," he replied, meaning every word.

"You saved the baby's life."

"You are giving me far too much credit. You would have done the same thing had I not been here."

Shaking her head, tears began to fall as she relived the moment of fear.

"No, I couldn't even move."

Afraid to hold her, he wiped away the tears from her face with his thumb and said, "You did fine. I know you would have done the right thing." As he gazed tenderly into her eyes, he said softly, "You are wonderful. Mark is a very blessed man."

Before she could return his reply, she heard her name called from the bedroom. Walking to be with her family, Rachel knew why his words had caused such an uneasy feeling inside of her—feelings that she seemed to have often in the present days. Mark would not be blessed. He was marrying a woman who was in love with his own brother.

Matthew had waited until the family had become acquainted with the newest Parker member before knocking softly on the door. He wanted to make sure everything was all right before he bedded down in the living area next to D.J. for the night. He would make sure that the fire burned brightly to keep the new baby warm. He was thankful that he had brought extra food over with him in case of such an emergency. He knew how unpredictable the weather could be. He would try to get to his parents' house to retrieve other supplies until they all could be moved back to their own place.

"Come in," McKenna replied.

Entering quietly, he saw Tucker sitting next to his wife and holding their child. He noticed the baby did not stir as he walked to where they were sitting and knelt down.

"Is there anything you need?" he asked, admiring the child. "D.J. and I will sleep in the living area where I can keep the fire burning. You will need to leave the door open to make sure it stays warm enough."

"We will, son," Tucker said. "McKenna wanted a little privacy to feed this little tyke first."

Hearing the words from her husband, the new mother laughed and said, "Privacy is not something that has happened around here lately." Looking directly into the warm blue eyes of the young man beside her, she said, "I am so sorry for you having to be a part of this. You will probably never want to have your own children and certainly not help deliver them after today."

Shaking his head, he told her with seriousness, "No, Mrs. Parker, it was the most wonderful thing I have ever experienced. I hope you won't feel embarrassment at such a godly miracle."

Knowing that he spoke what he felt, she realized what a special person he was. Not only had he relieved her embarrassment, he had shown her where his heart lay—only concerned about helping others. He was indeed a remarkable young man.

Leaning over, she reached out and took hold of his hand, "Thank you, for everything, and may God bless you richly."

"You're welcome. I'm just grateful that everything is all right."

Glancing at her newborn, she whispered, "Everything is perfect."

Standing to his feet, Matthew said goodnight.

I wish everything was as perfect in my world as it is in yours, Mrs. Parker, he thought to himself.

The following day, Tucker and Matthew headed toward the O'Malley place to pick up supplies. The snow had quit during the night, but large drifts remained in places, making walking difficult. The horses had stayed dry in the lean-to next to the house. Matthew was thankful that he had built it the week before.

After more than an hour of trudging through the heavy snow, the house came into view. The soft puff of smoke rising above it gave a welcoming feeling to the tired, cold men.

Walking through the door, Genie glanced up from the sewing she was doing in the rocking chair. Seeing who was before her, she quickly set it aside and stood to her feet.

"Tucker, Matthew, whatever is wrong?"

"Nothing," Tucker told her with a grin. "At least not now. McKenna and I have a new daughter."

"What?" she exclaimed in amazement. "She's not due yet."

"I know, but babies tend to have a mind of their own when it concerns McKenna. Not only is our little one here safely, but your son played a major role in delivering her."

"Matthew," she asked in unbelief, "is this true?"

Nodding his head, the young man told his mama, "Rachel did most of it. I just helped when she needed me."

"All right, both of you. Take off those wet things and sit by the fire to get warmed. I want to hear the whole story from beginning to end. You'd better wait until Ian gets in, or you'll have to tell it again. He just went to check on the livestock in the barn. That sure was some kind of storm we got. Left as fast as it came."

"Mama, do you think you could fix us some food to take back to my house. That is where Mrs. Parker, the baby, Rachel, and D.J. are right now. I have a few things but not enough for everyone."

"What?" she exclaimed again. "I may not be able to wait for that husband of mine to hear this story."

Walking toward the kitchen, the woman began to prepare a large basket of various things they had available. Noticing the coffee pot still sitting on the wood stove, she poured two cups of the hot liquid for the men to help warm them up. As she handed them their cups, the door opened and Ian stepped through.

"Well, if it isn't me dear friend Tucker. What brings ya' here on such a wintry day, laddie?" Glancing at his son, he said, "Your mama and I figured you were caught in the storm but reckoned you'd be all right for a short time. John and me were gonna come check on ya' shortly."

"Come on, Ian," Genie told him impatiently as she helped him remove his coat. "Take off those boots and sit down. I think we are about to hear a very entertaining story."

"Aye, me sweet wife, ya' know how I love a good yarn."

When the men returned to the house, Matthew noticed Rachel standing in his kitchen. He had been building cabinets and had most of them done. His heart leapt in his chest when he saw how well she fitted into the atmosphere.

"Matthew," she asked him as she checked the potatoes she had cooking on the stove, "I found your potatoes, and Papa found a small slab of bacon. Do you have a frying pan around to cook it up?"

"Yes, I only have a few pots and pans," he told her as he removed his outer clothing, hanging it neatly on the peg near the door. "Look in the bottom cabinet to your left. Mama sent them over one day in case I ever needed them."

Watching her open the door, he saw her smile as she retrieved it. "I'll have this cooking up in no time," she said.

Walking to stand near her, he opened the bag his mother had given him, placing eggs on the counter.

"Oh, that is perfect," she said with a beaming smile. "They will complete our meal."

"Mama sent some ham and bread for sandwiches later and some fresh milk also. We should be set until tomorrow."

"Give me a few minutes and it'll be ready," she said as she found another small frying pan to cook the eggs."

"Feed your mama first," he said with concern. "We had a sandwich at the folks' place."

"Yes, I will. Of course, D.J. will be standing here waiting soon. He's already asking when it's gonna be ready."

After everyone had eaten, Rachel tidied the kitchen, and the small group moved to the bedroom to spend time together. They talked of many different things and laughed frequently. McKenna, hearing her new daughter begin to whimper, knew it was time to feed her. As D.J. and Matthew rose to their feet to give her privacy, Rachel also stood.

"I think I need to take a walk for some exercise," she said. "Have you fed and watered the horses yet?"

"I did earlier, but I'm sure they need some fresh water."

"I'll go with you," she said as she walked to put her coat on.

Although he loved having her by his side, he knew it was not helping neither his mind nor his heart.

After putting on his own coat, he held the door open for her.

Standing on the porch to take in the beautiful view before her, she said softly, "This is incredible. Look at the snow glisten off the trees. It is truly a winter wonderland here."

Matthew, staring at her instead of the land before them, replied, "Yes, it is God's country. I was fortunate to be able to buy this land."

Turning to face him, she asked, "How many acres do you have?"

"I bought twenty-five acres and am planning on purchasing more after I am finished with the house. I have quite a bit of clearing to do so I will be able to farm it. I want to get some cattle to raise in the spring."

"What a fine life you will have," she whispered with a small, choked voice.

Matthew, unsure of what had caused the emotion, took her arm lightly and said, "We'd best hurry or you'll get chilled."

Seeing their breath in front of them, she nodded and walked beside him toward where the horses were. Neither spoke, although their minds were filled with the same thoughts—thoughts of their growing feelings toward one another and how hard it was to keep those feelings in check.

The rest of the day Rachel was determined to keep Mark in the foremost of her mind. He was, after all, to be her husband shortly.

I do love him, she continued to tell herself frequently, *and I will make him a good wife.*

The next day the Parker family was ready to go home. McKenna was gaining more strength, and Abbie Grace was doing well. After bundling her next to her papa's warm body, the Parkers headed to their own house. Looking over her shoulder, McKenna smiled. She would always think of this house differently from then on. It had already experienced its first act of love and was destined for happiness.

Rachel, who was also looking back at the house, could only wonder who would deliver Matthew's own children inside. A hollow place had entered her heart, and she could only pray that Mark and his love for her would fill it.

Chapter Fourteen

Mark and Rachel were sitting by one another and listening to Pastor Keller's words the following Sunday. A few minutes after he had closed in prayer, Timmy Atkins came rushing through the doors at the back, his eyes searching for Mark with panic present.

"Doc, my pa needs ya' real bad," he stated flatly.

Mark knew instinctively what was wrong with the man. He was in his forties and had been in a few days ago to the clinic with sharp pain in his upper right quadrant. He had already had several similar bouts and appeared to have gallstones. Mark had somehow known it would come to this—his first gallbladder surgery.

Turning to Rachel, he said in an apologetic voice, "I'm sorry. Can you ride home with your parents?"

"Of course. Don't worry about me," she replied, placing a hand sympathetically on his arm.

"I'll see if I can get Matthew to help. He's done so quite a bit lately." As he turned from her, Rachel could tell that he was thinking about his patient and what lie ahead of him. Watching him talk to his older brother a moment later, the two left, following the young boy to his ailing pa.

On the ride to the small house several miles away, Mark began to relate his fears to Matthew.

"This will be the first surgery I've done on the gallbladder by myself. I've assisted on several before, but it will be different alone."

"You will do fine," his brother said with confidence. "Let me say a prayer for you before we get there."

With a thankful nod of his head, Mark listened to the words that would give him what he needed for whatever he would face concerning his patient.

"Father in heaven, I ask that You give Mark the wisdom he needs today. Guide his hands and give him the assurance he needs to know that You are beside him, that he is not alone. You are the great physician, therefore, I ask You to have Your healing hand on this man. For I ask these things in Your son's precious name, Amen."

"Thank you," the young doctor said gratefully, feeling peace and a new confidence flow through him. He would use his ability and learned knowledge, and with God by his side, what better assistant could he have?

When they arrived at the small cabin of the Atkins, the door opened. Mrs. Atkins stood with a worried look on her face as she let the two men enter.

"He's hurtin' something awful," she told them as she led them to the small bedroom. The stench of the room almost made Matthew turn and leave. The man had obviously been sick several times and was now writhing in pain on the bed. Mark walked to him and placed a hand over his right upper abdomen.

"Is this where it hurts?" he asked, already knowing the answer.

With only a nod and a moan, the man shut his eyes, hoping to squelch the pain.

"We'll need boiling water, Mrs. Atkins. It would be best if we could use the kitchen table. It's higher and will be easier to work on."

"What is it, doctor?" she asked before leaving the room.

"Your husband has gallstones and won't get relief until we get them out of him."

"Oh my," was her only reply, unsure of what the doctor meant.

Following behind the woman, Mark prepared the table while the water boiled. He moved chairs to the side and cleansed it as thoroughly as possible with alcohol. Matthew, standing at his side, asked, "What do I need to do?"

"We'll have to help him get out here and onto the table."

As the men moved toward the sick man, Matthew noted that Mr. Atkins was smaller in frame and reached underneath to lift him.

"If you'll hold the door, Mark, I can carry him to the table."

Mark hid a smile as he noticed that indeed his brother had no difficulty lifting the man.

Placing him on the substitute operating table, Mark saw the two children out of the corner of his eye watching their every move.

"You'll need to take them somewhere while we operate," he told their mother.

"Adam Tyler, Luke, come on. Get your coats and let's go to the barn for a spell so they can fix your pa. We'll tend to the animals." The two little boys glanced at the strangers before them before dashing out of the house.

After both men washed their hands, Mark prepared his patient with the help of his brother. They removed his clothing and placed a blanket over him. He began to clean meticulously with alcohol. The man's continual movement made his work difficult. Reaching for his bag, he grabbed a dark brown bottle and a rag and poured a small amount of the liquid onto it. Placing it over the man's nose, he said, "Mr. Atkins, I need you to breathe deeply for a minute or so. This will help ease the pain."

Doing as he was told, the ailing man soon began to relax, and they watched as he finally closed his eyes, drifting off into a pain-free sleep.

"There, that should keep him out for a short while. I may need you to place it back over his nose when he starts to stir," Mark told Matthew.

"Whatever you need me for, just tell me," the oldest brother replied.

"You going to be all right with blood and foul-smelling bile?"

With a grin, Matthew replied, "Guess I have to be, don't I?"

With a smile for his answer, Mark began to work. He had laid out all his instruments. After retrieving the boiling water, he set it near him and held each instrument in the pan to kill as many germs as possible. After saying a quick prayer, he took his scalpel and began to make an incision on the upper right section of the man's abdomen, around his ninth rib, moving downward. While working, Matthew watched the intent features of his younger sibling and felt pride pass through him. He had all the faith in the world in him and would have trusted him with his own life.

"There it is," Mark told him with relief a short time later, finding the troublesome organ. "Can you clean away some of this blood? Rinse these rags out in the water first."

With a nod, Matthew dipped the clean rags into the hot liquid, careful not to burn himself. Waiting a moment for them to cool, he began to cleanse away the blood to aid Mark as he reached inside the man's abdominal cavity. Finding the gallbladder hidden beneath the liver, he made a small incision and reached his fingers inside. With a smile directed at Matthew, he said, "Just as I suspected—gallstones."

Gathering as many as possible, he removed his hand and placed them on the table. In total, he retrieved fifteen out of the man.

"Hard to tell what they look like," Matthew said as he studied the stones.

"It's because they are surrounded with bile. He should feel much better now. I think that's all there are."

With another rag, Mark wiped off his hands and reached for the cat gut to close the gallbladder. After retrieving the cooling liquid into a small bottle, he irrigated as much as possible and reached for the silk sutures. He began to work on stitching the skin together to finish closing the abdominal wound. Mr. Atkins began to stir, and Matthew was quick to place the rag over his nose. After a moment, the man began to rest again.

Placing a dressing over the incision, he straightened, rubbing his neck as a smile adorned his face.

"That should be it," he told Matthew with a sigh of relief.

"You did great," the older brother said with a slap on his shoulder.

"Thanks. Couldn't have done it alone though. Between the three of us, we did well," he replied, referring to the third as being God. "You can carry him back to his own bed now."

Picking up the man, Matthew walked toward the bedroom and carefully deposited the patient, pulling the quilt over him.

Leaning his hands on the table for a moment, Mark sent a prayer heavenward, thanking God for His assistance.

When Matthew entered once again, the two began to swiftly dispose of the instruments and clean up the small area. They worked well together, speaking little.

A few minutes later, they heard a timid knock at the door and saw Mrs. Atkins poke her head through the doorway.

"Is everything goin' all right?"

"Yes, it is fine. We are finished, and your husband is back in bed. You can come back in now."

With a beaming smile, she yelled toward the barn, "Come on, kids, they're done with your pa."

When she entered, Mark said, "I'll be back over later this evening to check on him. The main thing to worry about is infection. He can have water and some broth later if he is hungry, but nothing else. I will leave some morphine with you to give him for pain."

"Thank you ever so much, Doctor. All we have is a chicken to give ya,' but we shore do 'preciate all you've done."

"That's all right, Mrs. Atkins. Keep your chicken. I'm glad to help. Like I said, I'll be back later to check on him."

When the men were sitting in the wagon, Matthew laughed and told his brother, "You sure aren't going to get rich in this work."

"No, I've been putting enquiries out to see if there is something else available. I don't know how Rachel and I will survive on chickens."

Hearing those words pierced Matthew's heart, but he said nothing.

Moving his shoulders up and down, he said, "I guess I didn't realize how tense I was. My back is aching."

"You were doing some pretty deep thinking, that's for sure," Matthew told him. "Maybe you can talk Mama into bringing in the tub tonight for a nice, hot soak and John into carrying water."

"Now that, my dear brother, is a great idea," he said, wondering how he could bribe his youngest sibling into fetching him some water.

The following evening, Mark visited with the Atkins to check on his patient. The man was cool to the touch, and although in pain from the incision, he smiled and thanked the doctor for helping him. As the young physician left, he felt a measure of gratefulness to God for enabling him to be able to do what he could to help such folks—folks that reminded him of his own parents.

Matthew picked Christy up. They were headed to Cheyenne for lunch. He knew he had to end their relationship before it got any more serious on her part. He had tried to make it work, but it wasn't. With misery on his face, he led her to a table near the back.

Christy beamed a large smile at him, as they took their respective seats. Before he could tell her of his intentions, she asked boldly, "Don't you think it's time we talked of marriage? My mother keeps dropping hints about seeing me married."

Her words flabbergasted him, and before he could speak, she interjected, "I do care for you dearly, you know." She placed her hand over his.

"I would make a good wife for you and bear your children to fill up that big house."

Thoughts pulsated through his brain as she spoke of her feelings. He felt embarrassment flood over him with such intimate speech about her bearing his children.

Clearing his throat, he gathered his words carefully, and when she paused, he said, "That's why I invited you today. We need to talk."

Misunderstanding his meaning, she jumped up and quickly rushed to his side and squealed, "Yes, I accept," while kissing him fully on his lips.

Unwrapping her arms, shock registered on his face as he noticed the uneasiness of her actions, causing alarm on the other patrons in the restaurant.

"Please, sit down, Christy. Hear what I have to say first."

Returning to her seat, a smile of happiness filled her features as she waited for him to continue.

"This is not what I had planned today," he told her frankly. Watching the smile fade quickly, she asked, "What do you mean?"

"I asked you here to tell you that I won't be calling on you anymore."

Hearing his words, she began to speak loudly, "What are you talking about? You've kissed me, doesn't that mean anything?"

Trying to keep as calm as possible, he told her quietly, "No, you kissed me, if you will remember."

"How can you do this? Do you realize how embarrassing this will be for me, to my family?"

Seeing her true self, Matthew knew that she had only wanted him for a conquest; there was no love involved, it was pride.

"You don't really love me, Christy," he told her, astonishing her somewhat.

"What is love? Do you even know yourself, Matthew O'Malley?" she asked as she stood to her feet. "Don't bother seeing me home. I will walk to my father's bank and ride back with him."

Watching her walk away, he recalled her words and told himself, *Yes, I do know what love is, Christy. And I know why I could never give my heart to another woman; it's already filled with Rachel.*

Rising to his feet, he headed for the wagon. The drive seemed like a long one, but he sure felt as though a weight had been removed from him. No, he may never have Rachel for himself, but he knew that he would not settle for second best, and that was how anyone else compared to her. There would be no other for him, at least for the time being. God would have to heal his heart before he could turn his attention to someone else. He just didn't know how long that would take.

At supper that evening, Mark noticed his brother's unusual quietness and teased him, "So, where is your lady love?"

Glancing up quickly from his plate, he said quietly, "We are finished."

"I'm sorry, honey," his mother replied in sympathy.

Turning to look into her eyes, he told her, "I'm not. I knew she wasn't the right one for me."

"Don't worry, son, you'll find the one who God would have for you one day," he said, hoping to ease his aching heart.

With a look of despair on his face, he excused himself without replying, knowing the right one for him was marrying his brother in another month.

His mother, watching the retreating figure, felt her own heart break, realizing the dilemma he was in and yet kept it to himself. Rising to her feet, she followed her son into his room and closed the door.

Seeing her standing quietly, he intuitively knew she had guessed his secret.

"I'm sorry," she told him as she walked to embrace him.

"How did you know?" he asked as she looked into his beautiful blue eyes, so much like his papa's.

"It's written on your face, and I feel it in my heart."

"Does Mark know?" he asked in fear.

"No, and I'll never tell him. I will pray for you daily, that God will ease your hurt and replace it with His love."

"Thank you, Mama, because I don't know how I will face the days ahead knowing that Rachel is Mark's wife."

With no other words necessary, he watched as she walked sadly from his room, closing the door behind her.

Chapter Fifteen

The weather had taken a turn and had warmed up slightly. It had started to rain a bone-chilling drizzle that kept many inside. At the O'Malley house, Genie grabbed her husband's arm and told him, "Please, Ian, don't go out in this. Wait until Matthew is home to help you. He should be returning from town soon."

"Now, Genie, I'm thinking that maybe my lassie is worrying a tad too much about the weather. A little rain won't hurt John or me. Besides, I don't plan on admiring the scenery whilst we're there. I just want to get that fine tree that Matthew chopped down the other morning. It's a dandy and 'twill help us through the next few weeks. If he gets home any time soon, send the boy out. He knows where we'll be."

"Can't you wait until tomorrow? Maybe the weather will clear a bit, and with both boys helping, it will be much easier."

"We can't wait for the weather to clear, my love. It's been raining off and on for the last two days, and we need that wood before ole man winter strikes again. We need to be workin' whilst we can."

"You are one stubborn man!" she exclaimed in exasperation.

"That I know," he told her with a grin as he pulled her close, "and that's why ya' love me."

Genie felt uneasy as she watched the two put on their raincoats and boots.

"Please hurry," she told him as he planted a quick kiss on his cheek.

"We will. Lassie, if you'll just have us something nice and hot to eat for when we get back, I'll be a happy man."

Watching them drive away in the wagon a few minutes later, she smiled as she thought of days long ago when they had first built the house. The small soddy served it's purpose well while they were living in it, but it felt wonderful to be in a building with a floor beneath it. The children hadn't seemed to mind the small place, however.

Walking to the large picture window near the front door, she let her eyes take in the miserable weather and experienced an uneasy feeling pass through her again.

"Lord, protect them." were the only words she could send heavenward at the moment.

An hour had passed when she heard the front door open and saw Matthew enter, drenched.

"Quick, get out of those wet clothes before you get sick," his mama told him as she assisted him with his soaking overcoat.

"It's getting worse outside," he told her. "The rain is turning to sleet, and soon it will be turning to snow."

"Oh no, your father and John have gone to retrieve that tree you cut down. He was determined to get it up here so he could let it dry out in the barn for a few days."

"I've got to go and help them," he told her with concern.

"At least change into dry clothes and put your other boots on."

Nodding, he headed toward the room he shared with Mark to change quickly.

Just as he was on the last step, he saw John burst through the door and yell, "Quick, it's Papa. He's hurt."

Reaching again for his coat and boots, Genie entered after hearing the commotion and asked, "What's wrong?" Fear rose into her throat.

"We were almost out of the woods when a tree cracked and split, sending the largest section crashing down. It fell on Papa before he could get out of its way. I tried to pull him out, but he's trapped. It's laying on his legs."

"No," she cried as she began to reach for her own coat.

"Mama," Matthew told her as he grabbed her arm, "you stay here with Sarah. This is no place for you. Stay home and get the room set up with any supplies we may need. We don't know how bad it is. Please!" he told her with firmness.

Able only to nod in agreement, thinking of the small child asleep in the other room, she watched as the two brothers left in a hurry. Matthew ran to the barn to grab the chain that might be needed to remove the tree.

As they pulled up to the place where their father was, he saw that he was still conscious and smiled at them as they approached.

"Sorry, laddie, for makin' ya' come out in this weather to rescue your papa."

"How bad is it?" he asked with dread.

"I don't rightly know. I can't feel my left leg anymore, and the pain has stopped for now."

Nodding, Matthew placed the chain around the section near his injured father and ran back to the wagon to hook it to the axle. John, who was watching almost in a state of shock, heard him say, "Stay near Pa and help guide me while I pull the tree off him."

Slowly, the tree was removed and the boys carried their father to the back of the wagon. John sat beside him while Matthew grabbed the heavy tarp to keep him from the icy rain that had begun again.

"Be takin' it slow there, son," he heard his papa say. "The pain is becoming a bit sharper now."

Hearing those words, Matthew knew the seriousness of his condition. Never had he heard the man complain before about anything.

Going as slowly as possible, he prayed continuously and beseeched God on behalf of his father.

As they drew near the house, Genie ran out to greet them.

"Oh, Ian," was all she could say before the tears intermingled with the cold rain on her cheeks.

"Now, Mama, 'tis going to be fine. Just ya' wait and see."

The brothers carried their father into the house and placed him on his bed.

"John, go and get Mark. He should still be at the clinic."

Watching him leave, Matthew assisted his mother with the removal of Ian's wet clothes and helped him put dry, clean ones on. Genie was amazed at the levelheadedness of her oldest son. He had always been organized and methodical with his work, but only as she observed him today did she realize yet another special gift that God had given him—the gift of mercy.

"If you'll try and get some warm liquid down him, I'll stoke the fire to help stop the chills."

Both working in accord, they soon had the cold man warm, although he frequently grimaced with pain.

Later, the front door and Mark and John entered. Worry was etched on both of their faces as they headed toward their parents' bedroom.

"Papa!" Mark exclaimed with a measure of relief when he saw the small smile his father offered.

"Well, I'll be, I've not had this much attention for meself in a long time," he told them bravely.

"How bad is the pain, and where are you hurting?" his son enquired.

"It's me legs, son, especially the left one."

"Let me take a look at you and see," he said as he pulled back the cover to reveal a badly twisted knee.

"It's broken and will have to be set," he told everyone as he continued to probe with gentle fingers.

"Was afraid of that," Ian said with a small smile. "Didn't think it was supposed to bend that way."

"Oh, Ian, can't you be serious for even a minute?" Genie rebuked him.

Turning to look solemnly at her for the first time, he whispered, "I would, my dear, sweet wife, but I'm trying hard not to think about the awful aching."

Mark reached into his bag, pulled out a bottle, and emptied some powders in a small measuring spoon.

"Here, Pa, take this with some water and it will ease the pain. I'm going to have to fix that leg before I can splint it up."

Turning to look into the faces of his brothers, he asked, "Who wants to help me?"

Matthew, seeing the almost panic-stricken face of his youngest sibling, quickly offered, "I'll help you. John, why don't you ride over to the Parker's place and tell them what has happened. We could sure use their prayers."

Genie realized that her thoughtful son was offering her young-est an escape while they took care of their papa, and she smiled gratefully at Matthew.

With a quick wink, he smiled in return.

"That's a good idea, honey," she told her youngest son. "Why don't you change into some dry clothes and get the extra raincoat in the hallway. At least you will start off somewhat dry."

Needing no further excuse to leave this room, the boy dashed out of the room and up the stairs to do what he had been told.

Despite the medicine, the intense pain while his leg was set made the older man yell out sharply and lose consciousness. Both brothers were grateful. Mark could finish the job quickly without worrying about causing his father any more discomfort. It was not nearly as easy taking care of a loved one, he had discovered.

They had just pulled the covers up around him when Genie entered.

"Is he all right?" she asked worriedly. Sarah was now awake and stood beside her with eyes ready to pop.

"We won't know for a few days. Infection could set in; plus, the fact that he was in the rain for quite some time is not going to help. Keep him as warm as possible and encourage him to drink a lot of fluids."

Nodding at his instructions, tears began to trickle down her cheeks, and both brothers quickly strode toward her to offer comfort.

"And pray," Matthew told her tenderly.

"I have been. It seems that's all I can do now."

"It's the best thing to do now, Mama," he reminded her kindly.

"I'm going to stay the night with him and make sure he isn't in too much pain," Mark told her.

"That's not necessary, son. I won't leave his side."

"It's all right. I don't mind. Besides, I wouldn't get any sleep if I weren't with him anyway."

Nodding in agreement, they all stood a moment longer to watch the man they loved. Hopefully, he would rest for a while from the medication he had been given and would have relief.

"I'm going to take care of the livestock," Matthew told his mother a short time later, needing some fresh air to clear his mind.

As he walked by, Genie reached out and hugged him. "I am so proud of you. Thank you for helping your papa today. I'm afraid I couldn't even think straight."

"It was God who helped me get through it. I just wanted to run the other way and pretend it had never happened."

Hearing his honesty, she smiled and placed a finger against his cheek. "I love you, son," she told him simply.

"And I love you both, Mama."

Mark watched the interlude. His mother approached him and wrapped her arms around his waist. "Do you realize how proud I am of my children? What would we do without you to take care of us? I love you, too, my doctor son."

Hearing her voice break, he engulfed her tightly in a warm hug and said, "And you know I love you both also. You and Papa have guided us and shown us what real love is between a husband and a wife."

"Soon, you will understand this love yourself," she told him, unaware of the new feelings her words had released inside him.

Matthew finished feeding the animals and was leaning against the beam that stood in the middle when the strain from the past few hours surfaced and erupted from him. Tears began to fall as he recalled the thought of losing his beloved father.

Rachel, having ridden over with her pa, entered the barn and saw him as he wept openly, his back to her. Quietly she walked to him and placed her hand on his arm.

Feeling her touch, he swiped the tears with the back of his hand and turned to face her.

"I'm sorry for interrupting you. Is there anything I can do to help?" she asked in a soft, hurting voice.

Without a word, he gathered her into an embrace and held her for the length of several minutes. Hugging him back, she sensed that words were unnecessary between them. He was seeking solace, nothing more, and she happened to be the one to provide it.

As he pulled away a short time later, a small smile was shared between them before he said, "Thank you."

"You're welcome. It's the least I could do for you after all you have done for us," she replied, peering up into eyes darker from the emotion he was feeling.

Reaching out, he wiped a tear that had slipped unheeded down her cheek. Her eyes were filled with concern, and the vulnerability on her face made her more beautiful than ever. The walls of his heart were broken down, and his raw feelings for her seeped through.

Before he could help himself, he leaned over and kissed her parted lips. Although tentative at first, the kiss grew deeper before either realized what they were doing. Love flowed and entwined their two hearts together in a kiss that seemed to wipe away all other thoughts except their need for one another. Feeling his strong arms around her, pulling her close, she wrapped her own arms around his neck, never wanting to let him go. It was where she wanted to be...in the arms of the man she loved.

Mark's face appeared suddenly in her mind and she quickly stepped back. Placing her fingers against her tingling lips, she gasped in shock.

"Rachel," Matthew told her in agony, "I am so sorry. Please forgive me."

Watching her run from the barn, he felt new sadness fill his soul. He knew that it would be impossible to stay and watch his brother marry her. He thought he was strong enough, but he was wrong. The type of love he felt was the kind his parents had for one another, and it would only grow, not lessen, should he remain. He felt jealousy as he thought of Mark with Rachel and the life they would share together as man and wife. With new determination and resolve, he would wait until he was certain of his father's well being and move into his new house—a house that he might have to sell. He knew he could find a place to live and a job in Cheyenne if he needed to. And after feeling the love spread through him during that kiss, he knew he did need to put distance between he and Rachel if he was to retain any sanity.

Wouldn't it be ironic if he had been working so diligently to build a home for his own family when his own brother might actually live there with the woman he had originally built it for? He knew Dr. Hill would be retiring soon and that Mark would be offered the job before anyone else. Feeling more desolate than he ever had in his entire life, he fed the animals, his thoughts recalling vividly the kiss he had just shared. Somehow he had known all along that kissing Rachel would be different than when Christy had kissed him.

Genie walked into the bedroom the following morning carrying a cold glass of milk for her husband. She saw him try to smile at her despite the pain present in his leg. He was running a fever, and the coolness of the liquid on his lips was like a balm to him.

"Aye, that tastes good, me lovely wife."

"How is your leg this morning?" she asked, knowing how he had tossed and turned throughout the long night. The only relief he had known was when Mark had offered him morphine.

"'Twill be better in no time," he told her, avoiding her question.

Watching Mark enter, he came to sit on the foot of the bed. Seeing his father's flushed face, he knew he was battling infection in his body from the break.

"Drink a lot of fluids today, Papa," he said. "You will feel better after the fever has broken."

"'Tis not me hurting head that is bothering me, laddie," he told his son with a small grimace.

"Let me see how your leg is doing. Thankfully it was a clean break and the bone didn't pierce through the skin." After examining him, he resplinted the leg and asked, "Do you feel up to sitting in the chair?"

"Aye, son, if you think that is best for your papa."

A small chuckle escaped Mark as he told him, "I wish all of my patients were as agreeable as you."

With both Genie and Mark to help, they had him sitting up on the side of the bed. A wave of dizziness circled the man, and they waited for it to pass before aiding him toward the chair.

"Don't put any weight on that leg. You'll have to stay off of it for a few months to let it heal."

Hearing those words caused worry to pass over the older man's features.

"Months, me boy?" he asked. "Why I've never been still for more than a day, how can ya' ask me to sit quietly for months?"

"You have no choice. If you put weight on it too soon, it will break again and then your recovery will take even longer."

Not a person to be pessimistic, he turned toward his wife with a snicker and said, "Well, me lovely woman, looks like ya'll have to put up with the likes of me company for a bit."

Grateful that he was all right, she leaned over and whispered, "And that will be fine with me. I'm sure I can find things for you to do around the house."

"Now look what ya've done son. This woman will have me darnin' them socks of yours and knitting scarves before long."

Listening to his parents and hearing the obvious love they still had for one another, Mark smiled and left the two of them alone. As he started through the door, he said, "I'll return shortly to help you back into bed, Papa."

"Now don't be forgettin' me, Mark. I may be temped to get there by meself."

Knowing that his father was telling the truth, he would return shortly to ensure that he was back into the safety of his bed with help.

Matthew knocked softly on his parents' door, quietly opening it. He saw his father smile at him with a lopsided grin.

"Howdy, there, son. Don't be standing there. Come visit with your pa."

Hearing the cheerful spirit of his father, despite the intense pain that still lingered, he smiled in return. As he approached the bed, he handed his father a cane to aid him in his walking.

Reaching out for the object, his father whistled appreciatively before he said, "Mighty fine work here, me boy."

Spotting the gleam in his son's eyes, he asked with amusement, "And where, might I be askin,' did this little beauty come from?"

"None other than the tree that put you here," Matthew told him with a chuckle. "Thought you might like to have a remembrance of this and couldn't think of anything better."

"So, ya' went and retrieved it by yourself, did ya'?"

"No, I took John with me. The large limb that had fallen on you was still attached to the base of the tree, and we had a terrible time trying to free it up."

Running his hand over the smooth piece of wood, his papa said, "Your mama and I have indeed been blessed by the Almighty to have such fine children."

Placing his hand on his father's shoulder, Matthew told him, "No, it is we that are blessed to have such wonderful parents."

"Ach, now, son, ya' want to see your pa cry? If'n ya' keep this talk up, I'll be a sobbing like a wee one."

After visiting until he saw his father begin to grow weary, Matthew stood to his feet.

"Goodnight, Papa. I'll see you tomorrow morning."

"Goodnight, son. I'm beholden to ya' for my friend," he returned, gesturing toward the gift.

Genie walked through the door as Matthew was leaving.

"We have reason to be proud of those youngins, don't we, lassie?"

"Indeed we do," she replied softly, letting her thoughts dwell on each of their children.

Two weeks later, certain that his father was on the road to recovery, Matthew informed his parents of his decision.

"I still don't understand why you have to move yet," his mother told again. "You're new house isn't quite finished. Can't you wait until it's complete?"

"No, Mama. My mind is made up. It's time for me to be on my own. It's not like I'll be far, just a little over a half mile away."

Shaking her head, thoughts of Rachel suddenly popped into her mind. Was that why? Had something happened lately that she was unaware of? The thought did little to comfort her. Her heart hurt for her tenderhearted son. He had waited so long for God to bring the right woman into his life, only to discover that it was his brother's own fiancée. Now she knew why he had never been interested in any of the girls who had tried to catch his eye. He had been waiting for Rachel to grow up.

Watching him pack the next day broke her heart, not only because her own flesh and blood was leaving, but because of the sadness present in his face.

"I will be praying for you."

Looking deeply into the eyes of his mother, he knew that she had discovered his secret.

"I have to go," he whispered against her hair as he hugged her. "It may not be far enough," he admitted with sadness.

"I know," she whispered back.

"It hurts too much now. Maybe with time my feelings will change."

Unsure of how to reply to his words, she hugged him before letting him walk out the door.

He had not run into Rachel except at church. He purposely came late to the services and left early to avoid her. He knew that he had compromised both her and Mark in the barn and was not ready to look into her eyes and see the disappointment she held in him. He would apologize later for his actions. How he would stand and watch them become man and wife was something that he tried not to think about. For the time being, space was the best thing he could offer his broken heart.

Chapter Sixteen

Night was beginning to settle. The Parker family was sitting down to supper when there was a knock at the door. Tucker, rising from the table, walked over to answer it. Before him stood Mark with a worried appearance on his face.

"May I please speak to Rachel?" he asked.

"Of course. Come in."

Entering into the warmth of the home, he saw his fiancée rise to her feet and take a step toward him.

"Is everything all right?" she asked quietly, aware of demeanor.

"No, it's not. The Carter boy became sick a few days ago and died before I could get the chance to see him. I've recently heard that the whole family is sick now, and from what I can gather, it sounds like it could be typhoid fever. The Samuels' daughter is ill also. I'm afraid this could spread and be an epidemic. I wanted to see if you would help me go to the church and begin to set up a small hospital for all those who are sick. It could be spreading through all the children who were at school last week. I would ask Matthew, but he and John are needed around the farm now that Papa is hurt."

Running his hand through his hair, a worried expression on his face, he continued, "If it is typhoid, we'll have to be quarantined until it passes. I know this is a lot to ask of you, because you risk the chance of becoming sick yourself, but frankly, I don't know what else to do. School will have to be closed."

Hearing those words made McKenna's heart drop. As she, too, rose to her own feet, she saw her daughter turn to face her with a pleading look.

"I have to go, you know that, Mama," she told her mother.

"Yes, I know. Please be careful, and remember that you'll be in our prayers constantly."

Her father, coming to wrap his arms around his oldest daughter, felt his heart sink at the thought of her leaving to help.

"I love you, honey. You have to do what God tells you to do."

"I am, Papa."

Rachel moved to her bedroom to pack and felt the presence of her mother behind her.

"I'll do my best to take care of her, sir," Mark told the older man.

"I know you will, son. And I appreciate that. As much as we'd like to protect our children, we know that sometimes we have to let God watch over them."

The chill in the air made the ride seem longer to Rachel. Although snuggly wrapped up in the thick, warm quilt, a light snow had just started to fall and she shivered slightly. Noticing the shiver, Mark placed his arm around her and pulled her close.

"I'm sorry for asking you to do this. If anything should happen to you, I would never forgive myself."

"Don't be silly. That's what I am here for, remember? Besides, you have the same chance of getting the sickness that I do."

"Yes, but I've been around a lot more illnesses and have built somewhat of a resistance against these things. We'll just pray that we'll stay healthy."

A few moments of silence ensued before she asked, "Tell me what we need to do once we get to the church."

"I've already spread the word for the town folks to bring as many extra supplies as they can spare and place them in the building. They are taking food and water as well as blankets and such, so hopefully we'll be prepared for a few weeks if necessary. You and I will have to organize everything as we receive patients. I've sent a few men to Cheyenne for medicine that we may need. Mrs. Carter has volunteered to help in any way she can."

"It sounds like you've thought this through."

"We had an emergency like this while I was in medical school. At least I have some knowledge of what to expect. It won't be fun, and I'm afraid we're going to lose some patients, even children. Typhoid is not something that is easy to cure. Hopefully, people will come in when they first experience the symptoms. Their chances are somewhat better then."

Rachel, sitting and taking in his words, prayed silently that God would be with them over the next few weeks. She had never seen death before her and didn't know how she would react.

As they reached the church, they saw that several wagons were already present. Men were carrying supplies into the small building and lining them up against one wall. Rachel noticed another man working outside, splitting firewood to keep the place warm during their vigil.

"These are good people, aren't they?" she asked almost silently. Fear of what lay ahead, knowing that some of her dear friends and neighbors would die, troubled her heart.

"Yes, and if we work together as a team, many more lives will be saved."

"And you are a good man," she told him as he assisted her to the ground.

Without saying a word, he smiled a boyish smile that reminded her of olden days when they were just kids and played together.

Taking her arm, he assisted her toward the church. As they entered, warmth flooded through her and she began to remove her coat, hanging it up on the small pegs on one wall. She saw that all of the pews had been removed, and the room stood completely bare except for the woodburning stove in one corner.

"We'll start by separating the supplies. Place the perishables near the front and then gather all the blankets and begin to make beds near one another on the floor. We'll try to keep the sickest on one side of the room, separating them from those who are just showing symptoms."

Nodding in understanding, Rachel began to work silently and diligently. Within an hour, the room looked like it was ready for patients.

The town postmistress, Mrs. Carter, had asked to come and help them. She had lost her own husband in an accident over three years ago, and with no children of her own, she felt free to offer her services.

By the end of the week, more than ten people lay on the blankets that served as beds. They ranged in age from three years to a few grandmothers and grandfathers. Coughing and moaning could be heard throughout out the room.

Rachel, assisting a little boy of five to sit up, wiped the sweat from her own forehead as she lifted the cup to his mouth.

"There you go, Sam," she told him with a small smile. "I think you are feeling better today."

"I am, Miss Rachel. My throat doesn't hurt as much."

"I'm so glad. Maybe Dr. Mark will let you go home later today to be with your mama and papa."

"I hope so," he told her solemnly. "I sure do miss them."

Hugging him close to her warm body, she thanked God for saving the little tyke. They had already lost three in a week, and she didn't know if she could stand someone else dying. Tim Hudson had died yesterday. He was a young man who had a wife and son. The thought of them without their loved one broke Rachel's heart. She could picture the hard days ahead for the family. Little Rebecca Simpson had also died at the beginning of the week. She was only six years old. She was the youngest of five other children, but by the time she had arrived, the disease had taken its toll on her slight body, and they were unable to help very much. Rachel had held her in her arms when her suffering had come to an end. Tears streamed down her face, and Mark, noticing her anguish, literally had to separate the two. Overwhelming sorrow filled Rachel as she watched the little girl's lifeless body carried out into the bitter, winter weather. Her heart had felt as cold as the air that entered through the open door. The little girl had been in school the current year and had worked her way into her schoolteacher's heart with her loveable disposition. Rachel didn't know how she would handle the empty seat that would be present in school from then on.

Another had died this morning. It was an elderly woman whose body was unable to fight the ravaging disease. She had smiled tenderly at Rachel and told her that she was finally going home to be with her husband. Seeing the tears gathered in the young girl's eyes, the woman whispered that she was ready to die. She asked Rachel to shed no tears for her.

It had been a very emotional, as well as physically tiring week. Not only did they work ceaselessly, they took little time for themselves for sleep or food. Mrs. Carter had proved to be a godsend. She worked tirelessly without complaint, and her compassion as she bathed and fed patients was amazing.

As Rachel walked to the front of the church to begin preparations for a noon meal, she felt a wave of dizziness engulf her. Wiping the perspiration away from her forehead, she turned and saw Mark watching her. Standing to his feet, he walked closer and placed a hand on her cheek.

"You're sick, aren't you?" he asked with dread.

"I think so. I'm not feeling very well," she whispered hoarsely as darkness suddenly surrounded her and she began to slip to the floor. Quickly gathering her in his arms, he called, "Mrs. Carter, please help me!"

The older woman was quickly at his side. Preparing a new place in the corner, they soon had her tucked into the makeshift bed and pulled the quilt up around her chin.

"I'll get some medicine into her, and you try to get her to drink something cool."

As Mark walked toward the medical supplies, he remembered how light she had seemed in his arms. This past week had been hard on her. He felt responsible for not having made sure she had eaten and slept more. With only the three of them taking care of so many sick and the constant care they offered, he wished he had not been so wrapped up with their needs more than those of his fiancée.

Lord, please don't let her die, he begged inwardly, thinking of how many people loved her and needed her.

By evening, the fever was raging throughout her body. Rachel tossed and turned constantly and cried out several times during the night. Mark tried to devote as much time as possible to her while tending to the needs of the others. He had not slept in three days and was physically exhausted. He was extremely grateful for the postmistress and all her steadfast work and tenderness to the patients.

Two days passed and Mark feared for Rachel's life. She had eaten very little and could barely speak. She was in and out of consciousness, and he had to mop her hot forehead from the fever continually. The wracking cough plagued her weakened body and would not let her rest.

Standing, he walked to the door and opened it, stepping out into the brisk, cold air. Pastor Keller and her grandmother, who lived across the road, happened to be outside also. Spotting both of them in the yard, Mark yelled, "Reverend, would you do me a favor?"

"Certainly, Doctor."

"Your granddaughter has typhoid. Would you take a trip to the Parkers' farm and tell them that Rachel is very ill. They need to pray."

Concern etched the older man's face as he thought of the new member of his family being sick.

"We'll go right away. And rest assured, I'll inform others so that many prayers will be ascending the throne of God on her behalf."

"Thank you."

"How bad is she?" Susan Keller inquired with a heavy heart. "Do I need to come and help?"

"She is not doing well. No, you need to stay away from here. It is highly contagious."

Too emotionally upset to continue with words, Mark turned and headed back to her side.

McKenna was preparing supper when she heard the wagon pull into the yard. Excitement coursed through her at the thought of Rachel's return. She had heard various reports of those who had not been able to fight the sickness. She prayed often and anxiously waited for the epidemic to be over and for her daughter to come home.

As she opened the door, her smile turned to a frown of concern when she saw her new father-in-law and Tucker's mama climbing down from the wagon.

"Good evening, McKenna."

"Good evening, yourself," she greeted them with a slightly hesitant voice.

"I promised Mark that I would send word that Rachel is very ill. He asks that we all pray for her."

Feeling the blood drain from her, she was vaguely aware of the dear loved ones following her inside.

"I was so afraid this was going to happen," she whispered as the pastor assisted her to a chair. "She's rather frail herself."

"She is where God wants her to be, of this I am sure," he told her. "And it is much better to be in God's will and doing what He wants us to do than be out of His will and doing what we want to do."

"Yes," she replied as tears began to fall.

"We have to trust God, McKenna, that He will touch our precious girl," Mama Parker told her with tears in her own eyes.

The door opened then and Tucker, seeing the distraught look on his wife's face, feared for the worst.

"Is it Rachel?"

"Yes, she has the sickness."

In two large strides, he stood before her and gathered her in his arms.

The minister, placing his hand on Tucker's shoulder, knew that they needed their privacy and led his wife toward the door.

"We'll be praying for her, as well as many others. I'll also check with Mark on her condition as often as possible."

"Thank you," Tucker replied.

Taking McKenna by the hand, he led her to their bedroom.

"Let's go before God on Rachel's behalf." As they got down on their knees by their bed, petitions were laid at the feet of the Almighty as they prayed for their oldest daughter.

As they stood to their feet, she told him, "I need to go to her."

Taking her hand, Tucker replied quietly, "No, you need to stay here with Abbie Grace. We have placed her in our Father's hands now. He loves her more than we do. Now is the time for us to rely on our faith."

Nodding in agreement, knowing he was correct, she whispered, "It is so hard to leave it in His hands."

"Yes, God asks us to cast our burdens on him. He is more than able to carry them."

Mark had just given Rachel another dose of the strong quinine and felt her fingers on his own. Turning to look into her gaunt face, he heard her speak in a hoarse voice, "I don't think I am going to make it."

"I don't want to hear that," he replied rather harshly. "Of course you will pull through. You are made of tougher stuff than this sickness. Besides, there are too many people who love you and need you."

"I know. And I feel like I'm letting them all down."

"You will be if you don't fight with everything you have. Don't give up now. Tell yourself that you are going to get better."

"I've tried. I'm just so tired," she whispered as she closed her eyes.

Mark was not a man to cry easily, but he felt the moisture gather in his eyes as he let his gaze linger on her beautiful face. Even in sickness, she was still lovely to look at. Her long lashes, although light, fanned against her pale cheeks. He tenderly brushed an unruly curl back from her soft skin. He beseeched God from his inner being that He would intervene and save her. Because, despite what he felt in his heart, he knew that Rachel was right; unless their heavenly father did touch her with His healing hand, she did not have the strength to beat the sickness.

Matthew heard the knock at his door and began to descend down the stairs to answer it. As he reached to open it, he saw his mother standing before him. Seeing the look on her face caused him to ask, "What it is?"

"It's Rachel. She has the sickness."

Digesting her words, he suddenly felt as though his world were crashing down before him.

"How bad is she?"

"Your papa saw Pastor Keller in town and said she is not doing well. They fear for her life."

Watching the pained expression cross her son's face, she took a step to place her arms around him and whispered, "I am so sorry."

"Mama," he asked in anguish, "why do I still feel this way about her? I know she will soon belong to Mark, but she is all I think about. I don't know what I would do if she were not here. It's as if a piece of me would die if something were to happen to her."

"I don't know, son, why this love remains so fiercely in you—only God does. For now, however, we must pray and beseech God to save her."

"Mama, I pray for her daily already. Even though she will be with Mark, I only wish the best for her."

Hearing his words, his mother realized how deep her son's love was for Rachel. As she left a few minutes later, she asked God not only to heal Rachel's body but to touch her son's heart.

The night was a rough one for Rachel. The fever had taken over her body and sweat soaked her clothes several times. Mrs. Carter had patiently changed and bathed her in cool water to help relieve the warmth. She lay only in her petticoat now, and the thinness of her body was evident.

Mark, frequently checking on her, was fearful that she would be gone by morning. Around five o'clock, a worried Mrs. Carter approached him as he bent over a little boy.

"You're doing fine now, Sam. I think you'll be able to go home today."

Sensing her presence behind him, he rose to his feet when he saw the expression on her face.

"It's Rachel. Something's not right," she told him.

Walking over to her, he looked into her face and noticed the peaceful look that was present. Near panic spread through him as he bent to one knee and laid his fingers on her cool cheek. Feeling her breath against his hand, he stood quickly.

Turning to look into the worried face of the dear woman, he grabbed her and hugged her as he exclaimed, "The fever has broken! She's going to be fine now. She's sleeping."

"Hallelujah," the relieved woman said as she returned his hug.

"Let her rest a little while and then try and get some soup down her. It's going to take her some time to recuperate, but I'd say she's definitely on the road to recovery."

Word spread quickly about the returning health of the young woman. Not only was her family thankful to God, but many whom she had grown up with were relieved when she was finally feeling better.

A few of the children she taught brought her a bouquet of wildflowers. Thomas and Maggie McKelvey made her a card, wishing her well. These kind gestures made Rachel anxious to get back to her class.

By the end of the week, everyone was able to leave the makeshift hospital. The small rural community had survived the epidemic of typhoid. Lives had been lost, but each knew it could have been so much worse. They had the young doctor and his quick action to thank for that.

The wedding was in two weeks, and Rachel, thinking about her life that lay ahead, felt sadness inside her. She knew she and Mark would have a fine life together. He had rented a small house in town where they would live after they were married. She smiled briefly as she recalled how excited he had been when she saw it for the first time. He had walked around and told her eagerly where some of the furniture he had purchased would be placed.

Yes, he would be a good husband. Oppressing the thoughts that maybe that wasn't enough, that there should be more, she felt drained and decided to lie down for a little while. She had been doing a lot of praying concerning her marriage, desperately seeking peace, but trusting in God to work out things. Closing her eyes, sleep claimed her quickly.

One thing she had learned from watching her parents over the years was that when one made a commitment and gave their word on something, he did not break it for any reason.

Chapter Seventeen

The following week, her mother came into her room and found Rachel sitting in the chair near the window, reading the Bible.

"Good morning, honey, how are you feeling today?"

"I am so much better, even stronger than yesterday. I might even venture a small stroll in the next day or so."

Leaning over, McKenna kissed the top of her daughter's head before telling her, "I know it's early, but you have a guest."

Frowning, trying to think who would be paying her such an early visit, she heard her mama say, "It's Mark."

"Oh," the young girl replied. McKenna, turning to leave the room, pondered her daughter's word as she left to prepare breakfast. She knew what was bothering her but was unsure if she should speak of it at the present time.

A moment later, the young doctor entered the room and came to sit on the foot of Rachel's bed.

"Good morning, are you feeling better today?"

"Yes, it's amazing how much strength I've gained in the last few days. I was just telling Mama that I might even venture out of the house and take a walk tomorrow."

"Don't go too far," the doctor side of the young man cautioned her. "You were very sick and don't want to overdo it yet."

"I won't," she promised.

"Good. You have more color in your cheeks today."

"Do I?" she asked as she felt warmth course through her. She was uncomfortable with the compliment, even though it was from him.

"Yes, and I think you've put on a little more weight."

A slight pause ensued here before he reached for one of her hands.

"You know I love you, Rachel, don't you?"

Although she had heard the words before, she felt discomfort as he said them.

"Yes, and I love you too," she replied, not lifting her eyes to look into his.

"Do you, Rachel?" he asked suddenly.

"Yes, of course," she told him quietly.

"Are you still planning on going through with the wedding?"

With these words, she quickly peered into his face. "Yes."

"Mmm...I think we have a problem then."

"A problem?" she asked in bewilderment.

"Yes. How can you marry me if you are in love with someone else?"

He watched as tears pooled in her large, cornflower blue eyes and threatened to spill over. Averting her gaze from his, she looked unseeingly at the book in her lap.

"I'm sorry. I never meant to hurt you. I want you to know that I have not made this commitment lightly."

Looking up at him again, she continued, "I really do love you, you know."

"And I love you, but not the way real love should be between a husband and wife. I would say our feelings are more like a brother- and sister-type love. Mama actually opened my eyes the other day on what true love should be between a husband and a wife."

"You too?" she asked in amazement.

"Yes. Oh, Rachel, how did we get caught up in this mess anyway?"

"I've been thinking about that for quite some time. I think our parents just assumed that because we were best friends, one day we would fall in love and get married," she told him, feeling as though her heart had been released from the walls that had surrounded it.

"I think you're right. And we also convinced ourselves of that in the meantime."

Laughter spilled from each of them at the foolishness of the situation.

"How are we ever going to explain this?"

"I think our mothers are already aware of this. Mine keeps questioning me in a subtle way. I just haven't said anything to anyone about my feelings."

Reaching over to give her a quick hug, relief flowed through each of them as they began to speak again like the old friends they really were. There was a relaxed atmosphere present as they spoke.

"What are you going to do now?" she asked. "Will you stay and live in the house you have rented or move to Cheyenne? I know you enquired about a practice."

"I've actually had an offer for a partnership there. I was waiting to make a decision until I could talk to you."

"I will miss you," she told him sincerely.

"And I'll miss you, my little shadow, should I decide to accept."

A slow smile spread across her face, and her eyes twinkled at the endearment.

"How did you know I loved Matthew?" she asked a moment later in a discerning voice.

"There's always been an uneasiness about you when he's around, especially since our engagement. Your face lights up when he comes near you. I suppose I am partially to blame for your feelings. Something was always coming up, and I was practically throwing the two of you together."

"Really?" she asked in embarrassment, thinking of his remark.

"Yes, I don't know if the others have noticed it or if he has, for that matter."

"Please," she whispered in near panic, "you won't say anything to him about this, will you?"

"No, if you don't want me to, I won't say a word to anyone."

"You have been my best friend since I was eight years old, and I think you will always be my best friend," she said as she laid a hand on his cheek.

"I don't know about that. Things will and should change when you get married. I would assume that your husband may want that role."

"I guess you're right," she giggled.

As he observed the woman in front of him, Mark saw how beautiful she was, both inside and out. They had shared so many things through the years. It had been a happy childhood, but it was time to move on to what and who the Lord had in store for them.

"Do you remember the time I took you crawdad hunting late that night in the spring when you were about ten?" he asked fondly, chuckling at the memory that had suddenly appeared.

"How could I ever forget that? Mama was more than a little irritated when I came home with mud from head to toe. Papa had to retrieve the large tub and water for me to get cleaned up." Pausing, she let her mind linger back to that night. "Oh, but it was worth it. The fellow we eventually caught was the biggest I'd ever seen."

Laughing at her words, he said, "I don't think my family was too happy about it either. We were a mess, weren't we?"

Squeezing his hand, she said, "You helped make those years special. I'll never forget you for that."

"And I'll never forget you either, but I think it's time for both of us to see what the future holds and what is right for each of us. We can't live in the past forever."

"Yes, although the future doesn't seem very bright," she said quietly as she thought of her love for Matthew.

"We could have made this marriage work, I know. But think how different it will be when we are married to the person God has picked out for us," he answered her honestly.

"Can I ask you a question, Mark?"

"Sure."

"In the four months we've been engaged, you've never kissed me. Why?"

"I think in my heart that I knew it wasn't right. Not that you aren't attractive, because you are, but you seemed shy whenever I even thought about it."

"I know, there was always this feeling deep inside me, but it wasn't you," she added quickly.

"My little shadow, it was me though," he laughed aloud.

Joining him with a small laugh of her own, she said, "Well, maybe you're right."

"Somehow I don't think you'd hesitate if it was someone else," he told her suggestively.

Feeling the crimson flood her face, she couldn't find the words to answer him, already knowing the answer from the day in the barn.

Standing to his feet, he leaned over and kissed her on her warm cheek, telling her, "I hope that brother of mine wakes up and realizes how lucky he is someday."

"It'll be kind of hard with him not being around very much," she replied sincerely. "I never see him anymore."

"Yes, but circumstances can change quickly, as my parents frequently tell me."

"That reminds me, how is your father doing?"

"His leg is mending, although it will be a while before he can return to any hard labor."

"At least he still has John at home to help him."

"Yes, he's grown up fast since the accident and is a big help to both of my folks."

"Keep in touch with me, promise?"

"I will, and if anything new happens to you, be sure and let me know," he told her with a wink.

"Believe me, I will. Take care in that big city of yours, and don't forget to write."

"Guess you think I'll be taking that job then?"

"Of course you will. Was there any chance that you wouldn't?"

"You, dear Rachel, know me far too well."

"Thank you," she told him with genuineness in her voice, referring to the broken engagement.

"You're welcome. I'm just glad we came to our senses before we made a huge mistake. Goodbye, shadow."

"Goodbye."

"Mama," Rachel said as she grabbed her winter coat the next afternoon, "I'm going to take a quick walk and get some fresh air."

"It's cold out today, don't be too long. You don't want a setback now that you're doing so well."

"I won't.

Walking into the crisp coldness felt so good to Rachel. Most of the snow had melted, and the ground only had patches here and there. Inhaling deeply, she moved cautiously down the path that she and Mark had made many years ago. As she neared the stream, she gathered her coat and scarf up close to her and sat down on a nearby log, watching the slow movement of the clear, fresh spring water flow before her. She had not found the right moment to tell her parents of her broken engagement. Hopefully later that evening she would be able to inform them.

Closing her eyes briefly, she lifted her face to enjoy the feel of being in the open air again.

"Are you sure you're well enough to be outside?" the deep voice asked from behind, startling her.

"Matthew!" she exclaimed.

Walking near enough to sit by her on the fallen log, Rachel hastily scooted over to make room; butterflies in her stomach were beginning to dance at his presence.

"I'm sorry, I didn't mean to scare you," he told her.

"It's all right. I guess I was a million miles away."

"Thinking about the wedding, I'm sure," he said in a no-nonsense voice.

"Oh," was all she could reply, wondering why he didn't know that there wasn't going to be a wedding. Obviously, he had not seen or spoken with Mark yet.

"I heard you were real sick. They said you almost didn't make it. I'm glad to hear you are up and about again."

"Thank you. I am feeling much better now." Straining to keep a normal voice, she asked, "How is your new house?"

"Slowly getting things done. It's almost finished on the inside anyway. I can't say how long it will take to actually complete it."

"We've missed seeing you around. What brings you here today?"

Hearing those words from her stung his heart momentarily, almost as if she were not happy to see him.

"I guess I had to see for myself that you were all right. Why, do you want me to leave?" he asked in an uneasy manner, thinking about the kiss they had shared in the barn and her upcoming marriage to his brother.

"No, it's not that at all," she said quietly as she turned to look at the rippling water before her, feeling the uneasiness in the air.

Hoping to turn the conversation to a lighter tone, she added, "Mark says that your father is mending nicely."

"Yes, although I haven't actually seen that brother of mine yet to hear what he says on the matter. He was gone when I stopped by this morning. I think he's at the Smiths' house. Mrs. Smith is in labor with her first baby and is having some problems."

"I will have to pray for them," she told him sincerely.

Turning to face her, Matthew took her hand in his and looked into her eyes. "The real reason I'm here is that I need to talk to you and apologize. I'm really sorry for embarrassing you the last time we met. I don't know what came over me, but I had no right kissing my future sister-in-law. I just want you to know that I promise it will never happen again. That's why I haven't been around much lately. I think you understand. I have no desire to come between you and my brother. My intentions were not to hurt either one of you."

Not knowing how to reply, she could only nod as tears began to gather in her eyes.

Mistaking the tears, he rose to his feet and turned to leave.

"I'm sorry, Rachel, for everything."

As she watched him walk away, she felt her heart break in two and knew that the only person she had ever truly loved was leaving her for good. She had never felt such anguish as she did at that moment.

Standing to her feet, she brushed the tears from her eyes with her hand and saw him climb upon his horse. When he reached the small curve in the path, she realized that her love was worth taking a chance for. Even if he might not return it, she had to know.

"Wait!" she yelled as she began to run to him blindly through her tears. Stumbling over a large, exposed root of a tree, she fell to her knees.

Stopping his horse, he dismounted quickly and ran to her side. Assisting her to her feet, he asked, "Are you all right? Where are you hurt?"

"In my heart," she told him in misery, gazing into his intense blue eyes.

"What do you mean?"

"There isn't going to be a wedding."

"Why isn't there going to be a wedding?"

"Mark and I agreed yesterday not to go through with it."

Glancing around the small woods, he frowned, trying to grasp what she had told him.

"I don't understand. Did Mark hurt you? Did he let you down and break your heart because he didn't want to marry you?" he asked, feeling a new anger at his brother rise inside him.

"No, he wants to go to Cheyenne and practice medicine there."

"Let me get this straight. He wants to go to the city, and you don't, so you agreed to call the wedding off, is that it?"

Shaking her head slowly, trying to think of the right words, she said, "No, we both realized almost too late that all we feel is a brotherly, sisterly love. Not the love a husband and wife should have for one another. He's always been a good friend, and I think we convinced ourselves that it was more."

Relief and joy surged through his handsome features as he turned away to think about her words, making certain that he had heard correctly.

"I was willing to go through with the commitment I had made, but Mark told me…oh," she stopped, realizing what she had almost said.

"What did he tell you?" he enquired as he turned to face her again.

"No, never mind."

"Please, Rachel," he pleaded as he placed a finger on her chin and raised her eyes to meet his own darkened blue ones, "I have to know."

"It's silly really. You'll think it is anyway."

"Please," he prompted again tenderly as tears fell unheeded down her face.

"He told me I couldn't marry him when I was in love with someone else."

Elation swept through his heart at her words, and hope abounded within him for the first time in months.

"And who might that person be?" he inquired in a tender voice.

Shaking her head, afraid to make a declaration, she heard him ask, "Do you love me, Rachel? Tell me, is it me?"

"I tried not to," she admitted tearfully.

Gathering her into a loving embrace, he whispered, "I only hope it's half as much as I love you."

Pushing him away, she looked into his glorious blue eyes that were filled with amazement and asked, "You love me?"

"I think I have since you were about sixteen years old. I just didn't realize it until you were seeing Mark. Wait," he told her as he reached into his pocket and withdrew something. Opening her hand, he placed a yellow ribbon in it. Revelation filled her mind as she looked at him questioningly.

"You wore this at your sixteenth birthday party. You lost it when we were playing games, and I'm afraid I kept it."

"For three years?" she asked in amazement.

"I told you, I knew that I was waiting for you to grow up. Even then I wanted you to be mine."

A smile broke through and she squealed as she threw her arms around his neck and hugged him.

"I do love you, and not as a brother," she beamed. In a teasing tone, she said, "I won't keep you to your promise, you know."

As he frowned, trying to recall what promise she was talking about, she added, "You promised a few minutes ago never to kiss me again."

Watching as a slow smile filled his face, he leaned his forehead against hers, reveling in her nearness.

"Can I kiss you—a real kiss this time—to show you of my love?" he asked with huskiness in his voice.

"Oh yes," she whispered, watching as he lowered his head and his cold lips met hers for their second kiss, stirring feelings that she had never felt with his brother. As she pulled back to gaze into his eyes, she told him, "Although, this is not the first time we have shown each other of our love," referring to the barn.

"You're right. I felt so bad about that kiss. It was getting to the point of being impossible to be near you and not declare my feelings." With a gentle touch, he pushed her hair back from her face, marveling at the softness of her skin.

"That is why I had to leave so abruptly. I was certain that you had discovered my secret. My love seemed to grow more everyday instead of lessening, as I had prayed. Everytime we were together was both a wonderful and miserable experience? Do you know what I mean?" he asked as he continued to hold her, never wanting to let her go.

As she pulled back enough to gaze into his eyes, she smiled brightly before she said, "Yes, I know exactly what you mean. I felt the same way. Oh, Matthew, this is really happening, isn't it?" she asked him as she hugged him again, loving the feel of his arms around her.

"Yes, my lovely Rachel, and I think my heart could burst."

Each was content to let their love flow through them and savored the feel. A moment later, Matthew pulled back slightly to look into her eyes before asking, "Will you marry me?" Leaning downward, he placed his forehead against her own once more, basking in the knowledge that she was really going to be his now and forever.

"Yes, yes, yes," she replied quickly. "Any time, anywhere."

"How about this weekend?"

"So soon?" she asked, thinking about the possibility.

"You do have a dress, don't you?"

"Yes."

"And our parents have the reception meal planned, don't they?"

"Yes."

"Do you want to wait?"

Looking into his face, with love overflowing, she laid her head against his chest and told him, "No, I love you so much it hurts. I want to be your wife as soon as possible." Excitement surged through her veins, and she wanted to shout her love for this man from the mountains.

"So what you feel for me is different than what you feel for Mark?"

"There is no comparison. Do you know that in all the four months we were engaged, we never even kissed."

A new thankfulness passed through him again. "I'm glad. I want you to be all mine, forever and always, and no one else's. Especially not my brothers," he told her in a serious voice.

"I've never been Mark's. Not really. I think, deep down, we both felt it."

Feeling her shiver, he took her hand and told her, "We've got to get you back into warmth. I don't know what I'd do without you."

As they walked toward his horse, he kissed her several more times and said, "You have made me the happiest man alive. I came here with dread, knowing I was going to have to see you marry my own brother and having to accept it. I had even considered selling the house and moving to Cheyenne, where I wouldn't see you as often."

Placing a hand against his cheek, she told him, "Circumstances can change fast, just as Mark told me yesterday. I was pining away for you with little hope of ever telling you my true feelings and planning on marrying a man I didn't love. And now look at us."

"Do you want to ride?" he asked her, recalling her recent illness.

"Only if you do. I find I need to be near you," she told him with a quick grin.

After climbing up into the saddle, he assisted her. Feeling her wrap her arms around his waist, he placed his own hand over hers and squeezed. She was where she needed to be—with him. Placing her head on his back, Rachel hugged him and whispered, "I love you, Matthew. I can't wait to be your wife in the beautiful home you have built."

This time, with Rachel saying the words, he felt no embarrassment at her speaking of such things, only wonder and thankfulness.

"We will raise our children with love. It will be a wonderful life, and I can't wait either."

"Will you help me deliver your children one day?" she asked boldly.

"I wouldn't miss it for the world," he returned, meaning it with his whole heart.

The two couldn't stop smiling on the way to the Parkers' home. As Matthew assisted her to the ground, they walked hand in hand to tell her parents the news; there was still going to be a wedding, it was going to be Saturday. It would even be to an O'Malley, just not the one they had planned on.

When Matthew said goodbye to her later that evening, he hugged her, as if making sure he was not in a dream.

"Please, tell me again that you love me," he whispered against her hair.

"I love you, Matthew O'Malley, with my whole heart. You and only you, always you."

As he rode his horse home, he grinned and shook his head. *Soon, Rachel will be the rightful mistress here. You knew all along that she would be beside me, didn't You, Lord? It sure would have made it easier if You had shared this with me.* As he walked to put the horse away, he thought, *But she was definitely worth the wait.*

The next morning, Rachel heard a soft knock on her door and saw her mother enter and sit down beside her on the bed. She was studying her daughter's face before she told her, "Now *this* is how a woman in love looks."

"I know exactly what you are talking about. I want to sing and dance and tell everyone that I love Matthew O'Malley."

Shaking her head, McKenna said, "I was really worried that you were going to go through with your marriage to Mark. I knew it wasn't the right kind of love."

"Why didn't you tell me?" Rachel asked.

"Because you knew it already. It was pointless to say anything. I just prayed that God would open both of your eyes before the wedding."

"And if we hadn't?"

"Then I might have said something. I think Genie was about to talk to Mark also."

"She knew too?"

"Oh yes. She knew long ago that Matthew was in love with you, and it broke her heart to see both of her sons love the same woman."

"I need to talk to her and apologize."

"That would be nice, but I'm sure she doesn't expect one. We're both just grateful that things turned out so well and that Mark didn't get hurt."

"Yes, I think that's why I was willing to go through with it despite my feelings. I had made a promise and was ready to fulfill it. I wouldn't hurt him for anything."

"But don't you think that would have hurt him eventually? You can't start a marriage with secrets and deception. I know from experience that God can take friendship and turn it into love, like He did for your papa and me. But our circumstances were different."

"I guess it would have been wrong. I think God was trying to tell me all along that I loved Matthew and needed to break it off with Mark."

"I'm sure it was Him speaking to you, honey. Sometimes He whispers to us with His gentle spirit. We have to be quiet long enough to realize that it is Him speaking to us."

"That's exactly what He did, Mama. He whispered to my heart. I think He must have been doing some talking to Mark also." Rachel sat for a moment to think about her future before she exclaimed, "I could burst inside! I'm gonna be Matthew's wife. I can't believe how happy I am. I can't think of anything else."

"Somehow I think he's about to do some bursting himself," her mother told her with a quick grin.

"I love you. You are truly my own. I want you to have these now," McKenna said as she reached into the pocket of her apron, her lovely brown eyes filled with traces of tears.

Extracting the small pearl necklace that had been her own mother's, she placed it into Rachel's hands.

"I didn't get to wear these when I married your papa, but you need to have them for your wedding. And when it comes time for your sisters to wed, I hope you will pass them down to them."

"I wish I had known Grandma," the younger girl said as she touched the smoothness of the beads.

"She would have loved you dearly."

"Like I love you, Mama," Rachel whispered before she felt McKenna's arms gather her close. "You are truly the mother of my heart."

Chapter Eighteen

Smoothing the dress with her fingers to make sure no wrinkles were present, Rachel let her hand rest on the beads that lay around her neck. They represented something old for her wedding day. Her grandmother had given her a lace handkerchief to carry that would serve as something borrowed. With a smile, she knew what her something blue would be—her husband's clear blue eyes. The wedding gown her mother made her was something new.

She would have to be careful or her emotions would surface and she would find herself crying. Hearing the soft knock at the door, she watched as her father entered with a smile and a large parcel in his hands. Handing it to her with a grin, he told her, "It's from Matthew."

Unsure of what it could possibly be, she sat on the bed and slowly unwrapped the present. Inside was a new dress. On the top laid a note that read:

To My One and Only Love,

This is to replace the dress that you ruined when you helped me gather the hogs in their pens. I loved spending time with you then, and I eagerly anticipate spending the rest of my life with you from this day forward. I have waited for what seems a lifetime for you, but I always knew in my heart that you were worth it. I want to share the good times and the bad times, to grow more in love with you daily, and to wake up with you by my side each morning. I love you, Rachel, thank you for marrying me.

Forever yours,
Your Bridegroom

Although Rachel had chuckled when she saw the gift and read his first line, tears soon broke through, and she had to wipe them away to finish the love letter from the man whom God had given her. Feeling her father take one of her hands in his, she heard him tell her quietly, emotion filling his own voice, "This is a special day for you, honey. A day filled with promises of hope for a bright future. I can only pray that your life will always be one that will bring glory and honor to our heavenly father, because I know you bring joy to your mother and me. We are so proud of you and know that God brought the right man into your life at the right time. I loved you, Rachel, from the first time I held you in my arms and welcomed you into this world. Thank you for being a daughter any man would love."

Now Rachel was crying in earnest. Feeling the strong arms of her father around her, love abounded, and no words could be found.

For the length of several minutes, each was content to remain where they were. Both were thanking God for everything He had done over the years and for this moment.

Gently releasing her, he stood to his feet and wiped a tear that remained on her cheek.

"You are beautiful," he told her as he left the room, "Matthew is indeed a fortunate man to have you as his wife."

Sitting on the bed trying to gather her composure, another knock sounded before she saw Matthew open the door and walk in, closing it quietly behind him.

With astonishment on her face, she whispered, "You're not supposed to see me before the ceremony."

"I know, but I had to make sure that you hadn't changed your mind...that this is real."

Reaching out a hand to touch his cheek gently, her eyes shone with radiance as she said, "I love you and can't wait to become Mrs. Matthew O'Malley. Does that help?"

Relief flowed through him as he grinned and slowly kissed her parted lips. As he stepped back, he said, "Did you like your gift?"

Laughter erupted and she said, "I loved it. Only you would think of something like that. And your note made me cry when I have tried so hard not to today." Gazing into his eyes, she whispered, "But do you know what I love even more than your gift and note?"

"What?"

"You."

Hearing the door open behind them, the couple smiled when they saw McKenna standing in the doorway with Genie at her side. Without a word, the bridegroom stepped around them with a beaming smile plastered on his attractive face.

"Just making sure," he told them as he slipped by.

Their laughter followed him as he shut the door.

The simple ceremony lasted only a few minutes. Matthew had trouble keeping his eyes off Rachel, much to the amusement of everyone, including Pastor Keller. She looked breathtaking to him in her dress. Family, as well as friends, had gathered to witness the event, and the first to congratulate them was a smiling Mark.

"I am so happy for you two," he told them with sincerity. "I thought I might have to break my promise and say something to this brother of mine, but I guess he's got more sense than I gave him credit for."

As he hugged Rachel, he whispered, "Isn't this better than secondhand?"

"I'd never call you secondhand. Just for me. But someone someday will definitely think you are first."

"You're right."

With laughter, Matthew pushed Mark away from his new bride and told him, "Okay, that's enough. She's mine now, remember, little brother?"

"I think she's always been yours. We just didn't know it."

Smiling at her new husband, Rachel replied softly, "Yes. I just had to sift through the good to find the best for me."

Later, after the wedding, as Matthew carried his bride across the threshold of their new home, he watched her gaze as she appreciatively saw all that he had accomplished since her last visit.

"I'm sorry that it's not quite finished," he told her apologetically. "I figured I'd let you put your woman's touch to the rest."

"I don't care. It's perfect just as it is. I'll be more than happy to help in any way that I can," she added with a quick grin.

Chuckling, he told her, "It would have been a lot more fun building it if I had known that for sure."

"You did a fine job. Although the thought never crossed my mind that I would someday be mistress here."

"I love you, Rachel. So much that I feel like I'm dreaming. I promise to take care of you and provide for you and any children God blesses us with."

"I know you will. I think that's one of the things I've always admired about you. You care for people in a deep way. You feel with them when they hurt and rejoice with them when they are happy. Please don't ever change."

"I won't. And I can honestly say the same thing about you. I love how you do little things for people, unexpected things, like taking Widow Casey food when she lost her husband. Or staying at the Fergusons' with their children when his wife was sick, or when you helped deliver your little sister. I wanted to hold you and comfort you so badly then, but I was afraid you would discover my feelings. You are a special woman, and I am blessed to have you share your life with me."

Wrapping her arms securely around him, she told him, "And I love you with all my heart for a lot of other reasons too." With a grin, she added, "For always coming to my defense when I needed it. Remember when Bobby Perkins pushed me down and got my dress dirty when I was younger?"

"Yes, I remember. He only did it because he got mad that you didn't like him."

"Really?" she asked in surprise.

"Yes, he had been bragging about how he would get a kiss from you, and when you turned him down, it upset him."

"I never knew that. Is that why you hit him?"

Laughter flowed through him as he told her, "Well, that, plus I never liked his attitude about you anyway. I guess even then I knew which way my heart was tugging me. My head just didn't get the message until later. When did you know that you were in love with me?"

"At the skating party. I couldn't keep my eyes away from you, especially when Christy started showing you a little too much attention."

"She did?" he asked in thought. "I don't seem to remember anyone but you that night."

"And I was so jealous thinking about the two of you spending time together."

"You were feeling the same way I was about you and Mark then."

"Yes."

"I'm glad that God didn't answer my prayer," he whispered against her hair.

"What prayer was that?"

"After we went skating, I asked Him to remove my love for you if it was His will."

"For once I'm glad His answer was no," she told him in gratefulness.

"Follow me," he told her with a teasing grin as he took her hand and led her upstairs. As he opened the door to the room they would share, he heard her sigh as she saw the rocking chair sitting near the window.

"Oh, you remembered."

"Remembered?" he asked in amazement. "That's all I could think about whenever I was here. It's for all the babies you'll rock while you look outside."

"Your babies," she told him as she walked close to him and placed her hands on either side of his face, kissing him slowly. As she leaned back to gaze into his handsome face, she heard him say, "Let me show you just how much I love my new bride."

With a giggle, she snuggled up close to him while he lowered his head for a kiss that would begin their new life together as man and wife. There was no embarrassment for Rachel. It seemed to be the most natural thing in the world to become the wife of the man she loved.

Rachel felt strong arms wrapped firmly around her when she woke up the next morning.

"Good morning," she heard Matthew whisper. "I thought maybe you were going to sleep the day away."

Reaching her arms above her head and stretching, she smiled lovingly at him.

"And what is that smile for?" he asked in amusement.

"When Mark and I were engaged, I was always uncomfortable with the idea of him being with me when I had a baby. I didn't understand it at the time, but now I do."

Sitting up and leaning on one elbow, she gazed with adoration in his eyes, "It's because I really didn't love him the way I should have. When I think of you being with me, it gives me comfort, not embarrassment."

"I'm glad you want me near you during that time."

"Of course. You were wonderful when Mama had Abbie Grace. We will create them together, and I think we should bring them in the world together."

"I do like your thinking, Mrs. O'Malley," he told her with a playful grin. "What about Mark? Are you going to let him help during the deliveries?"

"Not if I don't have too. I think you and Mama can handle the job just fine. Maybe your mother, too, if she'd like to be there."

"You know," he told her with a mischievous look, "we could be facing that in about nine months."

"I know," she said as she placed a light kiss against his cheek. "Although I wouldn't mind it being just the two of us for a while. I kind of like having you to myself."

"I know. It seems like it's taken a long time for this to happen. I have been waiting for you for quite some time. Thank you for marrying me," he told her as he returned her kiss.

"Thank you for asking."

It was two days before Christmas, and the newlyweds were planning to get a tree to decorate that morning. As Matthew lay next to his sleeping wife, he impulsively brushed the hair from her face. Seeing her eyes flutter open, he smiled and told her, "Good morning, sweetheart."

"It is a good morning," she answered back. "Every morning is good with you beside me."

"You're right," he said as he leaned down to kiss her on the top of her head. "Do you still want to go and get a tree this morning?"

"Yes, our first Christmas together must be special."

"How about if we do something else this afternoon too?"

"What's that?"

"I thought that after lunch we might go ice skating. I saw our pond the other day, and it didn't look too rough. It must have frozen without the wind blowing. Would you care to try it out?" he asked, knowing how much she loved to skate.

Throwing her arms around him, she said, "Yes, that sounds wonderful." Kissing him quickly on his lips, she continued, "Come on, let's get up and begin the day."

Watching her excitement gave him pleasure. "All right, if I have to," he told her with a frown. "Although I do hate to leave the warmth of this bed. It's kind of nice having you in my arms too."

"I do love you, Matthew O'Malley," she told him as she reached for her shawl on the end of the bed.

"I'm so glad you do, Rachel, because I don't think I could have lived without you. Why don't you stay here for a little while longer?" he asked in a suggestive manner.

With a small laugh, she leaned down to look into his eyes, saying, "I guess we're not in that big of a hurry now, are we?"

"No hurry at all," he whispered lovingly. "We have all day."

After finding a tree near the back of the property, the couple carried it home. Shaking the snow from it, they set it in the corner of the living area, near the large window.

"Perfect," she said as she surveyed it. "We can pop some corn this evening and make some decorations to put on it. Hurry, let's eat now," she told him with a grin.

Not being able to fool him, he laughed and asked, "Now why would you want to rush us through lunch?"

Jabbing him lightly in his ribs, she said, "You know why. Come on, let's have something light."

Eating leftovers from the previous night, the couple put on their warm clothes and reached for their skates. Walking hand in hand toward the pond, they saw soft, large flakes of snow begin to fall.

"Looks like another storm coming in," he told her.

"I hope we will still be able to go to Mama and Papa's for Christmas."

Hugging her, he said, "We'll make it. Don't worry. I know how much you need to be with your family during special times."

Stopping to look directly into his wonderful face, she whispered, "But you are my family now. You are who I want to be with the rest of my life. I love my parents and siblings, but not as much as I need you."

"Oh, honey," he whispered back, "that's exactly how I feel."

Letting him hold her for a moment, she pulled away, grabbed his hand, and started to run toward the pond.

After putting on the skates, they both walked toward the frozen water and slowly began to make their way around the perimeter.

"It is better," she told him as she turned in a circle. "I'm so glad you noticed this."

Holding out her arms, she watched as he skated toward her, and the two flowed together in unison for quite some time, feeling the crispness of the air on their faces. Matthew had been holding her hands and skating backwards when suddenly his foot hit a rough patch of ice. Losing his balance, he fell on his back and pulled his wife down with him. Shifting slightly, she looked into his smiling face and heard him say, "This brings back memories of another time we were skating."

"Yes, it does. Only I think I was the one who caused us to fall then."

"You know, I wanted to kiss you so badly then. It was a good thing you began to stand, or I would have."

Gazing into his eyes, she told him with love, "And I wanted you to so much that it scared me."

Leaning down, she brushed her cold lips against his, and soon the kiss became passionate. Pushing her away gently, he stood to his feet and helped her up.

"I think, my wife, it is time to go home," he told her with a gleam in his eyes.

"I think you're right," she returned with a smile.

As they walked toward their house, Matthew asked her, "Do you remember when Pa got hurt?"

"I'll never forget it," she told him. "We were so afraid for him."

"We all were, but that wasn't what I was referring to."

"Oh, I guess you mean in the barn then."

"Yes, I loved you so," he said quietly.

"No more than I did you. While you were kissing me all I could think of how right this felt and then I remembered Mark and felt so guilty."

With a small snicker, he said, "And all I could think about was that I was in love with you so much that it hurt. I knew I had to put some distance between us, or I'd never get over you, even to the point of moving away."

"I'm so glad you didn't," she told him, surprised that he would sell the house that he had so lovingly built. "I can't believe you would leave your house because of me. You love that place."

"Yes, I hadn't said anything to anyone about it. My first step was moving away from home. It was tearing me up watching Mark leave, knowing he was going to spend time with you. And Rachel, I love you more than the house."

"To think that I was willing to go through with the wedding. Mama chided me later about it. She told me that a marriage should never be based on lies and deceit, and that was what I was willing to do. She said that she was going to say something to me if I was still as determined to proceed. I was wrong, and I would have hurt both of us."

"My mama knew what I was feeling. She said it broke her heart."

Smiling, she stopped and turned to face him, "I never dreamed it could be so wonderful."

Scooping her up in his arms, he carried her up the porch steps and through their front door.

"I did," he whispered against her hair.

Matthew was waiting rather impatiently for his wife to wake up. It was Christmas morning, and he felt like a small child in his anticipation. Shifting several times, he saw her smile; she still had her eyes closed as she asked, "Is there a particular reason you are waking me up while it is still dark out?"

"Merry Christmas," he told her, watching her eyes open and gaze into his.

"Merry Christmas to you too," she replied, opening her eyes to look into his. "Our first Christmas together."

Sitting up in bed, he said, "The first of a lifetime." Leaning down, he brushed his lips against her cheek. "I'm going to put some more logs on the fire and make some coffee. Wait here for a few minutes before you come down. It'll be nice and warm by then."

Wrapping her arms around the pillow, she said, "All right. I do hate to move from this warm bed."

Watching him leave the room, Rachel thought for the hundredth time how fortunate she was to have this man as her husband. Closing her eyes again, she began to pray. The day always seemed to go better when she asked for God's guiding hand before getting out of bed.

After a short time, she slid her feet to the edge, pulled on a pair of socks, and put a light shawl around her shoulders, padding down the steps. Standing near the tree was Matthew, holding a small box in his hands.

With a look of delight on her face, she walked toward him and he handed her the gift, saying, "Merry Christmas, honey."

Slowly unwrapping the paper, she opened the lid to the box and felt her amusement turn to wonder. Inside laid a gold necklace with a cross on it.

"Oh, it's beautiful," she told him, looking first at the necklace and then at his smiling face. "How did you ever think of something like this?"

"I saw it in the mercantile right after we were married and knew I had to get it for you."

"It's perfect," she said as she removed it and held it out for him to place around her neck. Feeling the coldness against her warm skin, she reached up to touch it before turning to face him. "Thank you," she told him simply, afraid that if she said anything else, tears might begin.

"You're welcome," he replied.

Watching her step toward their small tree, she reached down and picked up his gift. As he took it from her, she said, "You may be disappointed in this. It's not near as fancy as what you have given me."

Tearing the paper away, he saw a new light blue shirt. Lifting it slowly, he examined the sewing and asked, "Did you make this yourself? If you did, it's excellent."

Hearing the pride in his voice, she said, "Well, Mama did help when I needed it. I hope it fits. She told me she made Pa one for their first Christmas, and somehow it just seemed fitting that you have one too. I know the whole time I was working on it, all I could think of was how wonderful it would look on you with your gorgeous blue eyes. I thought I'd carry on the family tradition."

"I love it. I'll wear it today to your parents' house. So you like my eyes, do you?" he asked her as he set the shirt down and reached for her.

"Yes."

"Between us, I would think the chances of having blue-eyed children would be fairly obvious. I have always loved yours too."

"Children?" she asked with a chuckle.

"Yes, yours and mine." Glancing out the large window, he told her, "You know, it really is too early to get up. I think we need to return to bed and sleep a little more."

"Sleep?" she asked with a laugh, feeling him lift her into his arms and move toward the stairs.

"Eventually."

"Rachel!" Matthew called from the bottom of the steps. "Are you ready?"

"Yes, I'm coming," she replied, descending the stairs. With a gentle touch, he placed a finger against her cheek, still in wonder that they were married.

"I love you," he stated simply.

"I know, and I'm so glad you do," she whispered back.

Taking her hand, he said with a mischievous grin, "I've loaded everything into the wagon. The folks will probably be waiting on us."

Returning his smile, she replied, "They may think things in their minds because we are late but won't say a word. They both know what young love is."

She was right. When the newlyweds entered the house, the adults smiled at their spouses. It did their hearts good to see the love on their children's faces. Even Mark, who stood near the fireplace, felt not only joy, but relief when he saw them enter in the happiness that was evident. He realized how close they had come to making a big mistake. Genie, who was sitting near the fire, felt her husband put his hand lightly on her shoulder, squeezing gently. Placing her hand over his, she turned to look in his eyes, noticing a wink.

After removing her coat, Rachel went to lift Abbie Grace from her cradle. She was sleeping, but she couldn't prevent herself from cuddling with the baby. Hannah, she noticed, had come to stand near her.

"Are you helping Mama with her?" the oldest sibling asked as she took a seat at the kitchen table.

"Yes, Mama told me she wouldn't know what she would do without me to help her," she stated in a serious tone.

"I'm glad," Rachel said as she looked into the smiling face of her mother. They had been worried that she might feel some jealously toward the new baby, but their fears had been unfounded.

Matthew and her father entered the house laden with gifts and food. Her mother, spotting several items set on the table, told her daughter, "We didn't expect you to make anything, honey."

"I wanted to bring something." With an impish grin at her husband, she added, "You know how much I love to work in that wonderful new kitchen."

Seeing the smile on Matthew's face made her heart flip inside her. He had gone to stand near Mark and asked, "How is the new job?"

"Good so far. I am still trying to learn where the people live and frequently have to ask for directions." Leaning towards his older brother, he told him quietly, "Married life agrees with both you and Rachel."

Watching his wife, seeing the radiance about her, Matthew could only concur. He felt like he had been handed the moon. He couldn't help but notice how natural it seemed for her to have a child in her arms. She was talking to her little sister with a patient tone while she cradled the newest member close.

McKenna, seeing the baby begin to awaken, told her company, "Let me feed this little lady, and we can begin to get the food ready. I know how hungry everyone must be."

Taking Abbie Grace from her daughter, she whispered, "Come, visit with me for a few minutes."

Rising to her feet, Rachel glanced toward her husband, whose eye winked when he looked her way. Entering behind her mother, she closed the door and walked to the bed to sit near her. Watching as she unbuttoned her dress, she saw Abbie Grace begin to root in eagerness. With a small chuckle, McKenna told her, "I know, my love, how impatient you become when it comes to your meals."

Rachel reached over and lovingly touched the soft head as she began to eat.

Feeling her mother's eyes on her, she heard her ask, "How is married life?"

With a smile that lit up her face, Rachel told her, "Oh, Mama, I did not know it could be this wonderful."

"It is with the right person," McKenna replied.

"And he is the right person. I shudder to think of the harm that would have taken place had Mark and I married."

"You didn't though, that is all that matters."

As the women sat near one another, both in their own thoughts, they thanked God for bringing the two together.

Chapter Nineteen

Four months later, Rachel had just begun to make breakfast. Feeling a wave of queasiness in her stomach, she dashed to the door and ran outside, vomiting at the side of the house. Waiting until she was sure she was finished, she felt her husband's hand on her shoulder.

"Are you all right, Rachel?"

Rising to her feet, she said, "I am now."

Lifting his eyebrows in an inquiring manner, he asked, "Are you pregnant?"

"I think so," she told him with joy. "This is the third morning in a row that I've felt sick."

Picking her up, Matthew hugged her, all the while exclaiming in wonder, "We're gonna have a baby."

Setting her slowly to the ground, they walked hand in hand back inside the house. The excited couple talked nonstop about the future and becoming parents.

"I hope this little one is as good as Abbie Grace. Mama said she is the best baby and rarely cries. She's such a little sweetie too."

"I hope so, too, although I think if we asked, my mama would be more than happy to help us through the first few weeks."

Laughing, Rachel told him, "I think she'd be disappointed if we didn't ask her. Although, she may be too busy now that they have Sarah."

"Yes, they do love that little girl a lot. But somehow I think the thought of a baby around again will thrill them, especially when it's their first grandchild."

That night, long after Matthew had fallen asleep, Rachel knew her mind was filled with too many thoughts for her to sleep. She placed a hand on her stomach and with overflowing happiness realized that soon she would be holding Matthew's child and rocking it in the chair he had made before their marriage. Shifting slightly, she rose up on her elbow and watched her husband sleep. She had thought that he was nice before they were married; now she knew just how wonderful he truly was. He reminded her so much of her own pa. Both were soft spoken, extremely patient, and devoted not only to God but to their families. Love ran deeply, and they took their responsibilities seriously. Unable to help herself, she leaned over and kissed her sleeping mate on his cheek. Seeing his eyes open briefly and then shut, she felt him pull her closer to him before falling back asleep.

Lord, I am indeed a blessed woman.

It was little Abbie Grace's first birthday, and everyone had gathered together to celebrate. The blonde-haired little girl was trying to walk. Still unsteady on her feet, she would toddle a few steps and fall backwards. The adults clapped when she would fall, encouraging her to stand. After a few times of it happening, she made a game of it and fell intentionally, giggling while everyone fussed over her. Sarah and Hannah had become the closest of friends and were like two little mothers over the toddler.

McKenna, standing next to Rachel, gently placed a hand on her daughter's large abdomen. "Soon we'll be welcoming a new member in the family."

"Yes, and I can't wait," the pregnant woman told her.

"I know exactly how you feel, honey. It gets to a point where you are just plain uncomfortable and want to hold that baby in your arms."

Matthew, coming to stand near his wife, placed an arm around her. "I don't know, I kind of like seeing her waddle around."

"Men," she told him as she poked him in the ribs. "You try carrying a load like this around all the time. You would be ready for it to end also."

"I know, I just like teasing you. You have a special glow about you since you've been pregnant. You are more beautiful than ever to me."

Hearing her son-in-law's words, McKenna said, "That's exactly what your father told me."

"They have to say that, Mama. They know how emotional we are and wouldn't dare take a chance to say the wrong thing."

McKenna, hearing the cry of a young child, went to see what her daughter's latest incident was.

Facing his wife, Matthew whispered tenderly, "I meant every word. You are lovelier than I have ever seen you." Placing a hand on her stomach, he caressed softly. "This is the child we created together. Nothing could make me happier than to see you carrying our baby."

Seeing the sincerity present in his face, Rachel felt tears threaten.

Pulling her to him, he held her until he was certain she felt better.

Later that evening, he lay with a smile on his face. She was snuggled close against his back, and the baby was busy indeed. How she could sleep with all that activity inside her was a mystery to him. After several minutes, he felt what he thought must surely be hiccups from her stomach. Turning as easily as possible, he placed his hand to where the movement was occurring and almost laughed aloud. He noticed that Rachel never stirred. He fell asleep a few minutes later, knowing that life for him could be no better than this.

Rachel felt the strong arms of her husband encircle her from behind.

"I'm surprised you can still reach around me," she told him with a slight grimace, "or even want to."

"I will always want to hold you," he told her. Placing a hand on her stomach, he chuckled when he felt a strong kick against his fingers.

"Both of our Mamas feel it will be soon. They think the baby is in position by the way I walk, which is like a duck, I suppose."

"I always did like ducks," he told her as he turned her around to face him.

"I still can't believe you are mine," he whispered as he brushed the hair from her face, "and that you are having our child."

"Forever and always, I think, were the words you used before we were married."

"Yes, and I meant it then as much as I do now."

Over the next few days, Rachel could tell she was getting ready to deliver. The pressure was becoming unbearable, and it was getting harder and harder to walk or get comfortable. As she leaned over to make the bed, she felt a twinge pass through her stomach. Smiling, she placed a hand over her abdomen and whispered, "Today, little one, is this the day that I will get to hold you?"

As if understanding its mama's words, the baby kicked violently and shifted its position slightly.

Matthew had left to work in the barn. He said he wanted to stay close in case she needed him. Throughout the next several hours, the pains began to increase in strength and duration, and she knew that she had better tell him.

Ambling slowly into the building after bundling up, she saw him brushing one of his horses. When he saw her, he tilted his head and grinned, knowing the reason she was there.

Only nodding her head, a large smile broke through his handsome features, and he quickly opened the stall door to come and stand by her. With a gentle hand, he caressed her stomach and felt the tightening beneath his palm.

"Do you want me to go and get your mother?"

"Yes, and have D.J. ride over and tell yours too."

"How about Mark?" he asked with slight hesitation.

Thinking about his words, she shook her head and said, "Just warn him to be ready in case we need him, otherwise, no."

Feeling a small measure of relief because of the past, Matthew helped her back into the house.

"Lie down and wait," he told her as a bit of nervousness showed through for the first time.

"I will not. I've got the rest of the laundry to put away. I never got around to it yesterday."

"Please, Rachel," he asked as his blue eyes darkened with concern.

"I'll rest if I need to, I promise."

Kissing her quickly, he said over his shoulder, "I'll be as fast as I can. I don't want to miss this."

"You'd better not," she warned with a grin. "Remember what I told you after we were married? From the start to the finish, we see this little one through."

"Believe me," he told her with a twinkle in his eye, "I remember it well."

"Off with you now," she told him as another pain rippled through her stomach, proceeding around to her back.

Seeing her flinch, he quickly grabbed his hat off the table and left.

Forty-five minutes later, Rachel heard wagon wheels as they approached. She was pacing now, trying to ease the pains. Seeing the door open, she was grateful that her help and support had arrived. Matthew stood to the side to let her parents enter, noticing the anxious expressions on their faces.

"Honey," her mother asked in greeting, "how far apart are the pains now?"

"I'm not sure, but they are getting stronger."

"Why don't you lie down until Genie gets here? She's delivered lots of babies and will be able to get an idea of how you are doing?"

"I feel better walking."

"All right, for now anyway."

The three felt concern as she continued to pace, bending over and holding tightly to whatever object was in her reach when a pain started.

"Please get in bed," Matthew pleaded with her.

"I will when your mother gets here."

Following her words, the door opened and a smiling mother-in-law arrived.

"So it's time for us to see our grandbaby, is it? Let's have you get into your nightgown, Rachel, and see how things are progressing."

The men watched as the two women assisted her into the bedroom.

Smiling, Tucker asked the expectant father, "It's hard, isn't it?"

"What's that, sir?"

"The waiting. It's always the worst part."

"I feel so helpless. I wish there was something I could do to help and ease the pain."

"Just pray, son, that's all the women will let us do," he told him with a grin. "And from what I've seen before, I think that's all I want to do anyway."

An hour became two, and still the menfolk had heard nothing except the soft moans of Rachel. Ian had joined them and was sitting next to Tucker.

Whispered voices of encouragement were spoken frequently from both the mother and mother-in-law, each praying that the labor would soon be over for the young woman and she would deliver a healthy child.

Sitting quietly, each man looked up with expectancy as they heard the door open. Genie had a grim look on her face as she approached them.

"The baby is turned wrong, I'm afraid. I don't know if I can get it in the correct position or not. We'll give Rachel a little more time and see if her body won't move the child on its own; otherwise, we are going to have to call Mark."

When Matthew heard his mother's words, he didn't care who helped to deliver the baby; he just wanted them both to be all right.

Neither noticed the face of Tucker, which had gone white at their dear friend's words. Dread and fear filled his heart. He was reliving his first wife's death during childbirth, and now he was facing the same thing with his precious daughter. McKenna, realizing what her husband's thoughts were, appeared at his side, asking, "How are you?"

"Not very well," he whispered honestly.

"Pray, Tucker, pray for our daughter. Bring her and the baby before His holy throne."

Needing no further encouragement, he stood to walk to a vacant bedroom, closing the door softly behind him.

"She wants you in with her," Genie told her son. As he began to pass, she laid her hand on his arm and said softly, "Be strong for her. You can help her through this."

Nodding, and with determination in his step and prayer in his heart, Matthew went toward the room to be with his wife. Nearing the bed, he saw the small bead of perspiration on her forehead and how pale her face had become. Bending over, he leaned his forehead against hers and told her, "I won't leave unless you want me to, not 'til that little one of ours is here for us to hold."

"Thank you. I don't know how long this is going to take. Maybe you'd better grab something to eat."

"No, I'm fine," he told her with firmness, surprised that she could think of his well being at the moment. Food held no interest for the expectant father right then.

"How is Papa?" she asked, knowing of his past with her birth mother.

"He is praying, as we all are."

Unable to reply because of the next pain that spread quickly throughout her body, it caused an ache in his heart as he watched her suffer. After it had finally let up, he whispered, "I would take the pain if I could."

"And I would give it to you if I could," she told him with a small grin. "But somehow I think you'd give it right back."

"Yes, that's probably true. I'm not as strong as you. Are you afraid?" he asked quietly.

"I was, but I'm not now. This baby will be born today and I'll not rest until I hold it in my arms. God will help us."

Seeing not only new strength in her body, he saw it in her mind and thanked God. Matthew knew that it was their heavenly father intervening for them.

An hour later, Genie told her laboring daughter-in-law, "Let me check you again and see if there are any changes."

With concentration, she lifted the small covering from Rachel and began to examine her. Glancing at her son, her face spoke volumes. Things were not going well and help was needed—Mark's help. With unspoken words between mother and son, Matthew leaned down and told Rachel, "I'm going to get Mark. Is that all right?"

Rachel's first impulse was to say no, but as she leaned back to relax before the next contraction began, she knew that her strength was slowing ebbing away. For the sake of the baby, she would allow him to assist.

"Yes, please ask him to come."

Hurrying out the bedroom door, he spotted D.J. sitting in the chair at the kitchen.

"Can you ride and find Mark? We need him."

Nodding with understanding, the young boy quickly exited to retrieve their doctor friend.

Tucker, listening closely, felt his heart fall. He prayed earnestly again for his daughter and her unborn child while he cradled his sleeping daughter in his arms.

Mark arrived a half hour later and entered with only a small greeting toward those in the living room. As soon as he walked into the bedroom, he felt fear as he saw how weak Rachel had become. He only hoped he wasn't too late. Quickly removing his coat, he rolled up his sleeves and headed toward the basin to wash his hands. Standing at Rachel's side, he lightly touched her arm and told her, "Don't give up yet, shadow, you've got to fight for this baby."

"I'm trying," she whispered as another pain ripped through her stomach, making tears slide down her cheeks. Despite the intense suffering, she never cried out or even whimpered. Somehow he knew that this was how she would be in childbirth.

"I'm going to check you now," he told her, hoping to ease the awkward situation.

Nodding, she closed her eyes and reached for her husband's hand again for comfort. Matthew felt pity sweep over him as he watched another set of tears escape her eyes and fall to the pillow beneath her—tears that he knew had nothing to do with the pain.

As Mark examined her, he shook his head in frustration.

"The baby is turned sideways. I've got to get it in the correct position if we have any hope of it being born." *Or saving Rachel*, he thought to himself.

Wiping his hand off on a cloth, he told her, "Rachel, I want you to lie on your side. We are going to try and turn the baby with the help of your body. It's a new procedure I just learned."

Those present watched as Mark maneuvered Rachel in different positions, lightly pressing on her stomach. Each was praying that God would intervene and enable her to deliver the little one.

"All right, lie on your back and let me check you again," he told her, worry evident in his voice. He knew she couldn't take much more of this, and the baby's chances were growing slimmer.

Although she never complained, Rachel frowned and tried to prepare herself again for his touch.

Matthew, watching as he examined his wife, heard Mark say, "That's good. The baby is in the correct position now. I think it's the cord that's stopping the baby from moving down the rest of the way. Let me just try and ease it over the infant's head," he told them while he worked in deep concentration. Rachel shut her eyes as a strong contraction tightened her stomach, working its way around to her back. Finally, the pain eased, and she took a deep breath.

A smile appeared on his face as Mark watched as Rachel's eyes opened and she looked quickly into his eyes.

"Did you feel it move?" he asked her with a grin.

Nodding her head, he asked again, "Do you think you can push when the next pain comes and get this little one out?"

With new resolve, she nodded her head and prayed silently, asking God to help. When the next contraction began, she pushed until Mark told her to stop.

"Terrific, Rachel, a few more and we'll have a baby. Well, come on, Papa," he told Matthew, who had stepped back to stand near her head. "Get down here near me. You want to see your child born, don't you?"

Needing no further words, Matthew walked to stand behind his brother and watched in awe as Rachel pushed their little one into the waiting hands of his brother.

Deftly cleaning the baby off, Mark looked to Matthew as if to say, *Well, tell her what it is.*

"It's a girl, honey. A beautiful little girl."

"Not too little. No wonder you had such a hard time. You weren't made to have children this size, but she's perfect."

The newborn, obviously angry at being placed in a world that was full of light and not near as warm, began to cry heartily. Those present in the other room heard the cry and beamed at one another with relief on their faces.

Taking a moment to look into the women's eyes and seeing their tears, Mark felt his own begin to gather moisture. Never before had he felt like shedding tears at a birth.

"Oh, Rachel," her mama whispered, "she's an absolute angel."

Mark placed the infant in her waiting arms and indeed she did look like an angel. She had a mop of dark hair and deep blue eyes with her mother's long lashes. Hearing her mother's soothing voice, she quieted down and a dimple appeared on one side of her mouth as she appeared to try and focus.

"Welcome, my little one," the new mama told her quietly as she kissed her soft head.

Matthew, who was now on one knee beside them, had to wipe his cheeks several times as he witnessed the tender scene between mother and daughter—his daughter. Pride flowed through him as he gazed at the two special people God had placed in his care. He had never dreamt that being a father could feel so incredible. He thought that being a husband was the best it could be. Now he knew that he had been wrong. Love only multiplied when children were added.

Lifting her eyes to look at him, Rachel smiled and heard him whisper, "I love you, thank you for our daughter."

"I love you too. You're welcome."

"I think I've done all I can do here, folks, so I'll be on my way," Mark told those present. "The ladies can finish cleaning you up and get you settled in. Try and feed her soon before you tire out anymore. You've had a busy day."

Holding out her free hand to him, Mark came to her side.

"Thank you doesn't seem like enough right now."

"But it is. Besides, it was God who stepped in and saved your lives. He just used me to help. You tore a little more than usual, so you will be sore for quite a few days. You also lost a little more blood with the delivery. Rest and regain your strength for at least a week before you begin doing things again."

Matthew, hearing these words, knew that he would watch his wife carefully to see that she obeyed them. He realized that little kept her down when she wanted to do something. However, he would put his foot down.

Rachel, listening to his doctorly advice, nodded in agreement and suddenly remembered his words from long ago.

"You cried," she told him softly. "You said you never cried at births."

"I've never delivered my niece before. What is this little lady's name anyway?"

"Emmy," both parents said in unison.

"Emmy Claire," Rachel added as she looked into his face.

"She's a special little thing."

"Just like her uncle," she whispered to him. Bending down and lightly kissing his sister-in-law's cheek, he stated, "My brother is a very lucky man, and I think he knows it." Smiling slightly in return, Rachel found it hard to keep her eyes open from the exhaustion that had settled over her.

Matthew, hearing his brother's words, replied, "Indeed I do. Thank you, for helping me keep my family."

Walking around to hug him, Mark grabbed his coat. He had a lingering smile on his face and a lightness in his step as he exited the room to tell the others the good news.

Genie stepped in and told her, "If you'll give me a second to clean you up first, we'll see if you can get Emmy to eat before you rest, sweetie."

As McKenna assisted her daughter with the baby, Matthew's mother tidied up after the birth, tending to Rachel.

Both women grinned at one another continually as they watched the proud papa touch his wife and daughter at all times. Standing to her feet, Genie told them, "Okay, you two, we'll leave you a few minutes alone before we send in the rest of the clan to see their new offspring."

Hugs and congratulations were shared before the doting grand-mothers left the room, closing the door behind them.

"Isn't she beautiful?" Rachel asked in wonder.

"Just like her mama. I am so proud of you. I wanted to run and yet you never gave up. You did so well."

"I wanted to run too," she told him. "I've never felt anything so pain-ful. At first I wanted to die, and then I was afraid I was going to."

"So was I, honey. I've never been so worried in all my life."

"She was worth it though. Our little one is finally here."

Taking her hand and placing his hand lightly on the baby's small head, Matthew began to pray, "Father, how can we say thank You for what You have given us today? We saw Your almighty hand at work, and You performed a miracle in this very room. Help us to always strive to stay in Your will and raise Emmy to be a child of Yours. Guide us to be her example in the way we live our lives so that she will want to serve You. Thank You for Rachel, and help her to rest and recuperate quickly. We love You, Father, and praise Your name for Your faithfulness. Amen."

After he finished, he saw that his wife was fast asleep and gently removed Emmy Claire from her arms. Placing a feather-light kiss on Rachel's brow, he brushed her hair gently away from her face, pulled the covers up snuggly around her, and went to show off his newborn.

The small group gathered around the sleeping infant. Tucker, taking the baby in his arms, told them with wonder, "She looks just like Rachel when she was first born. She had the same dark hair and long eyelashes. Within a few months, her hair began to turn light until it was eventually the color it is now. I'll bet that's what this little one's will do."

"There is the distinct possibility of it turning red," Genie piped in, glancing toward Emmy Claire's father. "Matthew's used to be a pretty shade of auburn until it began to lighten."

"Ach, nothing wrong with being a redhead," Ian O'Malley spoke up with a snicker. "Kind of fancied the look meself."

As chuckles passed through them, they continued to admire the infant.

Placing a finger against the cheek of her new granddaughter, McKenna whispered, "You, little Emmy Claire, are a gift from God. May each one of us be the examples we need to be to show you how to live a life pleasing to Him."

"Amen," Ian said, hearing her words. "And a fine little lass you are. We're mighty glad to meet your acquaintance," he said as he reached to hold his first grandchild.

All smiled as they noticed that, despite all the attention she was receiving, the baby never opened an eye.

Eighteen Months Later

Rachel and Matthew laughed as they watched their daughter, Emmy Claire, toddle around the large tree near the house. She was unsteady but determined. When she fell to the ground, the grass beneath his hands tickled her fingers, and she looked to her parents with surprise, wanting to cry, but uncertain that she should.

"It's all right, honey," her mama told her as she saw her face begin to pucker slightly. Matthew, sitting on the swing next to her, stood to his feet and took the stairs two at a time to gather his daughter in his arms.

"Hey, little lady, you're fine. Why don't you come up and sit with your mama and me on the swing for a little while? You've been busy all morning."

With a chubby fist, Emmy began to rub her eyes, and Matthew smiled at Rachel.

"Yes, she'll probably fall asleep if she is still long enough."

Sitting down by Rachel, she took the child and snuggled her close to herself, adoration present on her face. After only a few minutes, the toddler's long eye lashes fluttered against her rosy cheeks and she was asleep.

"Isn't she adorable?" she asked Matthew in wonder, staring into the enchanting face of their child. Although they were closed, her blue eyes were crystal clear like both of her parents. Her dark hair had turned into a reddish-blonde color, much like her father's, and her cheeks were distinctly pudgy. As he took the baby from Rachel, a dimple was evident in her cheek as she nestled closer to her father, who had placed her on his shoulder. They watched in amusement as Emmy Claire plopped a thumb in her mouth.

"Of course she is, she looks like her mama," he told her with love.

"I think she looks a little like both of us, blue eyes and all," she added as she reached over and brushed a small curl from their child's face.

"I dreamed of this," Matthew told her as he recalled the days that seemed so distant in the past now. "When I was building this house, I would come and stand right where we are sitting and think of how life could be with you by my side."

Rachel could hear the emotion in his voice and placed her hand on his arm. As she looked into his eyes, she felt her own mist up and replied quietly, "I never imagined that life could be like this for me. I know we were always good friends while we were growing up. The four of us were constantly getting into some kind of mischief. But there was something different about you. Now I know what it was…God was placing a love inside me that only you could stir." With a quick grin, she added, "And along with that love came stronger feelings also—feelings of jealousy."

"I think I know exactly what you were going through," he returned with a grimace. "The difference was that Mark was involved. I wouldn't have intentionally hurt him for anything, but every time the two of you were together, I think a small piece of my heart chipped off...at least that's what it felt like."

"Matthew O'Malley," Rachel told him as she touched his face with her fingertips, showing him with her eyes an intimate part of her that was saved for him alone, "I love you more than life itself. It's a fierce kind of love that makes me feel like the sun is always shining on me, even when it's raining outside. It reaches my very soul, and I want to shout to the world that you are mine."

Bending slightly, Matthew kissed her, letting his lips linger for a moment. Emmy began to stir and he sat up straighter, patting her small bottom to help her settle into sleep once more.

"You put the pieces together again, but you already know that, don't you?" he asked her. "You were the only one who could have done that."

"Yes, it was all in God's perfect plan. As my grandmother often tells us, we just wanted to help Him a little."

After swinging and enjoying the warmth of the sun for a few minutes, Rachel asked, "Can you believe Mark is getting married next week?"

"No, it took him long enough to ask Sylvia."

Laughing, she told him, "He said that after our broken engagement, he wanted to be absolutely sure before he made any commitments. And he is now."

"She'll be a good wife for him," he said as he thought of the woman's nursing training.

"Yes, she's perfect for him. Although I think Mark is going to have to behave himself since she's got seven older brothers."

Chuckling at the thought, Matthew nodded his head. "Yes, he'll have to be a gentleman at all times."

"If he is like his older brother, that won't be a problem. You are always so considerate and thoughtful."

"No regrets?" he asked as he looked into her face.

"None, I am where I want to be and am married to the man I want to spend the rest of my life with—the only man that I have ever truly loved. You are indeed my best friend. I can't help but think of one of Papa's favorite verses. It's in 1 Corinthians, chapter two, and tells us, 'Eye hath not seen, nor ear heard, neither have entered into the heart of man, the things God hath prepared for them that love him.'"

Raising her face to look deeply into his eyes, she told him, "He prepared you for me long ago."

"And you for me," he returned tenderly.

"The road had a few turns in it, but I definitely found my journey home. And that home was none other than the one you built. My journey ends here with you."

"No, Rachel," he whispered with love, "our journey *begins* here."

Dwelling on their conversation for a moment, Rachel felt him rise to his feet, turning to take her hand to help her stand.

Seeing the familiar gleam in his eyes, she tilted her head to one side as she heard him state, "Emmy Claire is asleep."

"Yes," she said as a small smile began to appear.

"How about we take a nap ourselves after we put her to bed?"

"A nap?" she questioned as she stood to her feet and headed toward the door with a knowing grin.

"In a little while," was his only reply.

Holding the door open for the two she adored, Matthew bent down and placed a kiss on her cheek before he passed. "I love you."

"And I love you," she said as she closed the door behind them.

Love abounded in both of them, knowing that God had brought them together in His own way and in His own time. He had known even when they were growing up as children that one day they would be a family—a family that realized the most beautiful things in the world cannot be seen or touched. They must be felt with the heart.